# SMALL TOWN QUILTING BLUES

## A Novel

## BY CHARLIE HUDSON

ISBN: 1508650616
ISBN 13: 9781508650614

# AUTHOR'S NOTE

In a presentation that I created for the 2013 Lancaster Quilt Show, I talked about how I "crafted" the town of Wallington, Georgia, and the characters whom readers meet in my series of stories set in Wallington. As the series has progressed and I have added more characters, I have had requests to provide a listing of recurring individuals, particularly since several of them share the same last name. This is to be expected in a small town, although it can cause confusion. This list is included at the end of the book somewhat like an index. I begin the listing with our main character Helen Crowder and her family, then members of the quilting circle, and other "residents" whom I hope will become familiar to you.

# ACKNOWLEDGEMENTS

There are always people who provide extra details and expertise for my books. I want to say a special thank you to, Jennifer Ball of the Quilted Cat weblog. I ran across a blog post of hers when I was trying to learn about quilting cruises. She was generous with her time and while I, of course, added in lots of fictional things about the cruise, her information was the foundation. And speaking of cruises, my friend and local vacation planner, Tony Fiorie of Cruising Unlimited, was a big help, too. Tony has been on virtually every ship that leaves South Florida and he handles regular vacations as well. St Croix is a lovely island that we have personal experience with (as is St Martin). I also want to say thanks to Brenda Grampas of The Christ the King Lutheran Church in Largo, Florida with their Christian Outreach Center. I met her and the wonderful group of people who do hold an annual quilt auction as a fundraier for the Center. Their work and the engaging day I spent with them a couple of years ago inspired the section in the novel about the quilt auction. My husband, Hugh, once again kept me straight on the scuba sections as well as gave me the loving support that he always does.

Quilters of all ages and levels are of course such a special group of people with your incredible talent and passion. This series wouldn't exist without your inspiration. And where would any author be without fans? Thank all of you for allowing me to be part of your leisure reading.

# CHAPTER ONE

"Well, I'm just so excited, I can hardly stand it," Becky Sullivan said, snipping a thread. "Bob, God love him, has never been interested in taking a cruise. He finally bought that old car he's been talking about getting forever, and he and the boys are going to spend the week tinkering with it. All very manly kind of stuff while we ladies are basking in the Caribbean." Becky was working on a foal and mother medallion that would be the central image of the horse quilt she intended to have finished for the raffle that was part of the annual animal shelter fundraising dinner. Her readers—a plain brown pair this evening—matched one of the browns in the quilt fabric she was working on. That wouldn't have been a deliberate fashion choice by Becky, but Helen had noticed it.

"Sunsets, tropical drinks with little umbrellas in them, and one would hope a handsome man or two," Phyllis Latchley added, her voice merry at the prospect.

"Hmm, it is a quilting-themed cruise," Sarah Guilford mused, her gold wire-rimmed glasses halfway down her strong nose. "I'm not sure how many men go for those types of cruises—no offense meant to Max," she added quickly even though he was the only member of the circle that wasn't at the meeting.

Phyllis arched her eyebrows, blue eyes twinkling as they always did when the subject of fun was raised. "Oh, I'm sure there will be some men along on a ship that size, and then there is the entire crew. They can't all be women or twenty-something males."

Rita Raney patted her rounded belly. "If it weren't for little Tyler here, I can promise that I would be taking time off to go. Steve gets seasick, so we won't be taking a cruise together at any point that I can see. Going with you ladies would be fun, and with quilting as the theme, I wouldn't feel like I was just running off on a separate vacation." Her husband, Steve, might be prone to seasickness, but he'd bought her a beautiful handcrafted rocking chair for the nursery and she was working on a lap quilt especially for it. She'd found a fabric printed with old-fashioned children's toys and was using a striped pattern with medium blue for the borders and as the alternate strips within the quilt.

"The same for me," Alicia Johnson said with a smile. "Not that Hiram gets seasick, but I want to finish all my major projects and get started on decorating the nursery. I think that Katarina is going to like her multiple shades of pink. I've kept it pastel and subdued rather than anything fluorescent." She held up the crib quilt that was almost finished to approving nods. Squares of different dolls in pink dresses alternated with squares of a slightly brighter pink rose fabric, which she'd selected for the border as well. It was definitely something for a little girl.

Each of the young women had chosen to know the sex of their baby beforehand, and they were due no more than a month apart. They hadn't reached the awkward stages of their pregnancies yet, but both of the youngest members of the circle had that glow the other women recognized. Rita's Italian ancestry showed in her faintly olive skin tone and deep brown eyes, while Alicia's black hair and green eyes of a Celtic heritage were counterpoint to her ivory complexion.

"Speaking of babies, I saw Tricia and Russell at Always Fresh Farms," Deirdre Carter said, placing a tiny stitch in one of the cardinal appliqués she was adding to a square. Her middle daughter was moving into a new house as soon as school was out, and she had always been a bird lover. The quilt would include all of the native Georgia woodland birds. "My word, he seems to have grown another inch at least since I saw them last week. He is cute as a bug, isn't he?"

"Well, of course, I think so," Helen laughed, the feeling of warmth for her grandson rushing through her as it did at the mere mention of his name.

Deirdre descended from one of the earliest families in Wallington, and at sixty-three, she was the oldest member of the circle even though she was one of the most recent to join. Helen had felt honored when Deirdre had asked her to coffee one afternoon to see about joining. She was the last of a circle that her great-grandmother had started, passed through her mother's generation. Those women, for reasons never made clear, had refused to bring in younger members of their circle unless they were family members, and Deirdre had been the only one of the younger generation who had taken to the craft. Circles in town who knew the situation had all extended invitations to Deirdre after her mother passed.

Helen said, "I think he's going through one of those growth spurts. You turn around and don't have a thing that fits."

"That's why I always give new mothers baby clothes for twelve-month-olds," Mary Lou Bell chimed in, lifting her blue eyes from her project. "I explain that in the card—that the outfit is for the day they can't squeeze into anything. It gives the mamma time to get to the store." She was working on a bed jacket for a former teacher who had recently relocated to The Arbors, an assisted living facility in the hospital complex. Collecting heart rocks had been one of the woman's hobbies, and Mary Lou had found a pale yellow fabric with hearts in more than two dozen shapes and sizes—no traditional red ones in the mix.

Helen nodded. "That is so smart. What does Waylon have planned while you're on the cruise?"

"Nothing special," Mary Lou said with a grin. "When he's not working, he'll be glued to the TV for basketball play-offs, baseball, or golf. I swear, I never thought we'd have a sixty-inch television set with whatever all those features are, but he's been in hog heaven since they installed it. He declares that it's the best birthday present that I ever gave him."

"Between humongous screens and 3D, and whatever else they can think of, I guess the home theater idea will be catching on again," Deirdre said, looking at Katie Nelson. "Is Scott getting a lot of requests for that with remodels?"

Katie was sitting in one of the chairs with an apron in a stand quilting frame. It was the final piece to coordinate with an oven mitt set and tea cozy that she was giving as a house warming present to some cousin or the other. The dark green fabric was festooned with colorful produce. In what seemed to be a pattern this evening, Helen wondered if Katie had noticed that the background was nearly the same color as her eyes. Unlike Alicia, Katie's hair was blonde in the honey tone range. "Some for sure, and thank goodness he already closed in and converted the old carport when he built the new garage, or otherwise, I imagine we'd be going through another addition. He settled for a fifty-two-inch screen television for his man cave, I guess the term is now. He's got that ratty old recliner that he refuses to give up and a couch that I swear is going to fall apart one of these days, but it is on the other side of the house and I don't take company in there."

"And speaking of additions," Carolyn Reynolds said, smiling at Katie. "Clarissa Grigsby was in yesterday, singing your praises to high heaven. Claims she hasn't cooked a meal in a month. Says she still eats out at lunch a lot, but absolutely loves walking in her house knowing she can have a great dinner ready in fifteen minutes no matter what time she gets home. There were two new women in the store yesterday who heard her; I wouldn't be surprised if they didn't come to see you. They both work and thought that Katie's Kitchen Helper sounded like a wonderful idea."

Carolyn had brought a table runner that she was stitching for the silver wedding anniversary of one of her longtime customers at her store, The Right Look: Ladies and Children's Apparel. She had gotten photographs from the wedding, found fabric that was the same shade as the bridesmaids' lavender dresses, and put in a center strip of quilted white tulips that had dominated the wedding bouquet. The binding was a shimmery silver tape that made for a lovely effect.

"Clarissa is definitely great at spreading the word for me, and yes, Maggie, one of the women you're talking about, did come in today," Katie said. "She took a menu and said she would be back soon."

Katie's Kitchen Helper had been a hit in town from the day it opened. Scott had remodeled the old Farley house for his wife, turning it into a take-out business that included delivery for a fairly small radius but she was hoping to expand. She prepared whole meals for busy families with special menus for seniors as well as dieters who had difficulty in managing portion control. Her business tagline, "Stress less, cook less, and eat well," resounded with women who were constantly trying to juggle work and family and those older people who no longer desired to cook, but who did want an option other than frozen meals or dining out. The discussion about Katie's decision for her mid-life career change had taken place right in Helen's kitchen one night after circle, and now it was at least an initial success. What the year would bring had yet to be seen, but Katie had a solid business plan. She'd worked at one of the local banks for years before deciding to launch onto the entrepreneurial path.

Phyllis drew her needle through the azure blue fabric of the lightweight jacket she was finishing to take on the cruise. Parrots and palm fronds against a blue background was the perfect motif. She tied off a stitch, her posture indicating that she was done for the evening. "I know those of you who can't come on the cruise have good reasons, but we will miss y'all."

"We expect photos and a full report," Sarah said, moving the squares she'd completed into her tote. She was making a quilt using alternating triangles of beige, russet, and taupe for one of her sisters who was redecorating her den. "Shipboard romances included if there should be such a thing to tell." Her smile to Phyllis was affectionate, followed by a quick glance at Helen. Helen sensed the unasked question about her and Max, but didn't bite.

"Is Laura Baker really going to be there?" Alicia's query thankfully drew the group's attention to her.

Although it was certainly no secret that she and Max Mayfield were spending time together, Helen wasn't ready to make them a topic of conversation, and by tacit agreement, everyone in the circle was waiting for either Helen or Max to explain their relationship. The simple truth was that neither one could because they didn't quite know what it was themselves.

"She is indeed," Phyllis said enthusiastically. "Two days anyway, then she has to fly back for the start of her new book tour. I saw her when we attended the Lancaster Quilt Show, and I can't wait to be in this kind of forum with her."

Her wide mouth spreading into a characteristic smile, Deirdre slipped her needle into the new leather case that her sister had given her as a birthday present. "I have all of her books. I love the way she weaves in family and personal stories with her designs and instructions. It's almost like you were sitting right with her." Deirdre had a rich history of close family with six siblings, all of whom had children and grandchildren. Tiny crow's feet around her coffee-bean colored eyes were nearly the only wrinkles in her dark skin, and most people who met her didn't guess that she was actually the oldest member of the circle.

Alicia looked slightly skeptical. "Is it true that she started quilting when she was in the first grade?"

Helen nodded, satisfied with her progress on the red rose nosegay square. One of the women in the church needed an extra pair of hands for a quilt she was trying to complete as a wedding present, and Helen had volunteered to help. It was a lovely I DID PROMISE YOU A ROSE GARDEN design. "Oh, yes. Her mother's side of the family has traced their ancestry to one of the Jamestown settlers. They have a few quilts that date back to well before the Revolution. Talk about quilting flowing in their veins!"

"And from what I understand, despite arguably having one of the finest pedigrees in the American quilting world, if you want to use that term, she isn't the slightest bit snooty about it," Phyllis said, looking comically puzzled that her wineglass was empty. "Hmm, I must have poured that one too lightly."

Sarah laughed and pushed her glasses up on her nose. "That would be the day. Seriously though, it is about time for me to be getting home. Don't forget that we'll meet at my house next week for circle. I know it will seem odd with four of us gone, but we'll have a good time."

There were murmurs as the women exchanged comments, began to fold projects, and filled their totes. Phyllis and Katie looked as if they were going to linger. The rhythm for circle was well-established, not through some silly set of rules, but from learning what worked best for the group. They arrived at Helen's at six o'clock, bringing in bite-size food in a mix of savory and sweet. Next came settling into the large room that Helen had transformed into an ideal quilting room; it offered plenty of space for everyone to be comfortable. Unless they had a group project, they arrayed themselves, depending on the individual's preference or type of project brought for the evening, at the custom-built quilting table, on the couch, or in one of the chairs set in an arc. An hour or so later, there was a twenty-minute break for everyone to stretch and get munchies and beverages. They closed up around eight thirty-ish, although more beverages were available for those who wanted to stay and visit. Plenty of conversation flowed prior to that, the sort of candid discussions and swapping of gossip that was to be expected from women who had known each other for many years. Even Rita and Alicia, the two youngest by at least a decade and still fairly new to the circle, shared in the sense of sisterhood that lent itself like the fragrance of a favorite perfume.

"Oh good, your shrimp spread wasn't completely devoured," Phyllis said, as by habit, the women carried the leftovers to the oval pine kitchen table.

Katie was at the counter next to the coffeepot and mugs. "I've waited all evening for one of Lisa's chocolate and pecan bars."

Helen poured another glass of water and squeezed a lemon slice in. "Do you do much in the way of desserts at your shop?" she asked Katie.

Katie slid into the chair to Helen's left. "Not really. I don't have the kind of talent that Lisa does and her bakery is so popular that anyone looking specifically for dessert goes there first. What most people are looking for from me are meals that can get them through the week." She stirred cream into her coffee, holding the cookie from Forsythe Bakery over a napkin. "I don't think people do dessert after a meal regularly these days." She took a bite of the treat, the usual look of pleasure on her face at tasting one of Lisa's creations.

"I have to agree," Phyllis said, pulling the shrimp spread close to her, cracker at the ready. This was one of Helen's frequent dishes—incredibly simple to prepare and she'd developed the balance of flavor over years of experimenting with proportions of a Cajun seasoning and lemon juice that she mixed with the cream cheese and minced shrimp. "I think people keep sweets in the house and might serve them for company, but they often save them for a mid-afternoon or late-night snack rather than right after a meal."

"From what I've heard about food on board the cruise, we'll have all the late-night snacking opportunities that we could want," Helen said.

"And then some," Phyllis said with a grin, lifting her glass. "Oh, you mean food."

Katie laughed. "You are such a pill. I really do wish I could be going with y'all, but I'm just not in a position to leave the shop yet. I'll catch the next one."

Helen nodded. "If this is as much fun as I think it will be, this could be a regular event for us. I mean, of course I'd heard of quilting-themed cruises and Wanda has already told the cruise line that she'll stay on their roster as a substitute."

Katie raised her cup in a toasting gesture. "Well, here's to what I know will be a wonderful time."

The three women touched glasses to mug, Helen smiling with thoughts of how many nights they'd sat in this same way, sharing whatever good or bad news was important at the moment. The heartbreak of a divorce, the joy of discovering that there were second chances at love, the frustrations of adult children who were poised to make poor decisions, the pall of a disease that took a relative or friend, the ups and downs of everyday life—all of these subjects and more had ebbed and flowed through this kitchen.

Tonight was light-hearted, though, even when Phyllis took one more cracker with shrimp spread and raised her eyebrows to Helen. "It's too bad Max can't come with us on this one. Y'all do know we're all dying to find out what's going on."

Katie kept a straight face, although she couldn't quite hide the question in her eyes as well.

"Not ready for prime time," Helen said with a gentle smile. "There's no rush, and I've been devoting a lot of time to Russell."

Katie shot a look at Phyllis and held her hand up in a *Stop* gesture. "And that's just fine," she said warmly. "Neither one of you need to be in a hurry about anything." She turned to the sound of *click-click* on the slate-look porcelain tiled floor. "Why, hello, sleepyhead."

Tawny, Helen's chug, meandered into the kitchen from the adjoining den, stopping by Katie's outstretched hand for a head scratch. Katie pushed her chair back from the table and scooped the small dog up, its little pink tongue lapping away at her chin in greeting. Even though Tawny was affectionate to all of Helen's friends, Katie had a special fondness for the mixed Chihuahua and pug. "I'll be happy to take care of her while you're gone," she said and let Tawny hop down to make her way to Helen.

"Thanks, but Tricia is going to take her to their place," Helen said as Tawny stretched with her paws on the edge of the chair. "Having access to Tawny saves them from having to get a dog yet. That will no doubt come after they have the new house."

Phyllis poured a fresh glass of wine. "Having your dream house built— that's always a fun and safe topic," she said with a wink. "Or is this more the in-between house?"

"Probably in-between," Helen said with a laugh. "I think that ultimately they're looking to have three or four acres. Tricia has made noises about getting a horse someday, but now is not the time to be making a move like that."

"Well, with the plan they've picked out and the neighborhood, it will be really easy to sell if they decide to later," Katie said. With her husband, Scott, as one of the primary builders in town, Katie knew all the areas as well as, if not better, than most of the Realtors.

"They are having a good time with it," Helen said, sending Tawny over to give a doggy greeting to Phyllis who had cheerfully taken the signal to change the subject from Max. Helen didn't mind her probing, and they had been friends long enough to realize that Helen would share her feelings when she was ready. But that was definitely not going to be tonight.

# CHAPTER TWO

Helen settled into her chair in the den, Tawny on her lap, the cup of chamomile tea in a mug on the side table, the remote next to it. The television was tuned to *Sabrina*, the original with Audrey Hepburn, Humphrey Bogart, and William Holden. She knew the dialogue virtually by heart with no need to have the sound very loud.

Phyllis and Katie had insisted on helping clean up, the light work done quickly as they continued to talk and finally exchanged good-night hugs. The kitchen, remodeled into her dream one after she and Mitch became empty nesters, was quiet for the evening, the light on over the sink the only illumination. She decided she wouldn't have a second cup of tea; rather when time for bed came, she would swap to the television in the master bedroom and prop against the pillows where she would either make it to the end of the movie or drift into a sleep and awaken at some point to another classic. She wasn't fundamentally opposed to remakes; she simply didn't find that most of them had the same depth as the ones from her youth. She smiled to herself. If she asked her parents, they would probably think the same of 1950s and 1960s remakes of films of the 1940s.

Helen stretched her legs onto the matching footstool to her comfortable easy chair, which was upholstered in a medium blue to coordinate with the navy and pale blue striped couch to her right. The glow from the tall floor lamp fashioned after an old gaslight streetlight in a bronze finish cast soft light over her shoulder. The den that opened onto the kitchen had been the room where Mitch used to lounge in the nubby brown recliner that they'd gotten him one Father's Day, a chair that she'd felt a pang for in letting go when she redecorated the den to make it more of her own. Not that she had feminized it—that was never the idea. She'd transformed it into as much library as television room, bringing in additional quilts as art, all with blue in them to coordinate with the slate paint on the walls, the navy blue Roman shade on the single window, and the upholstery for the couch and chair. Mitch's death from pancreatic cancer had torn a hole in her soul; she'd been in love with him since they were in their teens. While they had jointly redesigned the country kitchen, her conversion of the living room into a quilting room and the den into a library/television room had allowed her to break loose of what had felt like being mired for almost two years after he passed away. Having her daughter, Tricia, and son-in-law, Justin, move from Baltimore to Wallington had been a gift she hadn't expected to receive, and with little Russell now—it wasn't that she didn't miss Mitch; that ache would never completely disappear. Time, when allowed to do so, did have the ability to heal. Not erase the pain, but cover it like the scar tissue of any wound so that it wasn't the raw openness of when it was fresh. She and Wanda sometimes spoke of this, their widowhoods thrust upon them sooner than either had ever anticipated.

Tawny twitched her ears, her warm little body relaxed in Helen's lap. Taking the abused chug was another thing Helen hadn't planned on, but within a few days of agreeing to Rita's request, she couldn't imagine why she had hesitated. Rita, who worked for Doctor Dickinson, had found the trembling dog that had been abandoned at the veterinarian's office, and she had been correct in assessing that Helen was the right person to adopt her.

Helen reached for the tea, took a sip as the character of Linus Larrabee, played by Humphrey Bogart, oblivious to his heart, began falling in love with Sabrina, played by Audrey Hepburn. Love in one's older years. With all she had—her daughter in Wallington, her son in Augusta, both married to wonderful spouses, a six-month-old grandson, wealth in the way of friends, a comfortable life, parents who were still blessedly active, her sister in Lawrenceville, and even a snuggly dog as a companion—did she need a man added into the emotional equation?

She couldn't resist smiling at the barely restrained curiosity of the circle, especially on a night when Max wasn't present. She had no doubt that each of them—well, maybe not young Alicia and Rita—had a firm opinion of the idea of Helen and Max as a couple. Outspoken Phyllis had naturally made her views known, although the others had been more circumspect with no overt comments. "The fact that at sixty-two he's not out there sporting some twenty-five-year-old as arm candy says something about him," she'd pointed out one night after circle when it was just the two of them in the kitchen. "And for heaven's sake, Helen, who would have thought we'd have a male quilter in our midst? Talk about having something in common."

Seeing Max Mayfield at the quilt show in Atlanta last year had been completely unexpected. Then discovering that he had become a quilter was close to being a shock, although that wasn't really fair to think of it that way. Him returning to Wallington after having been absent for forty years definitely topped the "surprise meter." A senior when she and Mitch were sophomores in high school, Max had left for the University of North Carolina Chapel Hill the summer following graduation and his visits to see his parents and his sister had been quick ins and outs, rarely planned much in advance since his job kept him traveling most of each year. Even though Helen knew his mother, Miss Edith, from the time she spent quilting with residents in The Arbors, they were not close friends. Helen had only vaguely known of Max's globe-trotting in the polite way of paying attention when conversations swirl around. That had changed in the late fall when Wanda had flitted off to be a substitute instructor on the quilting cruises for the winter season and Max had come to town to enable his sister, Angela, a history teacher, to accept an opportunity to go to Belize on an archeological dig. Having left his road warrior job and discovered the world of quilting, Max accepted Wanda's offer to manage her shop, Memories and Collectibles, during the three months she was gone.

The strong friendship between Helen and Wanda extended into Helen teaching classes at Collectibles and that gave her more time with Max than she might otherwise have had. Or was that a mere coincidence? Having a male quilter was unique enough so that they would have had events in common and, in all likelihood, would have met at The Arbors occasionally. There was an easiness in being around Max that was more than their shared love of quilting—no question about that. Although they'd been out for several dinners and frequently swapped making dinner for each other, they'd begun whatever their relationship was at almost the same time that

Russell was born and that had been Helen's true focus for months. If Tricia was running late or needed to go in early, Helen happily carried Russell to daycare or picked him up, and she never minded babysitting to allow the new parents to have a night out. Now, though, with summer coming up, her services in that capacity wouldn't be required as often.

Tawny stirred from her light sleep, interrupting Helen's thoughts. She hopped down, shaking herself and turning to look up with her bright brown eyes. Helen pulled her feet from the stool, a touch of stiffness in her knees. "You think it's time for one more trip outside and then bed, do you?" She took the empty mug firmly in her left hand before she switched off the television and the lamp. She paused in the kitchen to rinse the mug and set it upside down in the sink. Tawny had slipped out through the doggy door, and Helen heard the dog tag jingle as she returned, ready for her bedtime treat. Helen ruffled Tawny's ears as the dog delicately took the small biscuit. Then holding the treat in her mouth, Tawny trotted back to her bed in the den.

Helen turned the kitchen light off and moved down the hall past the bedroom that had been converted into a home office, Tricia's old room that had become the guest room, and the bath that was in between them. The master, small compared to new houses being built, was at the back of the house as it had been when the bungalow style was constructed in the 1950s, the remodeling they'd done expertly blended architecturally thanks to Jeff Lawson. In actuality, Jeff had explained he could give them a six-foot extension, but no further due to the required distance between property lines, and they'd decided that the extra small space wasn't large enough to deal with the cost and bother of the expansion. He was able to cleverly re-use their existing square footage, though, to provide a separate tub and shower with a bench in it rather than the combination shower and tub they previously had. All the other changes to the bedroom had been strictly cosmetic unless Helen counted the new energy-efficient windows, which had been installed throughout the house. Since that hadn't altered the appearance and she did appreciate the reduction in her utility bill, she didn't consider that to be a genuine remodel.

It was amazing how a fresh coat of paint and new linens could perk a room up, and they had agreed that white walls could be a thing of the past. Mitch had surprised her with a new ceiling fan featuring bronze-tones, walnut blades, and a round frosted globe fixture. Their furniture, antique walnut from his grandparents, was solidly built. Mitch had replaced the old mirror over the dresser with a thirty-two-inch flat-panel television. In the same way she'd done with the guest room, the quilt on the bed had served as the color palette for the room. While she would hate to have to choose a favorite, this was the last quilt that she'd made together with her mother and grandmother. The design had been mostly her mother's, and the memories of the three of them working around the old quilting frame were still vivid. Tricia had claimed the area underneath the frame as her "tent" as children so often did, and the radio had been tuned to the gospel music that Mamaw Pierce loved.

The design featured four nested stars, the small center one of the palest peach color, each larger star as if bursting from that one, a darker shade. They were on a field of pale green, bound by an interior rectangle created by a double border of dark green and deep peach strips, a half-inch wide. The outer binding was the same deep peach. Within that rectangle was a borderless rectangle where the star pattern was repeated in a smaller version; one "nest" of stars on each corner, these done in grades of greens, the center stars in the same pale green as the field.

With all the different color grades in the quilt, it was easy to repeat them in some variation in the room. Three walls were the same as one of the greens with the wall behind the bed two shades darker. Helen had searched for a long time to find peach-colored shades to replace the cream one on the bedside lamps. The padded valence over the dark peach-colored Roman shade had been the easiest with a deep green and peach striped fabric supplanting the venetian blinds and off-white drapes that had covered the window for years. The end result of the redecorating was a cozy room that balanced family heirlooms with modern touches. The room that she and Mitch had shared for too few years, a room where she could still occasionally feel his presence as if he were propped on the pillow next to her. Funny, how she'd moved to his side of the bed that first night alone, after the awful day when she'd come home from her vigil at the hospital. She'd breathed in the scent of him and never told anyone that it had taken her three weeks to be willing to change the sheets and pillowcases.

Helen shook her head at that sudden memory, tuned the television into the final twenty minutes of the movie, and allowed her mind to focus on the delightful scene where the character of Humphrey Bogart finally acknowledged his feelings for Audrey Hepburn. Romantic comedy with a great cast—was it any wonder that it was a classic? Life was filled with enough sadness and struggles. Sometimes you just needed to relax and be entertained.

# CHAPTER THREE

Helen swung Russell from side-to-side, his laughter following the movement as Tawny pranced around, wanting to be part of the play. The baby's eyes were the same sable brown that she'd passed on to Tricia. His hair, though, was lighter brown like Justin's, rather than the darker chestnut of the women. Of course, hair color in an infant wasn't always what it would be within a few years.

"Oof, he is getting heavier," Helen said, pulling him onto her hip and gently touching her finger to the tip of his nose to bring out another peal of laughter.

"He's right in line with the charts," Tricia said, depositing the loaded diaper bag onto one of the kitchen chairs. She snapped her fingers and lifted up Tawny who was as wiggly as Russell. "And you're still a sweetie."

Helen carried Russell, who was now interested in the string of malachite beads she was wearing with the green and taupe print scoop neck top she'd put on over taupe twill slacks. His slightly chubby fingers had found their target, and they were already on the way to his mouth, straining the beads to what hopefully wouldn't be the breaking point. "I'm glad they get along together," Helen said with a nod, skillfully diverting his attention from the necklace with a set of bright blue plastic measuring spoons that she dangled in front of his eyes. He quickly snatched them, the tablespoon clicking against his new teeth—two on top and two on bottom. "As much as I love the little scamp, I wouldn't want to have to be worried about growling, nipping, and so forth."

Tricia set Tawny on the floor where she headed for her water bowl. "She's such a good-natured dog, that it never occurred to me for a minute that she would be a problem with him." She moved toward Helen, her arms open. "Shall I take him or fix the tea?"

"Your call," Helen said, twisting the knob to turn the burner on under the cobalt blue teakettle.

Tricia grinned as Russell was attempting to fit all the spoons in his mouth at one time, sideways, his face puzzled as to why he was having difficulty. "You can hang on to him for a bit. Have a seat and I'll do the rest. We have cookies by any chance?"

"Unless Lisa Forsythe closes her bakery, we have great cookies," Helen said, gently bouncing Russell on her hip as she moved to the table. She pushed the chair back to sit sideways and give the baby plenty of room on her lap. He seemed to have figured out the one spoon at a time method and was busily alternating between eating the spoons and rattling them.

"Billions of dollars in research for new toys and he's happy with that," Tricia said with a laugh, taking out her favorite of Helen's mugs, the ones with a bright yellow background and white daisies all around.

"Big boxes are the other favorite if you haven't discovered that already," Helen said with a grin at Russell. "You buy this terrific new toy, and before you turn around, he's tossed the toy and turned to the box, his fantastic new place to explore."

"We aren't at that stage yet," Tricia acknowledged as the teakettle gave the first whistle. "Tea bags or steep it in the pot?"

Helen moved her head when Russell decided that she should share in his fun. A slobbery spoon in her mouth wasn't quite what she needed. "I'm good either way. I was thinking the cranberry and orange. The cookies in the jar are Lisa's latest recipe of cranberry and almond shortbread."

"Oh, those sound yummy. Let's do a pot then." Tricia went back into the cabinet—obviously in a yellow mood because of the four choices she had in teapots, she took out the one with alternating bands of deep and pale yellow. It was a pot that Helen's sister, Eloise, had brought her from a shop in Savannah. Tricia set the teapot on the stove to allow the steeping time and stepped into the combined back entrance, laundry room, and pantry to retrieve the highchair. Russell was with Helen so often she had a duplicate of crib, playpen, and highchair to save the trouble of hauling things back and forth.

"Up you go, little guy," Tricia said and transferred her son into the chair, the measuring spoon set still firmly grasped in his hand. Realizing food might be on the way he dropped the spoons as soon as Tricia belted him in and snapped the white plastic tray into place. He immediately began gurgling something completely unintelligible.

"We'll swap," Helen said and stood. "You get his juice, and I'll take care of us." She moved to the counter and took the cookies from the ceramic jar that Tricia had found at a garage sale. It was a pale blue, classic round shape with a knob on the lid and dark blue script on the side that said, "Grandmother's Cookie Jar Is Always Full." Of course, that had been true before Russell was born and the cookies had been kept in the cabinet. Helen's enjoyment of a good cookie and Lisa Forsythe's creative baking talent were a great match. It wasn't that Helen didn't bake anymore, but as often as she was strolling past Lisa's shop and as pretty as her displays were, it seemed only right to help support her business. Besides, Helen baked standard cookies—chocolate chip, oatmeal, peanut butter. While Lisa made those as well, her real flair was specialties such as today's delectable cranberry and almond shortbread, which were topped with a dark chocolate drizzle.

"You know, these are some of my favorite," Tricia said when Helen carried the plate to the table and went back to get the tea. "Although it's tough to pick an actual, single favorite of Lisa's."

"I agree," Helen said, settling into the chair beside Russell, who was clutching a graham cracker stick in one hand and had his bottle of juice close by. He seemed content with the arrangement. "So, you met with Scott about the new house? That must have been fun."

Tricia nodded as she blew a stream of air across the steaming tea. "Oh, it was. We've decided to go with the walk-out basement option, but he'll just do the rough-in for plumbing and electrical. We'll finish it ourselves. Keeps the cost down, and since we don't need that extra space to begin with, we can do the basement in stages after we move in."

Helen's eyes twinkled. "Hmm, you mean like getting the drywall up and electrical fixtures put in during a visit from Justin's folks?"

Tricia laughed. Her father-in-law had opened his own electrical business when Justin was in high school. "Not that they need an excuse to come down, but, yes, I'm sure that will be a part of the trip. You can imagine how thrilled Sue and Loyd were when we went to Baltimore to see them. They have other grandchildren in town, but they're all at least a few years older than Russell, so Sue hadn't done the rocking chair thing for quite some time." She bit into a cookie with that last sentence, slightly closing her eyes at the pleasure of the taste of the blended flavors.

"I love the design of your place," Helen said, reverting to the subject of the house that Tricia and Justin were having built. She slowly nibbled her cookie, not wanting to eat more than one since she was supposed to have dinner with Max tonight and he was even more of a regular of Forsythe Bakery than she was. She was betting that he intended to pick up something there. "The open floor plan with the kitchen, great room, and breakfast nook is really nice, and the dining room doesn't feel closed off, even though it's through that arched opening."

"I know. We debated for ages about having the great room smaller to allow for one bedroom and bath downstairs, but Scott pointed out that with the size of the lot and where the powder room was located, we could easily do an addition with a master suite later if we wanted to. I mean, having two master suites would be super if we could afford it. Right now, though, we think that the extra space in the basement is better for us. No one who's going to be visiting has problems climbing stairs, so it's not as if we need the guest room to be more accessible."

"I think that's a sensible approach," Helen agreed. "If you have the plumbing to hook into later and the space is available, an addition can be done for a fairly reasonable cost. All of those lots are right at an acre, aren't they?"

"Yes, and according to what I heard, for any new development, one-third-acre will be the smallest for single-family residences. They don't want to get into the density issues like in other places where the houses are so close they might as well be touching one another."

"I saw Clarissa Grigsby a few days ago. She was at the town council meeting where they approved Iris Place, and she said there were some people pushing hard for increased density. I guess that Tommy Hillman thinks we're lagging behind the times."

Tricia made a face at the mention of Tommy, a common reaction when the name *Hillman* was brought up. "That wouldn't surprise me in the least. I'm sure he views it as progress. If we listen to him, before you know it, we'll have a big batch of houses with the roads and schools not set up for it."

Helen took a sip of tea. "Well, the nice thing about Rita being in the circle is that we have reliable information about the factory, and it is still the largest commercial employer. The factory's expanding, although it's on a two-year plan, and allegedly some other related factory is looking to move into the industrial park. It's the same sort of thing—light industry. They're supposed to be making a decision in the next month or so, but the move wouldn't be until late next year. That means if the council has any sense, we have time to react to the housing issue correctly and make plans instead of finding ourselves with a lot of new people that the area can't accommodate."

Tricia reached for another cookie. Most of Russell's snack had ended up as a pile of crumbs, which he was happily scattering across the tray of the highchair with both hands. "It always is a balancing act, isn't it? Wanting growth, but trying to make sure it doesn't overwhelm you?"

Helen waved for her to stay seated while she stood to get a paper towel. "True, and so far, we've managed pretty well, but I suspect that has as much to do with the fact that we're far enough away from Atlanta so we're not attractive as a commuter community." She tore a paper towel from the holder, dampened it, and passed it to Tricia in exchange for her empty mug. Tricia nodded to a refill.

"You get people pushing for development, and they can roll right over the fact that it takes longer to adjust traffic flow and build or modify schools than it does to put up houses." Helen set the fresh mug in front of Tricia. "Speaking of building, will Scott have the house ready before the new school season begins?"

Tricia shook her head. "We had hoped so, but with the new school schedule starting in the middle of August, it's just too tight. It's going to be closer to the first week of October, which is still temperate weather. However, Scott promised to finish the garage first. So if we wanted to, we could move a lot of things into there and store them. That way, we could pack and move boxes of seasonal items and things we don't use every day over on weekends. When the real moving day comes, it will go more quickly."

"That's not a bad idea," Helen said, as Russell, blissfully sucking on his juice bottle, made soft sounds. "Where are you on picking out interiors like flooring?"

Tricia grinned and pointed to Russell. "Well, now that you mention it, we have a teacher's workshop on Wednesday, which means we'll get out at two o'clock. I'll leave the little tyke at daycare until regular pick-up time, and if you don't have plans, I thought we could go to Scott's office together. Justin honestly doesn't care about the cabinets or anything else as long as he has his two-car garage and gets a lot of say about the basement."

"Of course, I'd be happy to," Helen said without hesitation. No offense to men, but this really was something probably better done between women. It had been the same when she and Mitch had remodeled. Eloise had come over for a few days to help sort through choices about tile, cabinets, countertops, and paint colors.

"I mean, this probably isn't our dream house, but there is a good chance that we'll be in it for several years. Still, we want to keep in mind good retail in case we do sell later. That means I'm looking at mostly neutral colors." She flashed a smile at Russell. "If we decide two instead of three children and we like the neighborhood as much as we think we will, then we can always redecorate and do the addition in the future instead of moving again."

"That sounds like a good plan," Helen agreed and briefly wondered if Ethan and Sarah would be starting their family soon. After all, they had been married almost two years longer than Tricia and Justin. She'd been careful not to say anything, though—it wasn't her place, and a lot of women were waiting until their thirties to have children. She knew that Sarah enjoyed her job with the Augusta Tourism Council, but Helen had also seen that unmistakable look cross her daughter-in-law's face when she'd taken Russell into her arms. It was the expression of a woman who could see herself holding her own baby. Ethan had winked at Helen while his wife was focused on making cooing noises to her infant nephew.

"So, isn't tonight a date with Max?" Tricia's voice was tinged with a tease.

"He's making dinner," Helen said without inflection. "I don't know that you call that a date."

Tricia rolled her eyes in an exaggerated way and smiled knowingly. "As far as I can tell, the two of you are the only ones in town who don't think you're dating."

Helen wasn't sure she wanted to have this conversation. She got a reprieve when Russell took that moment to hurl his bottle to the floor and bang his hands on the tray, his face scrunched in preparation for a wail.

"Hmm, may be time to change a diaper," Helen said, pushing her chair back.

Tricia laughed. "Okay, I'll change the subject, too." She stood and retrieved the bottle as Helen lifted the squirming baby. "Let's check him and then I do need to make a run by the grocery store."

Tawny reappeared with the activity and stood with her front paws on the edge of Helen's chair. "Ah, everyone wants attention now," Helen laughed and gave the required head scratch.

"I'll get this one, and you take care of that one," Tricia said, reaching for her son and giving a nod toward Tawny. "At least with her, it's a quick trip into the yard and you do have the doggie door. How early is it that we can start potty training?"

"Not yet," Helen said with a grin. "Messy diapers are a way to find out if you married the right man. It's one of those things we don't explain to husbands beforehand."

Tricia dug in the bag for a clean diaper, Russell up against her shoulder. "Well, I won't say that it's Justin's favorite part of fathering, but he never hesitates to take care of it. Be right back."

Helen cleared the table, giving Tawny a dog treat rather than a chunk of cookie. Not ever having had pets in the house until she took in the precious little rescue chug, she was following the vet's advice about not letting her enjoy people food as tidbits. While the dog no doubt would have loved scraps from the table, not having them seemed to suit Tawny just fine.

Tricia returned with Russell dry and happy, his plump cheeks perfect for Mamaw's kisses as they went through the ritual of hugs all around before Tricia left. Helen stepped outside and stood on the top step as she usually did until Tricia backed out of the driveway with a final wave. She briefly said a word of thanks for having a son-in-law who had been willing to give up a promising career on the Baltimore police force to move with Tricia back to a town no larger than Wallington. She knew there were a lot of men who wouldn't have made the same decision. Although she hadn't minded traveling north to see them, Helen wasn't going to deny that there was great comfort in having her daughter and family less than a ten-minute drive away.

The ringing telephone reminded her that she needed to call Nelda Nichols at Collectibles about the group quilt project. Helen intended to finish her squares before she left on the cruise, and unless they changed the timeline, she would be back before the group started the assembly. The group often made quilts for different charity events. This one was to help raise funds for a new roof for Nelda's church. With part of the circle planning to go on the cruise and others busy with a variety of tasks, they'd decided to go with a basic patchwork design for this quilt instead of coming up with something complicated.

The showcase quilt for the event was a favored design that Nelda's daughter had created using an old photograph of the original church, which she'd transferred onto fabric. Fabric from some of the old choir robes were was also being used, and several of the older women from the church had kept pieces of the drapery from church remodels that had occurred during their lifetimes. The sentimentality of the offering was sure to bring a lot of ticket sales.

# CHAPTER FOUR

Helen made her way up the wide path that led from the parking lot to what had been one of the town's grand houses. Still grand, it had been converted into Memories and Collectibles on the first floor and Wanda Wallington's home on the second. The house had, of course, been modernized through its 160 years, always keeping in mind to retain as much of the old while incorporating modern conveniences. When Wanda made the decision to open her shop, Jeff Lawson, who specialized in historic preservation and restoration, had been diligent in making as few changes as possible to accommodate the commercial space, discreetly hiding additional electrical wiring behind decorative wooden boxes and extra molding that was indistinguishable from the original. The beautiful flooring, ornate moldings, magnificent staircase, light fixtures, and windows were mostly left in place, while necessities such as the cash register and computer sat on custom-built cabinetry that didn't detract from the period look. The kitchen, a commercial-grade one now because of catering that was sometimes required, was in the back of the house and not accessible to customers.

The columned Southern mansion porch was welcoming with rocking chairs and small round tables. The gracious foyer and four display rooms emanated the sense of age of when hoop-skirted women passed through them. The ballroom, which had always been the main feature of downstairs, was the quilting center, and Wanda had deliberately not jammed the aisles close together. The interior was designed to allow customers to move comfortably, and the three tall quilt racks that held one quilt on each side were mostly used for consignment quilts, which meant there was a constant rotation. The separate rooms for the doll collections, scrapbooking, and other items (candles, bath products, and general gifts featuring local artists' offerings such as handcrafted jewelry and decorative photograph frames) were smaller but also laid out well. Collectibles was set up for its intended purposes—first, to provide boutique shopping without the need to drive to Atlanta; and second, to be an enjoyable spot for leisurely shopping with friends and relatives, poking among the types of things that women loved and men rolled their eyes at, wishing they were at the hardware store. On the other hand, a man looking for a gift knew he could come to Wanda or Lillian McWherter, the only other full-time employee, and be guided toward that perfect present.

Helen was not there to shop or teach a class this morning. She called a warm, "Hi, how are you?" to Lillian, who was on the telephone, and carried her bulging tote and notebook into the classroom where Wanda was waiting.

"Coffee, I assume," Wanda asked with a smile of greeting in her blue eyes. Before her was a tray with a white carafe, two mugs, sugar and sweetener packets, and little containers of French vanilla creamer, today's flavor. There were no pastries in sight, which was good. The double chocolate torte at Max's last night would fill her sweets indulgence for a couple of days.

"Of course," Helen said, setting the notebook on the table and her tote in the chair next to her. She took time to prepare the coffee before she tapped the notebook. "I have the information for Susanna for the classes while I'm gone, and I have these great fabrics that I found last week at Delilah Carlton's yard sale." She took two sips of coffee then pulled a bundle of five different fabrics from the tote.

"Oh, look at this one," Wanda said, reaching for the purple paisley, then extracting another fabric from the loose stack. "Oh, my goodness, you have roosters!"

Helen laughed. "I knew you would like that." The almost yard of material, which featured four varieties of roosters on a flour-sack background, had probably once been kitchen curtains. Although Wanda didn't go overboard with a rooster theme, she did have several scattered about upstairs and a few in the shop.

"Are you planning to take these on the cruise?"

Helen nodded. "Some of them anyway—the roosters are yours if you want."

"Absolutely," Wanda said, refolding the piece and putting it to the side. Neither woman could begin to count how many pieces of fabric they had swapped between them over the years of their friendship. "Now, let's talk about the bon voyage party. Do we have a count on how many are coming?"

Helen drank some coffee, opened the notebook, and flipped half-way through it. "I'd say twenty-five, maybe thirty. All the women in the circle, plus a number of spouses, Tricia and Justin, you, Max, Lillie, Nelda, Susanna, and a few extra. Scott is doing pulled pork, Katie is bringing chicken, I'll pick up the deli platter and rolls, and everyone else is bringing different dishes. What did you decide on?"

Wanda looked around the room. "Chilled spiced shrimp, and we have plenty of condiments in the refrigerator. I thought we would take it easy on the decorations and not go completely overboard, if you'll pardon the pun. Mostly bright colored tablecloths, candles in seashell holders, and a couple of banners."

"That's enough," Helen agreed. "I'll come at four; that should give us all the time we need to set up. Max said he'd help with lifting and hauling, and Susanna will probably come early. I imagine Nelda will, too." She was the extra helper that Wanda depended on during the holidays and, on those rare occasions when Lillie was gone.

Wanda drained her mug and gave a mock sigh. "Even though I spent three months on the cruises, if I didn't have so much going on here, I swear, I'd been getting back on the ship. Y'all are going to have so much fun."

"Well, we certainly appreciate the insider information you provided, not to mention the cabin upgrades."

Wanda waved her hand dismissively. "All I did was let you in on the secret of which week in May is the least booked, so that put you right in line for an upgrade." She grinned. "You are really going to love having a balcony." She glanced at her watch, one of the items she personally collected. When her jewelry box with twenty slots was full, she would move some from her collection into the shop for sale. Today's choice was gold-toned with a crab shape as the face, and the links were seahorses connected tail-to-tail. She had picked it up in one of the ports of call during her time on Sunstar Cruises. In fact, Wanda was looking decidedly nautical with navy blue slacks and a red and navy striped top with tiny gold anchors embroidered around the square neckline.

"Listen, I have to make some calls. Do we need to go over anything else?"

"I don't think so," Helen said. "I want to make a few more notes for Susanna, then I'm off to tie up loose ends." She stood, as did Wanda. "You go ahead and when I'm done, I'll take the tray into the kitchen."

"Deal." Wanda came around the table for a quick good-bye hug. Then Helen poured the rest of the coffee into her mug, sat down, and added to her notes. She just remembered that she hadn't told Susanna that Yvonne McCloud's other niece, Ashley, would be joining them in the next class. Yvonne's niece, Charlene, who lived in town, had asked for quilting lessons as her thirteenth birthday present, and she'd had two of the six so far. Ashley's school was letting out this week, and she was coming for a visit. At not quite a year older than Charlene, she'd been thrilled with the idea of taking classes together with her cousin, solidifying the as-yet childless Yvonne's place in the "fun aunt" column. As much as Helen enjoyed quilting, Susanna was a true fabric artist who taught most of the classes at Collectibles. Helen was completely satisfied teaching only one or two evenings a week depending on the demand.

Helen's cell phone rang as she was unlocking the car. It was Tricia reminding her of their meeting at Scott's to pick out interiors for the house. "I'll meet you there," she said, calculating the time she needed for other errands and thinking what a full day it was going to be.

By the next morning, Helen's to-do list had every item neatly marked off, and no new tasks had popped into mind. Even though the bon voyage party was scheduled for that night and their departure for the airport wasn't terribly early, she didn't want to be rushing around, dashing to the store for that one last thing. They had all agreed that spending an extra night in Fort Lauderdale before the cruise would be a good idea, especially when Tony Fuller, one of only two travel agents in town, got them a great price on a small hotel near the beach. Despite there being multiple direct flights between Atlanta and Fort Lauderdale, there was always the possibility of delays and this way they didn't have to worry about missing the cruise. Waylon, Mary Lou's husband, was scheduled to take them all to the airport in his big Ford Excursion. Lynette, one of Phyllis's cousins, would be bringing them home after the trip. Her large van, which ordinarily hauled the middle school soccer team, was the perfect size. Her only request for serving as the group's return chauffeur was a bottle of Caribbean rum—some type that wasn't usually carried in the local liquor stores.

Before she picked up the party platter, Helen would drop Tawny off at Tricia's. It just made sense to leave the dog with them tonight instead of in the morning. In discussing the final arrangements, Helen had been surprised when Justin told her he was planning to install a pet door. "With us both gone during the day and that being what she's used to at your house, it will make it easier for everyone," he'd said to Helen's heartfelt thanks. "A lot of people need a pet door anyway, and with the backyard fenced in, it might be exactly that extra touch that certain buyers are looking for."

Helen finished her coffee and moved her luggage and clothes into the guest bedroom where she would lay everything out to be ready for packing in the morning. Tawny seemed to sense that something different was going on. She trotted at Helen's heels as if she needed reassurance that she wasn't going to be abandoned. "You'll be fine," Helen said affectionately as Tawny stood with her front paws as far up on the bed as she could reach, sniffing at the edge of the open suitcase. "You'll have a good time at the kids' house, and their backyard is as large as ours."

The entire day slipped by quickly as several friends who weren't attending the party called to wish Helen bon voyage.

Max pulled his red Explorer into the parking spot next to Helen's at Collectibles just as she was reaching in for the party platter, the bags of rolls already looped around her wrist.

"Hold on there, and I'll get it," he said as he swung out of the Explorer, his long legs having no need to step on the running board as she usually did. He was dressed for the occasion in tropical wear with a pair of lightweight khaki pants and a green shirt covered with colorful parrots. Her choice was floral—a V-necked short-sleeved top of red hibiscus and bird of paradise blossoms on a royal blue background and a pair of blue capris matched with red canvas slip-ons.

"I'll let you," she said with a smile, passing him the large tray with its plastic cover. "You look properly festive."

"As do you." The fingers of his strong hands touched hers in the process, and there was that familiarity that seemed to be making its way into their meetings more often lately. His gray eyes held that combination of warmth and laughter that she had becoming accustomed to, his smile wide. "All set for tomorrow?" He slowed his pace to match hers. He was an example of a man who didn't obsess about his health, but who also saw no reason to let his body go just because he'd topped sixty. He cycled much of the time and was at the fitness center four days a week. At almost six feet tall, he was toned although not muscled in the way that a young man might be.

"I'm good, thanks," she said tilting her head up slightly. "Waylon will be picking me up at ten forty-five, I think it is. He'll drop us off, and we plan to have a late lunch at the airport after we get through security."

As they entered Collectibles, Lillie smiled from behind the register. "Susanna and Nelda are here, and Wanda just dashed out for a minute." As a woman who looked a great deal like one of the shop's porcelain dolls, Lillie was a natural for costuming. Her choice for the evening was a vivid outfit of a bright yellow blouse with ruffled short sleeves and a multicolored skirt that could have come straight from an old Carmen Miranda movie, although she had opted for a green and yellow head wrap instead of the towering headpiece that the actress had been known for.

"Good, a tall man," was Susanna's greeting. "We have a stepstool, but we're going to need the ladder for the banners." At not quite five foot three, Susanna used the stepstool a lot. Helen assumed that Susanna, clad in jeans and a purple tank top, intended to change after they decorated the room. Her light hair was pulled into a pony tail, and as usual, she was devoid of makeup. Her stubby eyelashes, snub nose, and spray of freckles put her solidly in the "cute" category instead of pretty, but if there was a woman in town with a sunnier personality, Helen hadn't met her.

"Hanging banners is a specialty of mine," Max said, setting the party platter on the closest table.

"I'll put the rolls in the kitchen, then get the platter while you do whatever Susanna tells you to," Helen laughed. "Or do you need him first, Nelda?"

Nelda turned from the cabinet, her arms filled with tablecloths. "Not yet," she said, a shake of her head sending her large gold hoop earrings swinging. "I'll put these on, and we can do up the centerpieces." With an athletic body that came from having played tennis from a young age, Nelda was wearing what appeared to be a leotard considering its close fit. The coral pink color matched the striped sarong that she'd tied at one hip. People who didn't know Nelda well were always surprised to learn that she was closer to fifty than forty. The pixie cut that complemented her heart-shaped face and frosted hair helped convey the image.

Wanda came into the kitchen through the back door as Helen was storing the platter in the restaurant-size, stainless steel refrigerator. It slid onto the open space neatly beneath a shelf that held a large yellow bowl mounded with shrimp and covered with plastic wrap.

Wanda was in the same clothes she had been wearing that morning and grinned at the sight of Helen. "I had to dash out to the Oaks. Mamma was going to come to the party, but apparently, there's an extra bingo night this week. Who all is here?"

Helen filled her in while Wanda crouched to the lower cabinets and began taking out paper plates decorated with tropical fish and packages of yellow and red napkins with matching plastic ware. "These are all the heavy duty kind, so they should hold up to what we have planned," she said, passing them to Helen. "Plastic glasses or real ones?"

"No big messes to clean up—plastic and garbage bags," Helen reminded her with a laugh. "This is just for fun."

Wanda straightened, her grin still in place. "Then we should probably mix up the first batch of rum punch."

The result was judged to be excellent, and by the time Wanda and Susanna broke away to change, Max was put in charge of making the second, larger batch of punch, assisted by Phyllis who suggested the concoction could use a tad more pineapple juice.

Instead of a steady flow, everyone seemed to show up at once. The holiday mood permeated the entire downstairs of the shop—Radio Margaritaville being the evening's station of choice. *Bon Voyage* banners were strung above cardboard cutouts of palm trees and parrots. The heavy-duty plastic tablecloths popped with color, and the centerpieces were hurricane glass candleholders filled with sand and seashells surrounding a fat candle inside. The party was well underway, the food disappearing with excited chatter about the trip and plans for those who weren't going. Wanda said that it was like the midnight buffet they would find on the cruise ship. "Just tell me they keep a bar open, too," was Phyllis's comment.

"A lack of booze is not something that you have to worry about," Wanda assured her. "But do remember that you'll be stitching, too."

Phyllis waggled her fingers, having gone with a bright red polish to coordinate with her red capris, royal blue tank top, and scarlet macaw shirt.

"I'll be prudent until the quilting is done for the day." She grinned and then raised her eyebrows. "Unless it turns out that the ship's doctor is cute, single, and the right age. Then, my needle might slip, and I might have a little puncture or two that needs attention."

"Unless they've replaced him, I think the one on the *Sunset Voyager* is seventy, bald, and married with multiple grandchildren," Wanda said.

The volume to "Hot, Hot, Hot Calypso" cranked up as a conga line started to form and kept everyone moving for a while. It was, after all, a workday, and by nine o'clock, the little food that was left was sent home and clean-up went quickly.

Max walked Helen to her car, theirs the only ones remaining in the lot. They were parked beneath a streetlight, and Max paused while Helen took out her keys. "I know you said you were ready for tomorrow. Does that mean you have time for a drink or a cup of coffee, or is it too late for you?"

Helen had been thinking that they'd hardly had a chance to talk in the past two days. The evening was partly cloudy, a slight chill in the air after the crowd and energy of the room. "Actually a cup of coffee sounds good. As they say in the movie, 'Your place or mine?'"

"Well, I did buy a new French press, and my place is at least two minutes closer, so let's do that."

Helen suppressed a shudder when a breeze tickled her bare lower arms. Hot coffee did sound good. "That's fine," she said, sliding into her car while Max held the door. "I'm right behind you."

One cup of coffee would be perfect, and that way she could check that block—the Max good-bye block—off her pre-departure list, too. She smiled at that thought—after all, it wasn't as if Max was only a block to be checked off a list.

# CHAPTER FIVE

**M**ax's apartment was one of the new loft ones in the town square above retail space that spanned half a block. It was so close to Memories and Collectibles that he usually walked or biked. When Helen had heard about the construction of the mixed-use section, she'd wondered at the wisdom of what seemed to be an urban touch in Wallington. Not that downtown was terribly lively at night, but living above shops and restaurants wasn't her idea of an ideal arrangement. Then again, she'd never actually lived in an apartment since her college days. She and Mitch had married right after graduation and rented a small house with a yard, knowing that children would be quickly added to the family.

The designers and builders of the Uptown Apartments had obviously judged potential tenants more accurately than she had because the units had filled fast and didn't stay vacant for long when they went on the market. Well before Max had returned to Wallington, a friend of hers had been one of the first to move in, and she claimed it was one of the best decisions she'd ever made.

Since parking around the town square could be an issue at peak times, the developers had the foresight to build covered stalls for the tenants that required a pass key to enter as well as an adjoining public lot to help smooth the passage of their permit through the city council. From what Denise Grigsby of the *Gazette* had told her, some tax breaks had been added into the package to make it a win-win for everyone without downsides for the taxpayers as far as she could tell. That certainly wasn't always the case when town officials struck deals with developers.

Max stopped his Explorer several feet beyond the parking lot bar and walked back to swipe the key to allow Helen to enter. Since Max lived alone, she slipped her car into the second spot designated for his apartment. He'd taken a second-story unit, although it was the third floor if you properly counted the ground floor retail space. No matter how it was measured, Max's corner apartment did provide an excellent view of the square and the nearby city park.

Helen waited for him at the elevator. "The temperature has dropped a bit, hasn't it?"

"And this time tomorrow night you'll be in sunny South Florida," he said, holding the door for her to enter. "Have you checked the weather for the coming week? It's too early for tropical storms, so I assume you should have smooth sailing, so to speak."

"Becky gave us a full report on the extended forecast: clear skies, warm during the day, the occasional afternoon shower, but nothing worse than that predicted."

The hallway light was on in Max's apartment, and he waved his hand as they came through the tiny foyer into the open space. "Do you want to perch at the breakfast bar, take the table, or relax on the couch?"

"This is fine," she said, rounding the corner to take one of the pewter and black leather bentwood-style stools at the breakfast bar. The galley kitchen, in white cabinetry with stainless steel appliances and black granite, was more modern than Helen cared for. She thought it was described as "urban chic."

Max, who had been unsure of how long he would remain in Wallington, had taken a minimalist approach to furnishing the apartment. The layout was standard: the galley kitchen opened onto the den with the dining nook to the side and a short hallway from the den led to a bath on one side and a bedroom on the other. The slightly larger master suite was at the end of the hall. Max had told her that he had immediately set the extra bedroom up as an office, declaring that he wasn't expecting many overnight visitors. He kept two inflatable mattresses stashed under his bed in case nieces or nephews stayed over. The beige Berber carpet, white walls, and white wooden blinds throughout lent themselves to remaining neutral or adding color if preferred. Helen wouldn't have been surprised to have seen all leather and chrome for a decidedly masculine look, yet Max had either consciously or unconsciously used his design work in quilts as a basis for the décor. He'd chosen upholstery in solid colors of blues and greens for the sofa that defined the sitting area, a recliner to the left, and a club chair to the right. There was no footstool for the chair, and the coffee table in the center of the arrangement was paired with matching end tables in distressed medium tone wood. They were devoid of detail and had no drawers, giving a clean if not particularly interesting look.

Even though the large, flat-panel television dominated the far wall as was to be expected, Max's quilt, CETACEAN WORLD, provided the color scheme and hung to the right. He had created the design as part of a fund-raiser for a marine mammal conservation group, contributing the original quilt that Helen discovered had been bid up to $12,500 at the organization's annual dinner. This had been an occasion when he made a second, slightly smaller version to keep. Not being familiar with cetaceans other than to know they included whales, porpoises, and dolphins, Helen had asked Max to explain the different types. The blue whale in the round center medallion was encircled with a pygmy right whale, the familiar killer whale known as orca and often seen in marine theme parks, and the unique narwhal that had a single long tusk protruding from its head like a sea-going unicorn. The next circle out were the porpoises: a black and white spectacled porpoise; a harbor porpoise with a blunt nose; a Dall's porpoise, which was dark gray and white with blurry white stripes on its back; and a vaquita that he'd told her was probably the most endangered species in the world. The outer circle was devoted to dolphins: the bottle-nose that every-one knew, a spotted dolphin, a striped one, a spinner dolphin, one called a rough-tooth, and the unique Amazon River dolphin with its pale pink hue among the grays, blacks, and whites of the others. Wavy lines of seven shades of blue alternating from aquamarine to steel blue were repeated hor-izontally as the background. Those colors represented the "seven oceans" of the Arctic, Antarctic, North Atlantic, South Atlantic, Indian, North Pacific, and South Pacific.

When she asked him how he had found some of the more obscure images, he'd smiled and said that if you looked in the right places, you could almost always find someone who could create any image you wanted and transfer it to a piece of fabric. Even though he wasn't the kind of guy who dropped names as a way to impress people, his previous job had sent him around the world, including to some remote locations, and he'd made contacts on virtually every continent. She didn't think he'd been to the Antarctic, but quite frankly, she wouldn't be surprised if it turned out that he had.

Max interrupted her musing and held up one of three ceramic canisters where he stored his coffee beans. "How about Blue Mountain even though I know that Jamaica isn't on your itinerary?"

"That's perfect," Helen said, having learned that his limited indulgences included gourmet coffees and single malt scotch. He'd told her that thanks to the Internet, he didn't have to rely on the local groceries' fairly small coffee selection. They had expanded beyond the coffee basics, though, in recent years. Townspeople who had been displaced from New Orleans after Hurricane Katrina and who had chosen to stay well away from large bodies of water had convinced the stores to add Community Coffee with its dark roast and chicory flavor.

Max ground the beans and transferred them into the glass pot of the French press. He then carefully poured hot water, using the stopwatch mode on his cell phone to mark four minutes before he would gradually depress the plunger to allow the aromatic beverage to rise, the grounds sinking back to the bottom. He was actually the first person she'd known who used this method, and he'd admitted that it had been a source of irritation to his ex-wife who'd thought it was silly to take the extra effort when they had a perfectly good drip pot that you could set with a timer.

He pointed to the quilt and snapped his fingers. "I can't believe that I almost forgot. St. Croix is a port you go to, right?"

"Yes. Grand Turk, St. Martin, San Juan, St. Croix, and one other that I don't remember at the moment."

He smiled. "Then you really need to do the one-day scuba course, where they teach you the basics and take you into the ocean with an instructor."

Helen raised her eyebrows. "Scuba? At my age?"

He waved a hand dismissively. "First of all, you're younger than me; second, you're in good shape; and third, St. Croix has fabulous diving. You'll love it. Have you at least been snorkeling?" He poured the coffee into emerald green mugs embossed with turtle hatchlings and took the stool next to her, turning sideways to face her.

"No, it's something that Mitch and I talked about, but somehow our vacations never took us to the tropics. I suppose we thought we would go after we became empty nesters, and then, of course, there were other priorities with remodeling the house." If Max noticed the tiny catch in her voice, he didn't ask about it and she shifted the subject "You dive, then?"

"I try to take two trips a year," he said, sipping the coffee. "I missed last year with everything going on, but I was checking travel packages the other day. You remember how my sister Angela spent time in Belize last year on the archeological dig? She's still raving about the weekend they had on the barrier reef, so I thought I would try that next. There are several resorts that sound nice, or I might take one of the dedicated dive vessels that carry you far enough off shore so that you dive in areas that most other people don't have access to. I've done that a couple of times and enjoyed it."

Some of Tricia's friends belonged to a dive club in Covington, and they went on trips together. Neither she nor Justin had expressed an interest, and it wasn't anything that Helen had thought about, although she had seen it on the menu of optional activities for the cruise. "This one-day class—you actually go into the ocean? Isn't there supposed to be other training first?"

Max smiled. "You train in the pool first, learning how to use the equipment and getting comfortable with the feel of exploring underwater. The instructor will take good care of you, and I genuinely think you'll enjoy the experience. You've been to the big aquariums?"

"Yes, of course. Walking through the tunnels to see the fish and replicas of reefs seems more my style."

He laughed softly. "Well, give it some thought. After all, you'll have plenty of time for quilting, and you don't want to miss out on other adventures." He paused for a sip and winked. "Besides, my regular buddy that I dive with packed up and moved to Australia for the next three or four years. Not that I'd mind a return trip Down Under, but it is a long way to travel. If you learn to dive, I could tempt you with shorter trips."

"Ah," Helen said, not entirely sure if he was teasing or not.

He glanced into the kitchen and changed the subject. "I have torte left from last night if you'd like a slice."

"Oh goodness, no," Helen said, holding a hand to her stomach. "I can never resist Scott's pulled pork, and from everything I've heard, a great deal of what we will be doing on the cruise involves eating."

"It's been a long time since I was on a cruise, but I doubt that part of it has changed," he agreed. "Food is pretty much available twenty-four hours a day, but they usually have a nice fitness center, too."

"They do have one," Helen said with a smile. "And I have to admit that the idea of walking the decks as the sun rises over the Caribbean appeals to me. Maybe not sunrise every morning, but at least once or twice." She knew that Max shared her habit of being an early riser.

His gray eyes held remembered pleasure as he said, "One of the great things about being at sea is leaning on a railing with a steaming mug of coffee while you watch the sun come up, or swap that around and have a boat drink in hand while the sun goes down. And don't forget the brilliance of the stars at night."

He motioned, offering a refill. Helen nodded and leaned into the counter while he poured the last of the coffee into their mugs. "Goodness, should I feel badly that you aren't coming with us?"

"Not at all," he said and grinned in the way that she'd begun to notice more often. It was the kind of grin that was almost like a quick hug. "I've got a webinar to prepare for, a new quilt design to finish, and a couple of conferences with the Hawaiian quilting group that I work with. I'll be expecting plenty of stories, though."

"Stories, photos, and I assume a number of quilted squares shall return with us," Helen said lightly and lifted her mug, "and I will seriously consider the scuba part. If I get eaten by a shark, though, you have to take the blame."

He held his hand up in the Boy Scout Pledge. "Scout's honor, but I can almost guarantee that you'll be in far more danger from sunburn than sharks."

"A big floppy hat that rolls up is in my luggage," she said, pointing to her head. "And I have plenty of sunscreen set out for packing." Despite the caffeine, she suddenly felt the beginnings of a yawn. "Speaking of packing, as much as I enjoy your company, I do need to get home."

"It will be a full day for you tomorrow," he said and swiveled the stool to where he was facing her. "Have a wonderful trip, and if there are problems with transportation plans on either end, don't hesitate to call. My Explorer won't hold everyone, but I do have other resources that I can tap into."

"I appreciate the offer, and now, I'll say goodnight and see you in about a week."

Max walked her to her car, gave the chaste kiss on the cheek that he always did, wished her "Bon voyage," and stood by the parking spot until she gave him a wave in the rearview mirror. Tomorrow would indeed be a busy day.

# CHAPTER SIX

Helen wondered if her face gave away her excitement as a novice cruiser. If it did, she didn't care. The ship was amazing. As she stepped out onto the balcony, she felt a thrill imagining what it would be like once they were underway, the vastness of the Atlantic as they moved south into the Caribbean. The women had agreed to meet at the Welcome Party, and she'd already unpacked, surprised at the amount of built-in storage.

The snippet of photo in the brochure hadn't done the stateroom justice. The furniture was a cherry finish with Scandinavian lines, and the color scheme was a rich burgundy with teal accents. The carpet pattern of connecting rectangles was in more subdued tones of those same colors, and Helen immediately thought of what a nice quilt design it would make. The bed, on the far side of the room away from the door, had a large wooden headboard with a bench attached to the other side. The bench was topped with a long cushion so that it served as a small couch facing two burgundy upholstered easy chairs and a round coffee table, creating a cozy sitting area. A writing table and wooden armless chair were against the wall by the bathroom, the rest of the wall was the wardrobe with shelves and drawers behind the doors. Wanda had told them not to bother with taking up luggage space with robes. The ones provided on the ship, she said, were "snuggly comfy."

Sliding glass doors opened to a balcony, where there were two sturdy-looking white chairs, a small square table, and two matching chaise lounges with adjustable backs. Helen was glad that Tricia had given her an e-book reader for Christmas. It was another of those items that she'd thought she didn't really need, although when she'd mentioned it to Max, he assured her that as a former road warrior, it was a great invention. She had to admit that carrying the slim case instead of regular books was easier for travel. It wasn't as if she was giving up "real books," but this way she would have plenty of room for the new one by Laura Baker, which she intended to buy at the autograph party scheduled for the next evening. She didn't think that the other three instructors on board had new books out, although one of them was a prolific blogger from what she understood. Following blogs wasn't something that she had taken up yet, and she wasn't entirely sure why.

When she, Becky, and Mary Lou had signed up to take the maximum of four classes a day during their sailing time, which Helen knew she should stop using as a term, Phyllis had laughed and said she wasn't taking the first morning class. She fully intended to enjoy the nightlife that was offered. Helen suspected that pretty Mary Lou might well get lured into more of that than she was expecting to, even though, as Sarah had surmised, the cruise did seem to have a far greater population of women than men. On the other hand, if there were eligible men on board, she had no doubt that Phyllis would find them as one of her first priorities.

A knock at the door turned out to be an excited Phyllis. "Don't you absolutely love it?" she laughed, waltzing passed Helen. "Aren't the robes great, and how terrific are these balconies?"

Helen knew an actual response wasn't required as Phyllis danced a little jig, ending in a twirl—an interesting maneuver considering that she was wearing the jewel-decorated leather thong sandals she'd ordered for the trip. Her mid-thigh-length royal blue shorts were complemented by a matching blue and white striped top, a pair of dangling parrot earrings adding a touch of whimsy.

"When Wanda said 'upgrade,' she wasn't kidding," Helen said. "You all settled in?"

"Yes, and ready to explore. Coming with me?"

Helen smiled. "I'm certain that your exploring will be more like dashing. I think I'll meander. Maybe we'll run across each other before the Welcome Party."

Phyllis was already swaying toward the door. "Okay, see you in a bit."

Excited about finding her way around, Helen wasn't far behind her. She took the practical approach, however, first finding where the classes would be held the next morning. There were a few women poking about alone, as she was, while others were with companions. Enjoyment rippled through the air as surely as the breeze from the harbor, where a trickle of people could now be seen around the docks. Helen kept track of time, delighting in each level, trying not to seem too much of a novice in her amazement at the sheer size of the ship (although she understood it was not nearly as large as some). Until you walked it yourself, it was difficult to comprehend that you could have what was an entire village floating on a single vessel. Indeed, Helen had been to many a small town with a significantly smaller population than what was on the ship. She looked into every section that was open, made note of the well-equipped gym, and investigated the restaurant choices.

She stopped at the activities desk. "Are you locating everything okay?" The young woman behind the desk was petite with black hair in a short shag cut. The nametag fastened to her navy and white uniform said, *Amanda Rice, Asst. Dir, Activities.* "Have you had a chance to look over the different excursions that we offer while in port?"

Helen spent nearly twenty minutes in conversation with Amanda, who gave her a card with the name of the main scuba instructor on it. Amanda said she was an avid diver and loved the Caribbean; she agreed with Max's assessment that St. Croix was a great choice for diving. A trio of women who looked to be in their early forties approached, and Helen relinquished her spot and headed off to find Tommy the scuba instructor. When Helen found him, she tried not to think that he looked as if he had only recently graduated from high school. Here was a man whom she was thinking of entrusting her life to, and he most assuredly was not even as old as Tricia. He did have an adorable British accent, though, and explained that he was the third generation living in the islands. His parents relocated from England to the Grand Bahamas after World War II. He'd been practically born in the ocean and enthusiastically assured her that the one-day scuba course was immensely popular. In fact, he only had four spots left in the first class. Becky had promised to be her partner, or she guessed that "buddy" was the right word. Oh, yes, indeed, Mrs. Sullivan—was that Rebecca?— had been by to see him, Tommy said. If St. Croix was where they were interested in diving, that was the third port of call in the cruise and they could take the later class.

Helen left Tommy and made her way to the Welcome Party. Like Helen, several women were searching the crowd, looking to link up with their sister travelers. She heard her name and turned to see Becky, Phyllis, and Mary Lou near the railing waving to her. Becky, as was her style, had opted for khaki twill slacks with a bright red sleeveless shell that showed off her muscular arms. Her only jewelry was the gold horse's head pendant that she often wore. Mary Lou, of course, looked as if she were ready for a "Cruising Fashion" show in a V-neck emerald green knit top with a mid-calf-length wrap-a-around skirt in a tropical fish motif. Jade jewelry and a pair of dark green espadrilles finished the ensemble.

Becky was grinning. "Did you see the scuba guy?"

"Yes," Helen said. "He suggested we do the class for our first port of call. I told him that St. Croix had been recommended. He loves it there, too, but that's later, and if we go right away, I suppose we could take a second class if we wanted to."

"I'd just as soon take the earliest one if that's okay with you, then we can think about a second round if it's as much fun as everyone says. Plus, they offer horseback riding in St. Croix, and I don't want to miss that. We can go by and sign up for the scuba class after the party or in the morning. Did you see the gym? Isn't it nicely laid out?" Finding a place to work out would have probably been one of Becky's first concerns after the quilting.

"Better yet, I went ahead and booked us for dinner in the Chez Pierre section of the main restaurant," Phyllis said. "I assumed we'd be enjoying plenty of Caribbean fare and thought we'd work our way through the other themes as well."

"I'm good with that," Becky said. "I love the Copper Pot, but I do wish we had a little French bistro in Wallington, too."

"Oh, look, they're opening the doors," Mary Lou said before Helen had a chance to respond. She didn't have a lot of experience with French cuisine beyond quiche, crepes, and the wonderful coq au vin that was one of Wanda's specialties.

The female crowd—not a man in sight—moved into the room amid laughter and chatter. Three women smilingly greeted them and motioned toward the tables set up with beverages, hors d'oeuvres, and what appeared to be "goody bags." Helen noticed that even though much of the group was in the silver-haired range, about a third were younger, a few significantly so. The gift bags were labeled with a "Welcome to Quilting and Cruising" tag, the contents a mix of items from the cruise line and the cruise organizers. A bookmark featuring the cover of Laura Baker's latest book, a nail clipper, a tube of sunblock lip gloss, a plastic-coated ruler with inches on one side and metrics on the other, a plastic thimble, and a tri-fold brochure with the highlights of the cruise and a short bio and photo of the four instructors.

There was the sort of pause that occurs in a large gathering after the initial "oohs and ahs" are said. One of the greeters moved to the front of the room and rang a small bell. She was willowy, her light brown hair touching her shoulders, her voice melodious as she called for their attention. "Thank you, ladies," she said, a small microphone clipped to the lapel of her coral-colored pants suit. "It's a pleasure to see you all here, and I'd like to take a few minutes to officially welcome you." She introduced their four instructors: Laura Baker, Naomi Granger, Sonya Prince, and Melanie Wheatley. Each woman, in turn, gave welcoming comments and said she would be available for the next hour to answer any questions.

When the party broke up, Helen and the others decided to stop by their cabins for a quick change of clothes, then meet up to the restaurant. As Mary Lou and Becky peeled off into their cabins, Phyllis paused at Helen's door. "How much fun was that?" While Phyllis might be the genuine party girl of their quartet, quilting was still a deep passion with her. She was as excited here as when they attended the big quilting shows. There was something special about being surrounded by other quilters, whose love for the craft shimmered in the air, encasing them in a bubble of shared stories of how they came to be quilters, of amazing ideas for designs, and of an incredible range of talent.

"I think it's going to be great," Helen said, shooing Phyllis in the direction of her own cabin. "See you upstairs in a bit."

Wanda had explained that even though casual clothing was the rule for the cruise, shorts and flip-flops were not considered appropriate attire for dinner. So Helen slipped out of her slacks set. Realizing she was a bit sticky from wandering the ship, she spent a few minutes in the shower to restore a feeling of freshness then donned a deep purple, short-sleeved, empire-waist dress of fluid, easily washable jersey that fell just below her knees. Her low-heeled, black leather, open-toe pumps were comfortable and a classic style, the only pair of dress shoes she'd brought. The lovely set of polished amethyst beads with matching ball earrings Tricia had given her last year made the perfect accessory. Mindful of Wanda's advice that a light jacket or wrap was usually needed after the sun set, Helen draped a vintage shawl over her arm. Its design—a black background with swirls of lavender, blue, pink, and pale gold—could go with almost anything. She listened briefly outside the other women's doors but didn't hear anyone stirring. So she went upstairs to meet them at the restaurant.

Her first night at sea, the ship now its own island powering through the darkened waters more quietly than she would have imagined. Lights, people's voices, bits of music flowed as doors opened and closed. The breeze had intensified, and she thought how she was going to be glad for the wrap when they came out after dinner.

"Well, don't you look nice," Becky said, coming from the opposite direction. She ran both hands down her body. "Bob insisted that I buy myself something new. We were in Atlanta for the day, and I found a great sale." She grinned. "Don't tell Carolyn that I cheated on her. I usually get all my Sunday-go-to-meeting clothes from her."

"The outfit is absolutely you, and Carolyn wouldn't mind a bit," Helen said smiling. Becky's burnt orange slacks were slightly pleated, the buttonless jacket with narrow lapels was piped in umber, and the burnt orange and cream striped blouse had small umber buttons. The high neck of the blouse precluded the need for a necklace, and Becky was wearing modest gold hoop earrings.

"I didn't eat many appetizers at the party and am totally ready for what's supposed to be a four-course meal," Phyllis said, as she and Mary Lou made their appearance, exchanging compliments over each other's outfits.

"I am not eating snails, though," Becky said, as they made their way to the corner of the large dining room where a white arch stenciled with purple fleur-de-lis denoted the entrance to Chez Pierre.

Helen surveyed the different dining stations of the main room, sniffed the enticing aromas, and wondered if there was going to be any way to get off the cruise without gaining weight. On the other hand, it wasn't as if she planned to do this again soon, and amazing food was one of the points of a cruise. With that, she decided that if she declined the midnight buffet option, that should be demonstrating adequate restraint.

The placement of Chez Pierre made it seem almost like a separate restaurant, and when they were seated at a table by the wide windows looking out onto the water, Helen wanted to clap her hands in delight. Instead, she picked up her water glass and made a toast to Phyllis for making the reservations. Like Becky, Helen wasn't up for trying the escargot that Phyllis assured them was delicious. She made her way through superb lobster bisque, a marvelous salad with a delicious tarragon vinaigrette, lightly sauced snapper in parchment with julienned vegetables, and the best chocolate mousse she had ever tasted.

"As wonderful as this is, I'm voting that we sample all the different cuisines," Mary Lou suggested with a final sigh of appreciation for her peach melba.

Becky nodded, having given approval for her roasted lamb. "I could be convinced to come here every night, but I have to agree that swapping around is probably best. I have a feeling that everything will be terrific."

"I thought we might save the special restaurant, Star View, for our last night. That's the glassed-in one on the top level that features Caribbean Fusion cuisine," Phyllis said.

"You have my vote," Helen said immediately to a round of smiled consent, "and considering what I have consumed here, I fully intend to take a brisk walk around the ship in the morning before breakfast."

"They say the trio playing in the Ocean Waves Lounge is super," Phyllis said, her voice an invitation.

"This has been enough partying for me this evening. I'll be doing the gym early, and I have an excellent book waiting," Becky said, as Mary Lou gave a thumbs-up signal to Phyllis, indicating she was prepared for a longer night.

Phyllis sighed affectionately, her blue eyes teasing. "Okay, but don't even think about knocking on my door in the morning to see if I want to join you for exercising. I can be healthy at home."

They laughingly parted, Becky making a direct line for the cabin level, while Helen adjusted the shawl over her shoulders and moved to the railing away from the dining room and toward the ship's bow. She was alone for the moment in a dimly lit spot, sounds from around her muted. It was an almost startling silence compared to the constant whirl of the day. In the stillness, she could hear the engines deep in the ship's interior and the sound of the ship moving through the water, tiny white waves breaking against the hull. She looked up at the stars out here, away from land, with no urban lights to obscure their extraordinary brightness.

It brought to mind her childhood when she and her sister, Eloise, would spend the night at their grandparents' farm, ten miles from the nearest town. The other houses were separated by enough distance to give this same sense of isolation. Papaw Pierce would tell them to forget the television and take them outside, pointing to constellations, explaining the origins of the names. Sometimes, there would be a half-moon like tonight, and the glittery stars would sparkle against the black sky, evoking a feeling of wonder at the beauty of it all. Funny, now that she thought about it, those nights must have been an unconscious inspiration for A STARRY NIGHT and BIG DIPPER DREAMS, the quilts that she'd made for Ethan when he was going through the phase of wanting to be an astronaut. The little boy décor of Tommy the Train had given way to space ships, a painted ceiling with glow-in-the-dark Milky Way decals that Mitch had patiently applied, and Helen's two quilts covering the bunk beds.

Mitch. Oh dear, there it was, one of those flashes that still came upon her unexpectedly. The cruise they planned to take, merely trying to decide which destination they would choose. They would have stood here in this same way, Mitch's arm probably around her waist, her body pressed against his. She released a long sigh—not of sadness—more of a loving acknowledgment to the husband who had been taken too soon from everyone who cared about him. She blew a kiss into the dark, smiling at the image, and turned from the railing, fatigue nibbling at her brain and body. Her cabin had a nice assortment of teabags along with small packets of coffee, and she was certain there was a chamomile among them. She had no doubt that she would sleep well.

# CHAPTER SEVEN

Helen and Mary Lou were in the same class on honing their skills with machine appliqué. Becky was in the hand appliqué session, and Phyllis would appear for the second class where the intent was to machine stitch a tropical tote. There were between twenty-five and the maximum of thirty women in each of the three rooms with the plan for the instructors to rotate through the classes. That way the women didn't have to make choices based on the instructor. The schedule was set for classes during the days at sea, although the rooms were open for anyone's use during other hours except for one to four a.m. when the cleaning crew cycled through that part of the ship. Helen had been surprised when she'd read that, but Wanda had explained, "The idea is for everyone to have as much fun as possible. You have to take into account that some people are early birds like you, some are night owls like Phyllis, and some are cruisers who have been to the ports before and prefer to stay on the ship instead of taking excursions. You get a real mix of attendees."

After chatting with a number of the quilters, Helen better understood the open scheduling. One woman, on her tenth cruise and familiar with all the ports, said she'd rather spend time completing the quilt she planned as a surprise for her youngest granddaughter. "The record-setter is a woman from Boynton Beach, Florida," she told Helen. "She's not with us this week. I think her next cruise will be her twenty-fifth. She lives with her oldest son and says this is the best way for them to get along. They each get a frequent break. She's been doing this for so long, she gets major discounts. And she's a teetotaler. You'd be surprised how inexpensive a cruise can be when you don't drink."

Helen had made a mental note to ask Wanda if she remembered the woman. The morning had been no different from at home where she rarely slept past six. Her eyes had fluttered open at five-thirty, a brief disorientation as to where she was. Trying to go back to sleep was out of the question—not with a chance to see the sunrise on her first full day at sea. Wrapped in the ship's comfortable robe, a mug of steaming coffee in hand, she walked onto the balcony and watched as the last vestige of the sky's pearl gray was replaced by pale pinks that deepened, the orange orb of the sun emerging from the water until the glare turned bright yellow, too intense to keep staring directly at it. Stirred by the beauty and her own intention of balancing the wonderful food she wanted to enjoy without guilt, Helen quickly donned tights, a long-sleeved T-shirt, and sneakers for an invigorating walk along the path laid out for just such purposes. She nodded in response to other walkers. While the gym was well-equipped and she suspected Becky was in there, she preferred the feel of the wind, the sensation of the sheer openness of the space. At breakfast, she skipped the Belgian waffle station, instead taking liberally from the artistically arranged platters of fresh fruit and having a made-to-order omelet packed with vegetables and lean ham.

"It's a bit different having the sewing machines, isn't it?" said Mary Lou, settling onto the chair at the machine on the table next to Helen. If Mary Lou had a late night, you wouldn't know it by looking at her face. She was her usual self, wearing a short set in canary yellow with white piping around the scooped neck of her blouse and the pockets and seams of her shorts.

"I know, but it makes perfect sense with this setup. You wouldn't make a lot of progress in three days with all hand-quilting, and if I can, I want to take a quilt top back as a special memento. Who knows for sure if I'll come on another one of these?"

"That's too ambitious for me. Other than the tote, I'm going to dabble in all the different classes. I want to learn technique instead of finishing a full project. Oh, did you get by the Sea-to-Sew Shop? It's really well-stocked."

"I plan to stop in this afternoon before the autograph party," Helen said, as Sonya Prince waved her hand at the front of the room for their attention.

Helen assumed all three rooms were basically arranged in the same manner with three rows of tables, five deep, two machines per table for a total seating of thirty. There was enough space to easily move among the tables, and two long arm machines were available against the back wall, one to the left and one to the right. A few paces from the machine on the left side of the room were four ironing boards with full-size irons. The right side held four open tables, slightly shorter than the ones with the machines that could be used for laying out a pattern, cutting, etc. Those tables did not have chairs, although there were extra chairs stacked in a nearby corner. Each side of the room also had a portable design wall, the medium fifty-four-by-fifty-four size from the look of it. That was something Rita had mentioned that she might buy since their house didn't have space for a dedicated quilting room and she liked to keep her dining room table set with a cloth, napkins, a centerpiece, and candles. Max had told her he'd been using a design wall for years.

"I wasn't expecting such a high-end machine," Mary Lou whispered. "I may have decided what my birthday gift will be."

Helen had to admit this machine was well beyond the rather basic model that she had at home, a machine that she was sentimentally attached to because it had been a Christmas present from Mitch. In truth, though, she had plenty of room for two machines, and this model was one year newer than Max's. In addition to the extension table and a free hand system, the stitch library was extensive and the walking foot was nice. The memory function could be useful as well as the automatic buttonhole function. There had been a discount coupon for the manufacturer in their welcome bag, and that might be the deciding factor.

In the familiar way of classes, the women's chatter quieted as they focused on their machines—conversations devolved into snippets rather than sentences. Sonya weaved around the room in response to questions or to pause and see how someone was coming along. Notwithstanding Helen's inclination for hand appliqué, she could see that with practice, the technique they worked with that morning could rival handwork. Sonya had explained that properly using a stabilizer was how to eliminate puckers and pulling at the fabric. That and becoming confident in pivoting around points and curves were important aspects to success. Helen had selected a basic starfish shape and a cutaway stabilizer to work with, knowing that she could use the square she intended to complete later in a number of different quilt ideas. She selected a zigzag stitch with a width about one-eighth-inch wide and took her time, knowing that once she had the physical feel of the steps, she could worry about speeding up the process.

When the session ended, there was a short break. Phyllis grinned a greeting when she passed Helen returning to the classroom. "Up at the crack of dawn, were you?"

Helen swept her hand toward the railing. "Technically, I suppose it was before. The sunrise was gorgeous."

"I plan to catch one of those, but it will be because I'm just going in to sleep after a full night of partying," her friend said, arching her eyebrows. "Contrary to popular belief, there are several men of the appropriate age on board. You simply have to know where to find them."

"I'm not really surprised," Helen laughed. "You can tell us all about it during lunch."

"Maybe not *all*," Phyllis said in that tone she used so often when the subject was men. "I wouldn't want to shock poor Becky." She tossed a happy wave and disappeared into the room adjacent to the one Helen and Mary Lou were in.

With Phyllis, one never knew if she was serious or teasing, and Helen had learned from a lifetime of friendship that either could be the case. On the other hand, Phyllis would also drop anything she was doing at a moment's notice if someone was in need. She was a frequent visitor to the long-term care facility where her grandmother had lived. She'd spent hours every week quilting with her grandmother until she was no longer able to handle a needle, then it was reading aloud to bring cheer through her favorite books. Unlike so many people who would have declared their duty over with the passing of their loved one, Phyllis continued her visits, focusing particularly on those residents who seemed to have few, if any, close friends and relatives. This was a side of Phyllis that not everyone understood.

"Oh, I see you went with the floral fabrics," Mary Lou said, holding up her packet of underwater prints mixed with solids of greens, blues, and yellows.

Pre-ordering the fabric packs for some of the classes had been part of the registration process, and Helen had debated about which one to select, deciding that tropical flowers were something she was likely to see a great deal of and would be a fitting souvenir. Of course, had she known at the time that she was going to be talked into taking a scuba class, maybe she would have chosen the underwater one instead. Well, that was certainly something she could get at a later time. The top for the lap quilt she was planning as part of the Borders to Borders class was a packet of seashell fabric; pink, beige, and pale yellow striped pieces; and corresponding solid colors. She had in mind to donate the quilt as part of the annual fund-raiser to benefit the animal shelter, but, as was frequently the situation, that could change in an instant depending on what occasion for gift-giving popped up. That was something she thought virtually all quilters had in common. You would find a fabric that spoke to you and then discover that it was the exact match for an individual or event that you hadn't thought about when you acquired it. She'd lost count of the number of times that had happened to her.

Despite her belief that she couldn't possibly be hungry, by lunch, Helen was looking forward to what enticements would be presented. As Helen and Mary Lou entered the dining room, they spotted Becky and Phyllis at a table with a trio of women. Becky jumped up and came to them with an excited smile. "Oh, come see who we're sitting with. You are so going to love this story."

Phyllis introduced them to Allison and Vanessa Cuthbert and Georgina MacDougall. They were unquestionably related. "Let's hit the buffet, then you can hear all about this," she suggested to general nods.

Three generations of quilters in a family wasn't all that unusual, although it was heartening to see the tradition continued.

After they had all filled their plates Becky lifted a hand toward Georgina. "Do you want to start?"

The older woman smiled and patted her mouth. "Actually, as soon as she finishes that bite, I think Vanessa should." Her voice held the sound of the Tidewater region.

If Helen was an accurate judge of ages, she would guess Georgina at not quite seventy. Her daughter Allison looked to be in her early forties, and granddaughter Vanessa couldn't be much more than twenty. They were all petite, none of them taller than Mary Lou. Their eyes were the same shade of green, and hair color ranged from ash to honey blonde to frosted. They were thin, just a shade shy of skinny—bird-like came to mind. Their bodies were toned, however, and Helen wouldn't be surprised to learn that race-walking or cycling was another activity they shared. The daughter and granddaughter probably had once been cheerleaders or gymnasts.

"We're from close to Richmond, and I'm a senior at the University of Virginia," Vanessa said, confirming that geographical hint. "Majoring in sociology with a minor in English. I'm planning to work in a nonprofit," she added and inclined her head toward her grandmother. "I've written a paper on the quilting tradition in our family. Since quilting has always been important to us, and we know that my great-grandmother quilted, I thought it would be fun to see how far back we could trace that, why it was a tradition in my family, and how that related to the Americana craft in general."

Helen could see the application from a sociology perspective. Family strength was an underlying element for many quilters.

"Mamma started me with quilting when I was nine," Georgina said. "My grandmother passed away when Mamma was a teenager, and for some reason, it never occurred to me to ask anything about her as a quilter. We had a section from a really old quilt that was in a frame because of its age, but no one could remember exactly why we had it, only that it was something we should keep and take care of."

"The Internet is a wonderful thing," Vanessa said with a fond smile to her grandmother. "You can find an amazing number of connections that you might not otherwise."

Helen's curiosity was starting to tingle. Becky was right; it was an intriguing story. Vanessa had discovered that quilters dated back in their family to the mass immigration of the Scots as a result of the destruction of the clan system after the Battle of Culloden in 1746 when Bonnie Prince Charlie and his forces were defeated. Two quilts were among the limited personal belongings that crossed the Atlantic with her ancestors. As those were worn to tatters, pieces were kept to be incorporated into a new quilt. Furthermore—one of those academic phrases that slipped out—when the family set down new roots, the father was fortunate to have changed his agriculture leanings into success as a blacksmith. Their status as middle class was solidified, and quilts from his wife were acknowledged as some of the finest in the area. Her products found their way into many fine homes, and she carefully crafted a new quilt incorporating the pieces from the ones brought "from the Old Country" and framed the other scrap. The new quilt depicted the family's journey and fresh start in their adopted country, a quilt that was described in a letter to a cousin whose marriage had taken her to Ohio. As was the fate of so many, however, the Civil War tore the country apart, and the MacDougall family was not immune from tragedy. That quilt handed down from previous generations, the framed piece, and a few other items deemed precious were hidden from constant marauders then finally entrusted to a neighbor who was fleeing the chaos to go west to Ohio. There a cousin took possession of the bundle of keepsakes. In the more than a century that followed with untimely deaths, marriages, and remarriages, the origin of the quilt faded, but the quilt itself had remarkably survived and been preserved. Fascinated with the letters she'd discovered, Vanessa had tracked the quilt to the distant relatives in Ohio and arranged to have it restored to the direct descendants of Maureen MacDougall.

Allison spoke up as Vanessa paused for a sip of water. "You know the television show, *Uncovering Family Heirlooms?*"

"Oh, yes, it's a favorite," Helen said quickly and brightened. "Y'all are going to be on the show?"

"They're coming next month to film the segment," Georgina said proudly. "Vanessa's professor knows one of the show's staff members."

"Well, it's certainly a great fit," Helen said, embracing the tale, thinking how easily the heirloom could have been destroyed or never found, and yet, it was brought to light through a set of circumstances that might not have been set into motion if Vanessa had been a biology major like Tricia instead of going into sociology.

"Goodness, all this talking and we're coming up on the afternoon classes," Georgina said, seeing several groups of women flowing toward the door. "Will we see y'all at the autograph party later?"

Helen pushed her chair from the table. "I'm looking forward to it. I have all of Laura Baker's books, and I waited to buy this one because I thought we might be taking the cruise."

Phyllis nudged Vanessa as they fell into step. "With minoring in English, can we expect to see the saga of the family's quilt in a book soon?"

The young woman's laugh reminded Helen of Tricia. "I did keep careful notes, and I wouldn't count that out as a possibility. But graduating this coming summer is my first priority."

"Finding a job comes in as a close second," Allison said when the parties split for their respective rooms. "A pleasure to meet y'all," she added in parting.

"You, too," Helen said, struck by the thought that while none of their quilts could match the extraordinary circumstances of the MacDougall one, there were cherished family memories attached to several that had come from her grandmother. She should sit with her mamma and gather as much information as she could to chronicle how the quilts came to be. After all, who knew how many generations they might last? She didn't expect that Russell would be an only grandchild for long, and there was a strong likelihood that at least one grandchild would take to quilting. A journal of the family tradition—now that was a product of the cruise that she hadn't planned on, but what an excellent idea it was.

# CHAPTER EIGHT

Helen wasn't surprised to see that she seemed to be the oldest in the scuba class, although seven of the ten were closer to her age than to that of the young couple who appeared to be in a newly married state. Not quite the honeymoon glow, yet still those lingering touches as if they couldn't get enough of one another. She hoped it was a sentiment they would keep even when the touches became less frequent, when a slow smile over a cup of coffee and a kiss blown as one headed out the door conveyed the strength of their love.

"Isn't this cool?" Becky's reminder of their real purpose cut through Helen's dip into incurable romanticism.

"I feel a bit awkward," she admitted. They had been through the initial part of the class with only the mask, snorkel, and fins as Tommy and Claire, a lithe Bahamian who looked as if the scuba gear was second nature to her, had explained the principles of diving to them. They had taken great care with fitting the masks and working through the need to breathe in and out of their mouths instead of nose as was normal. Deep, even breaths were the key, no need to be in a hurry, let the body relax. Those who were unfamiliar with snorkeling swam a few laps up and down the pool to get them comfortable before they approached the gear waiting on the side of the pool for the next step.

Becky had swum alongside her, "Don't duck your head and get the tip of the snorkel in the water," she said helpfully when Helen had come up with water pouring through the tube and into her mouth. "Just lay your face in the water and float like when you were a kid." Becky had been snorkeling on a previous vacation and assured Helen that she was doing fine.

With everyone now familiar with snorkeling, they stood in the shallow end of the pool, strapped into their vests with a tank on the back, the regulators held loosely in their hands as Tommy grinned. "Okay, you are about to accomplish the most difficult step in diving."

Helen felt her forehead pucker. What, this soon? They were only in the pool.

"Taking that first breath when you are underwater can be very unsettling," he continued. "But, and I cannot emphasize this too much—you never hold your breath in diving, You breathe in and out through your mouth, just as we have done with the snorkel. So, put the regulator in and take a few breaths. Here we go."

Helen fitted the mouthpiece, stretching her lips and clamping down probably more tightly than she needed to, the sound of inhaling and exhaling noticeable. She sank onto her knees, the water coming over her head and suddenly realized that she couldn't inhale. Oh Lord, something was wrong with the equipment. She popped up, yanking the regulator out and taking the mask from her face.

Tommy moved in front of her immediately. "Couldn't inhale?" His eyes were encouraging, his voice calm. "It's a very common reaction. You learn to hold your breath underwater as a child, and your mind isn't ready to let go of that. We'll take a few seconds, and it will be fine." Helen saw that Claire was speaking with another woman who'd had the same problem.

After a few moments, Helen tried again. Tommy's confidence in her did the trick. Helen mimicked him, replacing her mask, putting the regulator in again, taking three breaths in-out-in-out-in-out, the air flowing easily. This time she went under, her eyes locked onto Tommy's, the momentary paralysis gone as if it had never happened. He gave her the signal they had demonstrated of the forefinger and thumb in a circle to indicate that she was "okay," and she turned slightly to see Becky breathing away, waiting patiently. The entire process had taken only a minute or two.

"You didn't have any trouble," Helen said as they emerged, their difficult step completed.

Becky grinned. "I had been warned about that beforehand. One of the women in our morning class loves to dive; she's planning to dive in all the ports. Says she only takes the tropical quilting cruises so she can enjoy both activities."

Helen realized it was silly to be embarrassed and refocused her attention on Tommy for the rest of the lesson. That afternoon, they would be going ashore to a scuba company that was taking them on a real dive. "With conditions like we have today, it will be like swimming in an aquarium," Tommy cheerfully reported. He also advised against eating heavily at lunch since even though the seas were calm, people sometimes reacted differently than they expected to in the smaller boat that would take them to the dive site.

They were docked on the Dutch side of St. Martin where an agreement centuries before had divided the island with the French, thus the dual designation of St. Martin and Sint Maarten. Phyllis and Mary Lou were headed to the famous shopping district in Philipsburg where jewelry and other stores lined the narrow streets. The district, where there was no sales tax and deals were to be had, would be jammed with bargain seekers. From what they'd been told, Europeans flocked there to avoid the high sales taxes of their own respective countries.

The dive shop was close to the pier. The forms they'd filled out were in Claire's folder, and different sets of gear were waiting for them when they arrived. It reminded Helen somewhat of the surf shops in Myrtle Beach where they had vacationed occasionally when the kids were young. It was smaller, of course, and not devoted to touristy souvenirs, but the sense of cheerful adventure surrounded the staff as they double-checked the fit of gear and answered questions about what the divers might see. Sharks? Oh no, not unless they were lucky. Helen was pretty sure that she didn't consider that as something to look forward to.

Despite the heat of the day, which had them all sweating and "glistening," as one woman put it, the staff suggested that they put their short wetsuits on, pulled just to their waists, because the boat ride was a scant fifteen minutes and it was easier to don the tight suit in the shop than on a moving boat. Helen wiggled into hers, thinking it was like the days of her youth before pantyhose replaced the need for girdles. Heavens, she was probably the only woman in this particular group that remembered those.

Once they were on the way, though, Helen set aside thoughts other than how beautiful the setting was. Azure, aquamarine, turquoise, cerulean, multiple shades of blue applied to the water and sky alike—blues that could not be pinpointed as a single color, shades that merged and flowed together, lightening here, deepening there. Mountains in the distance looked as if they stretched to meet sandy beaches, dense foliage in greens with scattered houses seen. Like many of the islands, St. Martin had only a few towns and small villages nestled amid acres of untouched land.

"And here we are," Tommy said as the captain brought the boat to a stop and the mate secured the line to a large orange mooring ball. Helen peeked over the side to see fish on the reef system below. Tommy issued final reminders about respecting the reef, that careless strikes from their fins could damage the fragile coral. "Please remember to not take anything. Just relax and enjoy yourselves."

"Easy for him to say," was Helen's thought as she took the step off the boat into the water following Becky. She stayed calm at the tiny jolt, bobbing back up to the surface, grabbing the line floating behind the boat. Claire was away from the rope, counting the students as they queued, waiting to descend in a group. She asked for the "Okay" sign from each, and Helen was comfortable enough to flash the signal. Tommy came in last, his regulator at the ready after he, too, did a quick check of everyone.

"Let's go under then," he said cheerfully, pressing the button to release air from his vest and enabling him to sink below the surface.

Becky patted Helen's arm, nodding that she was ready, and the water closed over their heads, their feet pointing down at a large patch of sand where they landed, placed into a semi-circle resting on their knees. The cloud of sand stirred by their movement quickly dissipated, and Helen realized that while her anxiety was not completely gone, her breathing was even, and the sights around her were incredible. A school of some sort of yellow striped fish passed by them, as tiny ones of bright blue, yellow and purple, and silver darted away. Red, yellow, and green coral decorated the reef that was almost within touching distance, not that she would do that.

Claire and Tommy divided the group just as they had in the pool, then they faced each student exchanging the "okay" signal in preparation for their underwater tour. Although the equipment still felt rather awkward, the weightlessness of the water took hold, and when Helen came off of her knees and stretched out into the horizontal swimming posture they'd practiced, she couldn't help but smile. That was to smile as much as she could and keep the mouthpiece firmly clamped in place. Everything was working correctly, and oh my, another school of fish, and a lovely multicolored one flitted in front of her eyes, gone before she had a good look at it. She glanced over at Becky to her left, the younger woman bringing her hands together in soundless clapping. Tommy's hand pointing up caught her attention. A turtle! A turtle rising from behind a rock, languidly swimming toward the surface. It was about the size of a hubcap and so graceful. What were those large silver fish that zipped past them? She recalled seeing a fish book on the boat; she would have to look them up as soon as she could. Oh my, what a strange-looking fish that was—long and skinny. With happy amazement, Helen realized that she was diving, scuba diving, in the ocean. As they toured the reef that meandered in more or less a long S-curve, she stopped worrying about what might happen. She relaxed and let go, delighting in the colors, shapes, and movement. It was like being in the huge aquariums they'd visited except she was inside, right there with the fish and other creatures. How pretty the coral and tube-like things were. When Tommy tapped the face of his instrument to tell them to check how much air they had left in their tanks, it was hard to believe that she was at the half-way mark. She knew that was fine, but where had the time gone? Tommy was soon leading them slowly upward, her excitement building to be able to express her pleasure. Mindful of the possibility of falling backward as the crew assisted her onto the boat, she waited until she was safely seated to remove the regulator, the mate helping her unsnap the vest and slide out of the gear.

He must have read the expression on her face. "A good dive?"

"Oh, yes," she said

Becky held her hand up for a high-five. "Can you believe that? Wasn't that great?"

Helen laughed. "Was I nervous about this earlier? Why?"

Becky brushed her fingers through her wet hair. "Oh, man, I never thought anything could compare to horses for me, but, wow, that was really something."

"Okay, everyone," Tommy said to the smiling faces. "Terrific job—I was impressed with how well you did."

He took them through a quick discussion of what they'd seen, answering a flurry of questions, while the crew and Claire set them up for the second dive that would bring their adventure to a close.

Helen was mildly amused at how eager Becky was to plunge in again, even though she too felt entirely differently at this stage than she had only hours before. What would it be like to go through the whole course? How long did it take to be as comfortable as the instructors were who had pirouetted and tumbled about as they shepherded their charges through another reef system that was a short ride from the first? This site had what they called coral heads—large segments of rock and coral with expanses of sand between them. Tommy pointed to an area that looked like a small hill, and then with a sudden motion, the hill moved, a big stingray emerging to "fly" away, no doubt annoyed at the intrusion. Helen had learned that one of the colorful fish she'd admired was a queen angel, another a rainbow parrot, and the funny-shaped long one was a trumpet fish that could change colors as part of camouflage. There were more schools of fish on this reef, and so many tiny, bright ones in one spot that it looked almost like a shower of glitter. No question about it, there would be an underwater themed quilt in her near future.

It wasn't until they returned to the ship and she stepped into a hot shower that she felt the twinges in her back, neck, shoulder, and legs that Claire had mentioned to her. "You've been using new sets of muscles all day, plus there were a lot of little bursts of adrenaline with the experience. Some aches will kick in, and you may experience a little stiffness in the morning, but it isn't anything to worry about. A couple of aspirin or your preferred pain reliever will do the trick."

Dinner—tonight's decision was Italian—rippled with exchanges of what they'd done. Mary Lou's necklace with a quarter-carat round diamond in the center and five "points" encrusted in diamond chips creating a star-effect was lovely and the price definitely less than she would have paid even on sale at home. Phyllis had been in the mood for a new outfit, having made the decision to pack light and bring clothes home as mementos. She laughingly said her choice today was in honor of Helen and Becky. It was a gauzy azure blue tunic that fell to her knees. On it was the depiction of a reef complete with corals and colorful fish very much like what they'd encountered. She'd paired it with a matching narrow ankle-length skirt in a shade darker solid blue, and the effect was stunning.

"We want to hear all about your day," Phyllis said, after they ordered an antipasto platter.

Helen had to admit that she was ravenous. She inclined her head to Becky. "She took to it like the proverbial duck to water, but I was a little nervous at first."

Becky smiled, her eyes spilling excitement. "Well, I did have the advantage of having been snorkeling before. The class part in the morning was okay, but when we actually dropped into the water, man, that was something else." She made an imaginary circle around Phyllis. "We saw that, and that, and that."

Phyllis plucked at the tunic. "These fish?"

"You bet," Helen joined in. "And a sea turtle and a stingray. It's just really hard to describe how beautiful it was. Remember the tropical reef exhibit at the Atlanta aquarium? It really was exactly like that. Oh, no sharks, though," she added.

Becky grinned. "Somebody asked about that, and Tommy, he's the main instructor, said they don't see sharks very often on the close-in reefs. They come out mostly as it gets dark."

Helen held up her hand. "As much fun as I had today, I don't feel in the least deprived by not seeing a shark."

The dinner flowed in the smoothness of friends happily sharing their experiences, the opposite sides of a coin with the bustle of bouncing from shop to shop and the quiet of the underwater world where the only noises had been the bubbles exhaled by the divers.

"The trio in the lounge last night was great, but there's a torch singer in the piano bar that I was told is fabulous," Phyllis said during a light dessert of lemon-infused sorbet. "How about we catch her, then we can do one of the later sets with the trio?"

Helen shook her head gently, hiding a yawn behind her napkin. "Maybe tomorrow, I'm beat. I can't believe how much energy you have after being out all day."

Phyllis tilted her head, that devilish look in her eyes. "Honey, we're only here for a week, and as much as I love Wallington, interesting night life is not something we have a lot of. This ship is as good as going off to somewhere like New Orleans, and I'm taking full advantage of it."

Mary Lou touched a finger to her new necklace. It sparkled even in the dimmer light against her classic burgundy-colored, silk blend sheath, which fit her body in a way that showed her trim figure without being overly tight. "I have to agree that it is nice to dress up. I'll go hear the singer, but that may be it for me. We'll see."

"They're showing a Helen Mirren movie that I haven't seen yet, so that's where I'm headed," Becky said. "Then it's off to bed for me."

Phyllis made shooing motions with her hands. "To each her own. You early birds remember to tip-toe past my cabin in the morning."

They hugged and kissed in parting. Helen did not linger by the railing tonight. She wasn't sure she had the energy to climb stairs to go up to the upper deck—a soothing cup of chamomile tea on her balcony sounded like a better option. In one sense, it wasn't only fatigue. As she'd thought about the day, how amazing their brief stays underwater were, it had brought Max to mind. When he said he would be happy to have another dive buddy, had he meant that as merely a throwaway comment, or had he been serious? She could certainly see why he enjoyed diving, and it wasn't a hobby they could very well engage in around Wallington. She assumed he would plan trips to the Caribbean considering all the direct flights from Atlanta. Did he envision her going along for a vacation to let her take a full scuba course?

She mused about it while the tea steeped then carried it out to the balcony, the hot beverage's warmth substituting for a wrap. Even though the overhead view from the balcony wasn't as spectacular as being higher on the ship, and she couldn't see the moon from her angle, there were plenty of stars in the segment of sky in front of her. The breeze was mild enough so that she was comfortable with her hands curled around the mug, which she held chest-high, breathing in the mixed scents of tea and ocean. A delicious calm settled over her, the dark beyond the lights of the ship impenetrable. She couldn't see through it, and thousands of years ago man had looked to the moon and stars to navigate, then taken that basic knowledge and created technology to make it easier. Here she was, trusting in both that technology and the skilled captain to get them to where they were going. It was a bit like the future, wasn't it? You charted a course, and despite not being able to see ahead, you moved in the direction that you believed was correct. Yes, a storm might blow in, but for the moment, it was peaceful and quiet. With another big yawn, Helen smiled into the night. How glad she was that she'd come on this trip.

# CHAPTER NINE

It amazed Helen that the days of the cruise were whizzing by despite the fact that it was definitely relaxing. The sensation as if time was literally dissolving had to be because of the variety of events, one that followed another, and the constant flow of other quilters as they met each other and shared stories, techniques, and learned about their often diverse backgrounds. Maybe it was the almost sensory overload of food and tropical settings with slight variations in each port. All she knew was that here they were, with only two stops left and then they would be on the way back to Fort Lauderdale.

It was sunrise—that spectacular sky she'd come to enjoy every morning, the flavorful coffee slowly sipped in anticipation of what the day would bring. It wasn't that she was being lured into wanting "a life in paradise" with dreams of chucking away what she had and escaping to one of the charming islands, although perhaps if she faced snow-bound winters, she would feel differently. This was more the chance to remember the need at times to break away from the familiar and reach out to sample what was, from a practical point, a mere day's travel away if she wanted to fly instead of taking a cruise. She'd noticed a number of direct flights from Atlanta when they were in the airport, and if she didn't want to cross the ocean for whatever reason, there were the beaches of the entire Gulf and southeastern coast reaching down into the tropical Florida Keys. She didn't plan to dash about on vacations as much as Phyllis did, but actually taking one or two a year was certainly within her ability. Without recognizing it, she had set aside the notion of traveling after Mitch died. They'd talked so often about where to go together that it hadn't seemed to be something she wanted to do alone. This trip was helping Helen see that she might be ready to travel a bit, too. She had possible traveling companions in Phyllis and even her sister, Eloise, whose sons were becoming a larger part of her catering business.

Helen swallowed the last of the coffee, ready for her morning walk and an early shore excursion of snorkeling. This was one day where their group was to be completely scattered. Becky was definitely going horseback riding, Mary Lou had signed up for the island art and museum tour, and Phyllis was, not surprisingly, on the tour that included the rum factory. Helen planned to snorkel, then catch a ten-minute boat ride back to the ship, dash in for a quick shower, and return to the island. She wanted to poke about the little town of Frederiksted in St. Croix and tour the nearby botanical garden. The small town's market was set up just outside the pier, and the little fort was just steps away.

Helen had her morning routine down, and within minutes, she was briskly making her way around the ship, gazing out across the extraordinarily blue water to the still-silent town. According to her research, this was the west side of the island. She saw a few vehicles slowly driving on "the wrong side of the street," as she thought of it. Despite the fact that St. Croix had been part of the U.S. Virgin Islands and an American territory since right around World War I, the British style of driving had never been changed. That seemed odd considering that Spain, Holland, Denmark, and even the Knights of Malta had flown flags at one time or the other over the islands after the native Indian tribes had been dispersed. She'd read that the Danes, who had established the first towns and plantations on St. Thomas, then St. John, and finally St. Croix, were the ones who left their mark architecturally, and the islands continued to be a favorite destination for Danish tourists. Well, St. Croix certainly offered an escape from their snowy winters.

The larger town of Christiansted was on the east side of the island. On the west side, Frederiksted was really only two streets wide from a commercial perspective, the main street lined with mostly restored buildings and a lovely walking area across the street fronting the water. The fort, painted a deep red, was to the left as you looked toward the town, and a series of beach bars and restaurants stretched beyond that. There were fewer houses than Helen would have imagined. She could see several houses dotting the mountains, though, with what must be incredible views. Living right on a beach would have advantages, but what would it be like to step outside with the panorama of the Caribbean all around? The airline magazine had contained advertisements for renting houses like that rather than staying in a hotel, and Helen could see the appeal.

Helen's plan for the sequence of her activities played out exactly as she intended, although by mid-afternoon when she waved cheerfully to the van driver who had taken them to the St. George Village Botanical Gardens, she was feeling the effect of the full schedule. The snorkeling had been wonderful, as promised, with the water as calm as a lake. The reefs, festooned with beautiful corals and what she was told were lavender sea fans, had been teeming with tropical fish, although none very large which was fine with her. She had the chance to once again see the parrot fish with the rainbow of colors that gave them their name, the eye-catching queen angels, brilliant yellow and black ones called rock beauties, and schools of snappers that had thus far managed to stay off a dinner menu. In what Helen took to be sort of a parting gift from the underwater world, a pair of eagle rays swooped across one section of the reef before they disappeared into the distance. They were smaller in size than stingrays, darker gray and had white spots on their backs.

After snorkeling, Helen headed on to St. Croix's sixteen-acre botanical gardens. Although they could hardly compare to gardens such as Georgia's own Callaway Gardens, the area was still nicely arranged and the variety of trees, shrubs, and flowers was intriguing as green parrots squawked, hummingbirds flitted about, and numerous species of butterflies hovered among hibiscus and other tropical blossoms. Their guide was a recently retired history teacher who had relocated back from Virginia to be with her aging parents. She was also an herbalist with fascinating tidbits about homeopathic treatments and beauty products that were common throughout the Caribbean. They strolled at a leisurely pace, a few individuals breaking away to go off on their own. Helen asked for the guide's card when the tour ended at the gift shop. She thought that perhaps Juanita at Always Fresh Farms might be interested in some of the lotions and soaps that the guide had mentioned. Juanita's concoctions had become quite popular, and she might want to experiment with some new ones.

As expected, the walk through Fort Frederik didn't take long, and Helen had smilingly moved among the vendors, not overly interested in their wares. By this time of the day, the crowd had thinned, most shoppers presumably having struck their bargains earlier in the day. In fact, several of the stalls were empty. She bought a silver cuff watch for Wanda with pieces of polished abalone embedded in it and a pair of blue Larimar earrings for Tricia. The stone, found predominantly in the Caribbean, was similar to turquoise in a softer shade of blue.

As for a souvenir for herself, some lovely scarves being sold by an old woman near the end of the line of booths caught Helen's eye. The scarves beckoned, draped on hooks so that they moved with the mild breeze coming off the water. As she approached the booth, Helen realized the old woman seemed to be in a heated discussion with a young woman. The discussion broke off when they sensed Helen's presence. The young woman turned away toward the back corner of the booth, anger still stamped on her face, as the older woman turned and smiled broadly at Helen, a gold tooth prominent among others that had not seen much dental care. It looked as if her hair was cropped short, and she had a scarf of gold and orange tied around her head in a modified turban with a section draped over her left shoulder. The cotton caftan she was wearing was a deeper orange with streaks of multiple shades of gold overlaid as a print. The woman might be five foot two if she stretched, her brown face creased with wrinkles, her eyes like mahogany. It was a warm face, though, despite whatever the emotion had been in the brief eruption with the young woman who was now striding away, one final scowl sent over her shoulder.

"A scarf to remember your time on our island is what you need," the woman said in a voice with the distinctive island lilt Helen had come to recognize. "I make them myself. The dyes are from our own plants, a technique from my great-grandmother that we have kept a family secret."

The beauty of the scarves may have attracted Helen, but the idea of handcrafted, especially if what the woman said was true about it being a family tradition, was irresistible. What a fitting follow-up to her visit to the botanical garden. "There's no hurry, lady, and Mama Marie will tell you anything you want to know about my scarves, except the secret, of course."

Helen could sense that the woman—Mama Marie—wanted to share her personal history, and she spent almost half an hour hearing of the plants involved in the process, how the widowed woman with children to feed had first come up with the idea of scarves for the wealthy ladies of the plantations. They could not be of ordinary material, but needed instead to have a silken feel. It had taken much experimentation to achieve that feel as well as the striking depth of colors in the fabric that would stand up to many washings. "You seem like a nice lady. I can make an extra bargain if you buy more," Mama Marie said, as Helen thought of how easily they would be to pack and how perfect for the women in the circle who couldn't come on the trip.

"You have a deal," Helen said, and Mama Marie grinned widely at the prospect of selling half her stock. Some of the prints were Impressionist-like in whorls, while others were more distinct with leaf or flower patterns. All of the colors were vivid. Helen glanced over at the square table in the corner where a gorgeous purple piece protruded from a small paper bag. She didn't see a corresponding purple scarf among the choices. "That's really pretty," she said and pointed. "It is another one?"

The woman turned, puzzled, then back at Helen and smiled again. "Oh, no, I sold those this morning." She reached for the bag and brought it over. "When I make the scarves, there are bits left at times—see?" She pulled short lengths of material out, not realizing what this meant to a quilter. She must have read the expression on Helen's face. "You like this?"

"Goodness, yes," Helen said, thinking of how many quilts she could incorporate the fabric into.

Mama Marie beamed. "For you, my nice lady—it is yours; take the bag as my gift."

Helen pulled an extra ten from her wallet. "No, please, I would be glad to pay for it."

The woman waved her hand in refusal. "You be sure and tell all of your friends when they come here to find Mama Marie."

Helen cocked her head, suddenly thinking of Susanna, the fabric artist, and her successful online business. "Mama Marie, do you have the ability to get to a computer? You know about selling through the Internet?"

Mama Marie placed the scarves into a bag, adding the bag of remnants. She shrugged and then lifted one finger. "My grandson, Kevin, he is a smart young man—will be finishing college this year. He said the same thing to me." She glanced down the street, a frown briefly tugging at her mouth. "He's a good boy, not like some of the grandchildren who don't know to stay away from bad people." She shook her head sharply as if ridding a thought, and her smile was back in place. "Kevin, he said he could run the computer and send my scarves all over the world. I do not know how this could be."

Helen laughed, taking her package. "Well, I think Kevin might be right. If you have his telephone number and don't mind giving it to me, I have a friend named Susanna who can call and talk to him about it."

Mama Marie shrugged good-naturedly, no doubt assuming that Helen wasn't serious. "Sure, why not?" She wrote in a cramped hand on the back of Helen's receipt, patting her hand when she gave it to her. "You have a good trip to your home."

"Oh, I'll leave you my name and number in case he wants to call me first," Helen said in what was almost an after-thought. She had no idea if connecting Mama Marie with Susanna was the least bit practical, but it might be. Helen's willingness to leave her telephone number would be an indication to the grandson that she hadn't been merely making polite conversation. Not that she understood how to do anything with Internet sales, but perhaps the younger generation who were comfortable with Internet marketing could work something out. After bidding farewell, Helen noticed that more of the stalls were beginning to close. She ambled the short distance to the ship, where clusters of passengers were coming from all directions. As she neared the entrance to the pier, she had the strangest sensation of being watched. She slowed and swiveled her head, thinking that one of their group might be hailing her, but despite familiar-looking faces, no one was reaching out to her. Hmm, that girl behind a knot of women seemed to be staring. Did she know her? Helen took a tentative step and it clicked into place—the young woman from Mama Marie's stall. Had Helen forgotten something? Seeing Helen looking at her, the woman pivoted sharply and dashed across the street. Odd, but before she could give it more thought, Becky's voice cut through the air.

"Hey there, how was your busy day?" Becky, her green cotton top damp with sweat and a bottle of water clutched in her hand, waved from the front of a white van taxi. "You done with everything?"

"Yes, and it was great. You look as if you had fun."

"Fabulous," she replied, falling into step and walking with Helen onto the ship. "The husband and wife who run the stables are wonderful—left the cold of Connecticut for a vacation here and promptly fell in love with the place. They bought the stables from an older couple ready to sell, and it was the proverbial match made in heaven. They've been at it for about five years now, and they've expanded into a small ranch as well as the stables. The horses are well cared for and truly gentle—not that I need that, but a lot of people do," she added and swept her hand toward the mountains. "It was great. We started at the stable in the valley close to the rain forest, went up through the trails, down across the road onto a beach for a drink break, then along a ridge with a view to die for." She swigged the last of her water. "I need a cool shower and a colder drink."

Helen glanced at her watch. "We're dining with Georgina, Allison, and Vanessa again this evening. We took the second seating since all of us had plans in different parts of the island."

Becky paused at the door of her cabin. "Yes, and I want to hear about the snorkeling, but I've got to tell you that I worked up an appetite. I think that one trip to the ice cream bar is in order. You want to join me? It won't take me more than a few minutes to shower and change."

Helen laughed and patted her stomach with her free hand. "That, I'll pass on. We're having Spanish cuisine tonight, and I've been told the flan with a cinnamon caramel sauce is not to be missed. I can't manage two desserts in one day."

Becky unlocked her door. "Okay, see you at dinner if I don't bump into you before then."

Helen realized that she was sticky, too, despite having had a shower earlier. Maybe another shower was in order, but, first, she wanted to lay the scarves out to get a better idea of which one to give to whom—or should she let each woman pick? She also was eager to look at the scraps of fabric. On the other hand, since they weren't dining until the second seating, she could pop up to the quilting shop. It had been quite crowded the few attempts she'd made to go in, and this might be a lull as passengers straggled back from excursions and the early diners would be getting dressed. Yes, that would be perfect. The shop wasn't large, although it was nicely stocked from what her quilting companions had said and it wasn't as if she was dripping with sweat. Besides, an extra set of going up and down the stairs would be good for her. There was no way she was going to resist the flan tonight, and she had promised Phyllis that she would try the octopus that was alleged to be delicious. She might as well burn off a few extra calories in preparation.

# CHAPTER TEN

"Hi, do you mind if I walk with you?"

Helen, who was walking off last night's flan, turned her head at the voice. She'd heard the footsteps coming up and moved a little to the right to provide room. The girl—no, young woman—looked to be a few years younger than Tricia. The nearly waif-like face, slender body, and height shorter than Helen by a couple of inches, she looked familiar. Her jet black hair in a short layered cut seemed a bit too dark for her complexion, although it could be natural.

"Sure, I've got about another twenty minutes to go," Helen said lightly, now placing the woman. Usually she was just starting out as Helen was finishing her daily walks. They had nodded in passing before. "You're on the same deck as we are, I think."

"Yes, the stateroom right by the stairs," she replied. Like Helen, she was wearing navy blue tights and sneakers. Her bright red tank top, however, was far from Helen's over-sized T-shirt, which came almost to her knees. Then again, she wasn't a grandmother by any stretch of the imagination. "It's hard to believe that the cruise is practically over, isn't it?"

"I agree," Helen said. The pink and gold of sunrise had already smoothed into another morning of soft blue with a yellow sun mellowed by thin coverings of clouds that would soon disappear to intensify the sun's glare and harden the color of the sky.

"You're with the quilting group, aren't you?"

"Yes, there are around one hundred quilters total. I'm with a group of four from our quilting circle in Wallington, Georgia. I'm Helen Crowder."

"Georgia, that's your accent," the girl said in a flat Midwestern voice. She pointed to her chest. "Des Moines, Iowa. I'm here with a girlfriend who won the cruise in a contest and her sister had to back out at the last minute." She grinned before Helen could comment. "It wasn't a bad thing, though. Mandy's sister got a big promotion at work and had to go to a conference in like San Diego instead."

"Well, I'm glad to hear that your good luck wasn't due to someone else's misfortune."

"Oh, I'm Brianna, by the way."

They were approaching the flight of stairs to the top deck. Brianna stepped back to let Helen precede her, both women silent as they climbed.

"Have you always been a quilter?"

An older couple several yards ahead moved slowly, taking in the fresh air at a pace that would give them a gentle workout. "Yes, it was something that I learned from my grandmother and mother, and I'm happy to say that my daughter, Tricia, is taking it up again. That is when she can fit it into her schedule."

"Oh, wow, that's nice," Brianna said with what sounded like a slight catch to her voice. She gestured toward the open water. "I knew they had themes for cruising, but I guess I never thought about quilting being one of them. I've seen the groups coming out of the classes, and we were at dinner last night with some of the women. It looks like everyone is having a good time."

The breeze was stronger at the higher level of the ship, and it wicked away the thin film of sweat Helen was feeling. "It has been a lot of fun. Do you do crafts?"

Brianna shook her head rapidly, then slowed a little, her tone edged with a note of hesitation. "Uh, not exactly. Do you mind if I ask you something?"

Helen dropped her pace and turned her head, alerted to an unspoken plea that she instantly recognized as a lead-in to something potentially serious. "It's a beautiful view up here, isn't it? Why don't we pause for a few minutes? You have a question about quilting? Or perhaps something else?"

The young woman swung toward the railing, a definite sheepish expression now visible. "Uh, yes, both, I guess. I hope you don't think that I'm intruding."

Helen's curiosity was piqued. "I'm not sure what you mean, but I do hope that I can help." Helen positioned herself with her right foot against the railing, angled to face Brianna who nodded as if Helen had already answered a question.

"I've noticed that, even though most of the women I've seen are older, there are some around my age. Did everyone start quilting like you did—when they were really young?"

"Goodness, no," Helen said. "Quilting is often passed down through generations, but a lot of women—and increasingly there are men, too—don't take it up until later. That's one of the great things about it—there are so many simple patterns to follow that you can begin at almost any age and be able to produce something in a short amount of time and then build on those basic steps." She cocked her head waiting for what she thought the real question was.

Brianna smiled slowly, almost as if seeing something in the distance other than seagulls. Then she shifted her focus to Helen. "That's good to know. See, it has to do with my gran."

"She's a quilter?"

"I think so," the younger woman said quietly. "See, the thing is that, well, I haven't seen her since I was little—I mean like about five years old."

Helen kept her voice soft. "She lives a distance from you?" She thought that would be a safe way to put it.

"Not exactly," Brianna said. "It's no more than two hundred miles, but well, my mom . . . well, something happened a long time ago and my mom left home and they haven't really spoken since then."

"Ah," Helen replied.

"Look, I don't want to get into this long story," Brianna said quickly. "The truth is that my mom doesn't have what you'd call great judgment when it comes to men and that's just all there is to it." She held up one hand. "It's sad in a lot of ways, but it was something that I learned to deal with pretty early on."

Helen felt an outpouring of sympathy for what wasn't said and simply nodded her head.

"I've been on my own since I graduated high school, and my mom took off with this guy about six months ago—they were out in New Mexico the last time I heard from her. She left some boxes with me, and I finally started going through them." Her voice was open, any hesitation gone. "I knew my grandfather had died, Gran raised my mom, and that there weren't any other children. I didn't really remember Gran, and for a lot of years, I didn't understand how often my mom lied to me about different stuff. Once I was on my own, I was pretty busy working two jobs and going to school so I didn't think much about anything else. But then when I started going through the boxes that Mom left with me, I found some things that should have been given to me: old birthday cards, Christmas cards, letters."

Helen thought she knew what was coming and kept silent. She didn't need to probe.

"Gran had written and sent cards for like three years, offering to let Mom come back or to take me in, if Mom would agree to get help—although there weren't any details about what kind of help she thought Mom needed. I guess that after trying and either being turned down or ignored, Gran gave up." Brianna drew in a deep breath and then exhaled. "And in one of the cards, there was a photo of when I was like maybe three years old. I was sitting next to Gran on a couch, and she had this quilt she was working on. I was holding a pillow with flowers and butterflies on it."

"That does sound like your grandmother might have been a quilter."

Brianna nodded. "I tried to remember and couldn't, but it was like little flashes would come to me—you know—images of colors and things. Quilting is really common in our part of the country and well . . ." The pause was short. "I looked her phone number up on the Net. It's the same one as in the letter. I've been thinking about giving her a call. I don't know exactly what I'll say to her, but it's been on my mind a lot lately, and then, well, when I saw all you ladies together, it seemed as if, well, maybe I ought to. And then, you know, if she does quilt, maybe that would be a good way to like start the conversation."

Helen resisted her first impulse to say, "Good Lord, child—just call the woman! Of course, she wants to hear from you." She brushed strands of hair from her cheek. "I think that would be a wonderful idea. I know it must feel awkward since you don't know what happened, but I'm willing to bet that she'll be thrilled to hear from you and quilting could be an easy way to bridge the gap."

Brianna gave a grateful smile. "Yeah, it was feeling weird, not knowing quite what to say. I like the idea of using the quilting as a way of transition." With that, she glanced at her watch. "Oh, golly, you need to get going, don't you?"

"Yes, I probably should," Helen said, sensing that Brianna's initial worries had been laid to rest.

"Look, I really appreciate you talking to me like this." She smiled and pointed at the deck. "I think I'll go one more round before I head down. Oh, can people like me maybe come in to one of the classes like at the end to see what it's about?"

Helen smiled. "Sure, we've had other passengers pop in to ask questions. I'll be in the middle classroom. If you want to get there right at eleven-thirty when we break for lunch, I'll be glad to introduce you to some of the other ladies and show you what we're doing. If that doesn't work for you, we go into the afternoon session at one and finish around four."

"Thanks a lot—that would be perfect," Brianna said with a wave of her hand. "I'll see you either before lunch or later this afternoon. Enjoy the rest of your walk."

"You, too," Helen said, waiting for a moment as the young woman strode away briskly. What an interesting encounter. Mitch used to tease her about being a magnet for "troubled souls." He said that it was the emotional equivalent of a dog whistle that normal humans didn't hear, yet the signal constantly drew in those who needed a shoulder to cry on, a sympathetic ear, and words of comfort. Although she didn't think of it quite in the same way, she knew he had a point in that she was often startled at the people who would seek her out for an intimate conversation at her kitchen table. It was a far wider circle than her close friends, and she also knew that one of the main reasons was that she kept confidences. There had even been a few occasions when she was able to softly correct some wild rumor being tossed about without revealing a confidence that had been shared. Lord, what tears there had been a few years ago when Maddie Roberts was convinced that her husband was having an affair with Lisa Forsythe when the truth was that he was sneaking around to plan a wonderful surprise party for Maddie's birthday. Not telling Maddie the truth had required significant restraint, but she'd managed to calm Maddie down enough for the surprise to be a smashing success. When Maddie had expressed embarrassment at her own lack of faith, Helen had assured her that the incident would never be discussed.

Unfortunately, there had been plenty of genuinely sad situations—the women within the circle had their own share. Brianna hadn't needed to reveal details of the estrangement between her mother and grandmother.

Helen had seen similar circumstances, and despite not knowing Brianna or the grandmother, she sensed that this was one of those times when the wounds that had been inflicted could be healed fairly quickly, whether quilting was involved or not.

Helen didn't linger in the shower, wanting to arrive at the classroom a little early. Being early for a class was a habit she'd picked up as an instructor, but it also afforded her time to fit in some extra socializing while waiting for the room to fill. There were fewer than a dozen women clustered around the door as she approached, barely avoiding a collision with one of the young staff members who was coming out, looking down at a slip of paper in her hand.

"Oh, I'm sorry," Helen said, stepping to one side.

"No, miss—it was me," the girl said hurriedly. "I wasn't paying attention. My apologies."

Helen smiled to indicate it was not important and turned as Becky called out her name. She was looking forward to the "Bits and Pieces" session since like every quilter she knew, she had a container filled with odds and ends, scraps of fabrics, appliqués, ribbons, and all sorts of things that she had no immediate need for, but that she wasn't about to throw away. The point of this class was to take all the items from an assigned bag and put them together to make a design—whatever flowed from seeing the bits and pieces with nothing preconceived in mind.

"This is exactly the class that I need," Becky said, sliding into the chair next to Helen. "I am such a stickler for patterns, and I've always been reluctant to try any type of design on my own, which is really rather silly when you consider the history of quilting. I'm hoping this will jog loose whatever it is that keeps me from being more creative."

"You quilt beautifully and that's creative," Helen corrected her.

"Thank you, but I always consider that as skill instead of art, and it's okay to recognize that I'm not spontaneous. I mean, that's one of the reasons most of us get such a kick out of Phyllis. She has enough extra spontaneity to make up for those of us who color so carefully within the lines."

"She does that for sure," Helen laughed and snapped her fingers. "Speaking of real creativity, though, I love those pieces of fabric from that lady in Frederiksted that I was telling y'all about at dinner. I haven't decided quite what I'll use them for, but I'm thinking of doing a special design to commemorate this trip."

Becky's smile held a hint of amused exasperation. "See, that's what I mean—you get a bag of scraps and right away your brain starts envisioning designs."

"Good morning, ladies," Sonya said to signal the beginning of the class. Like the other sessions, lively talk punctuated concentrating on the task at hand. This was a group undertaking. Sonya had divided the room into four sections, giving each a "grab bag." They were to take the first forty-five minutes to decide on a design for a lap quilt top. Keeping the design phase to under an hour would allow the women time to sew one or two squares during the class and ask for volunteers to then put the entire quilt top together, which would be passed on to a quilting circle in Fort Lauderdale. They would complete the quilt, which would in turn be donated to either a homeless shelter or one of the area hospitals. Sonya had already stitched a square with the name and date of the cruise to be incorporated in the bottom right corner just as if it was a signature in a painting. This part of the project had been kept a secret from the class, and Helen was delighted with the idea. Laughter erupted along with the chatter as the groups quickly sorted the array of items that included multiple packets of fabric that could be mixed and matched. There was no group leader designated; although after having spent days together, the women knew who the design-minded quilters were and, happily, all of them were open to suggestions so no one was left out of the process. Despite Becky's protestations of not being creative, she was quick with a pencil and roughly sketched out the design as suggestions were settled on.

Swatches of kite fabric, doll fabric, rocking horse fabric, rainbow fabric, six lengths of different-colored braided cord, and a bicycle appliqué soon became the TIME TO PLAY quilt top done in three horizontal rows. The cord, with the mixed colors, served as the border for the squares, and in keeping with varying the colors, there was enough solid fabric in the packet to alternate blue and green for the sashing.

"It's going to be really cute," Becky said, stitching away at a rainbow square. "Are you going to stay later to help with the finishing touches?"

Helen snipped a thread loose. "Yes. It won't take long, and I want to swing by the quilting shop and talk with Serena, the lady who runs it. Wanda thinks highly of her. She's originally from Dahlonega and still has family there. Wanda is hoping she'll come for a visit and wanted me to make sure she knew she had an open invitation."

Becky pulled her square from the machine, smoothing it with her fingertips. "Goodness, I don't think I've been to Dahlonega in years. You know, I've been considering a weekend getaway, and they have some great cabin rentals there. We could catch the Appalachian Jam, enjoy some hiking, and I'm sure there's a stable where we can rent horses."

"It is a nice historic district," Helen said, her stomach rumbling, signaling it was near lunchtime. "I have a wonderful book about the town that was written by a great-granddaughter of one of the founding families. It has local recipes along with the usual photographs." She snapped her fingers. "Shoot, speaking of books, I have to run back to the cabin. I forgot to put my e-reader on the charger, and it's way low on power."

"If you want to run and do that while you're thinking of it, I'll take your square with mine, press them, and see you at lunch," Becky said.

"Okay, thanks," Helen said, sliding her chair back quietly. Most of the women were moving around as they completed their tasks. The deck was sparsely populated, which was to be expected with people scattered about the ship engaged in the many activities available to them on the at-sea day. The passageway was empty except for a slender young woman who was a couple of steps ahead of Helen. She had a towel draped across her left arm and seemed to be looking for one of the cabins. She cast a glance at Helen, and an odd expression flashed across her face. It was the staff member she'd nearly collided with outside the classroom. Helen hoped she wasn't feeling embarrassed over the earlier incident. What a coincidence to see her again.

Helen had been impressed with all the staff she'd met. "Oh, hi, are you down here with us now?"

"Uh, no, miss—I'm just helping out the regular steward. An extra towel," she said with a half-smile and nodded toward the cabin down and across from Helen's door.

"They are comfy towels, and it really is a lovely ship." Helen used her keycard to unlock the cabin as the woman knocked softly on the other door.

Helen found the charger for her e-reader, plugged it in, and then suddenly remembered that she hadn't taken her vitamins that morning either. Goodness, was she so locked into the routine she had established that the slightest deviation caused her to forget everything? Shrieks of laughter came from outside—no doubt other passengers were popping into their cabins to get ready for lunch. Her stomach gave one more signal that it was time to make food a priority and she left, thinking that maybe she'd go with a big plate of tropical fruits and a little grilled chicken or shrimp skewers. After all, she could indulge in only a few more meals of the incredible culinary offerings, and while there was no shortage of good food to be had in Wallington, mangoes, papayas, and star fruit weren't something that you could find on a regular basis.

# Chapter Eleven

"Is it possible that every dinner we've had has actually been better than the previous one?" asked Mary Lou, who could eat a surprising amount considering her petite figure. She had braved the spicier Thai seasoning for her shrimp and declared it to be right on the edge of eye watering.

Helen's preference for complex flavors over heat led her in the direction of the basil and ginger duck—a meat she rarely got the opportunity to eat. Duck wasn't something she wanted to bother cooking; it was the type of food she had on special occasions in a restaurant. Becky stayed with a chicken curry, and Phyllis opted for the whole grilled fish.

"This reminds me of the first time I did a whole fish—in the oven, mind you—for my sister, Jeanie, and Darcey who was, oh, either seven or eight years old. It was a beautiful dish. Came out just like the photo in the cookbook. I had no sooner put it on the table than Darcey started tearing up. Didn't like it 'looking' at her. So no problem, I thought. I took it, sliced the head off, and set that aside. Then the child started crying because I'd 'beheaded' the fish."

The story was told with Phyllis's usual comic expressions, and as they all laughed, she waved her fork. "Fortunately, I had some left over shepherd's pie to get her through dinner. But right then and there, I decided that the child needed to learn that food doesn't always have to be fried or ordinary. Jeanie's never been what you would call overly skilled in the kitchen, and we all agreed that I would give Darcey a few cooking lessons including learning how to cut up a whole raw chicken. I'm not going to say that her ultimate decision to go on to culinary school was because of me, but I'm pretty sure I had an influence."

That set a lively discussion into motion about experimental dishes that had either turned into mealtime disasters or served as sudden inspiration for variations not originally intended. When they exited the dining room, Mary Lou and Becky set off for the lounge with the piano player that had become Mary Lou's favorite.

Helen was surprised. "You're not going with them?"

Phyllis shook her head, the dangling silver teardrop earrings set with amethyst chips swaying with the motion. "Actually, I have to pace myself a bit tonight. I have an engagement later. Are you still doing your nightly promenade?"

"Absolutely. Come with me and tell me what you're up to. I'm going to assume it involves a gentleman."

"Oh, very much so," Phyllis said, the purple print skirt she was wearing swirling around the top of her ankles in the stiffer breeze on the upper deck. The long-sleeved purple peasant blouse she had paired with the skirt seemed to be enough protection for her since she hadn't brought a wrap or jacket with her. "As a matter of fact, this will be the third evening we've spent together."

Helen, having selected a gauzy tunic over a tank top and her all-purpose black mid-calf jersey skirt for attire, used her wrap as she had most nights. "That sounds intriguing. Are you going to fill in the details or am I supposed to pull them out one-by-one?"

Phyllis's laughter pealed out into the open air. "He's Avery Lyon, the head of security for the cruise. A delightful sixty-three edging up on sixty-four, retired Navy, divorced, partly because he's a borderline workaholic. He hits six feet on the button, is nice-looking without a single feature that one could call handsome, and has a great sense of humor. Oh, he was a military brat—father was Navy, too, and his parents retired to Jacksonville."

"You must have met practically the first night of the cruise," Helen said. Fifty-plus years of friendship meant she could tell when Phyllis had a genuine interest in a man.

"The afternoon of the second day," she replied, slowing to pause at the railing. "An errant napkin blew from under my glass and he captured it as I was trying to retrieve it. Could we stop for a few minutes? The sky is incredible, isn't it?"

"I do love it," Helen said with a tiny sigh. "It brings back memories of camping trips with the kids. We made the round of the big lakes. That lasted all of two summers if I recall correctly and then it was on to other interests." She didn't try to hide the nostalgia in her voice—the other advantage of half a century of sharing joys and tragedies was that they literally had no secrets between them.

"Has the cruise made you miss Mitch?"

"Yes. I don't mean in a depressing way, just that this was one of so many things that we were supposed to do together." She turned her head to her friend. "I'm glad I came, very much so, and now that I've had a taste of cruising life, there may be more in my future. Still, I do wish that we could have done some traveling like we'd planned."

"Life does throw us some curves and knocks us off of our feet sometimes, doesn't it? I used to look at you and Mitch, watch you with the kids, and be so happy for what you had. It wasn't how things unfolded for me, and I came to accept that, but when you gave me the news about Mitch's cancer, I felt a part of me crumble with the pain I knew you were in."

Helen felt a surge of affection more than the press of tears, aware of the genuine emotion that Phyllis was expressing. They might have very different approaches to life, but they were sister-close in many other ways. "Thank you for saying that. The truth is that you haven't been dealt the best hand in the world either."

"What's the saying—there isn't anyone in the world that doesn't have a burden to carry? You know, discovering that my husband was a lying, cheating rat was probably as much a blow to my ego as it was anything else. I suppose on some level, I always knew that ours was more a physical attraction. There simply was not enough substance to sustain a marriage after the early romance wore off. It was as much the trashy woman he chose to run around with as the fact that he was running around that kept me from even thinking about giving him a second chance." Phyllis's sigh was longer than Helen's had been, more exasperated than sad. "Losing my husband wasn't a real loss when I'm being honest about it."

They were both leaning into the railing now, much as Helen had done that morning with Brianna. It was such a natural posture to take—to fold her arms on top of the railing, to stare out and up at the expanses, feeling the rhythm of the ship around her. It was the sort of stance that easily brought reflection—perhaps it was the vastness of sky and sea or the unspoken acknowledgment that centuries of humans—well, millennia in actuality—had ventured thus, crossing these very waters for pleasure or gain, to explore the unknown, to begin new lives.

"There's something about being here that makes you think, isn't there?" Phyllis's rhetorical question made Helen smile. "And since I'm taking one of those detours into serious conversation, I have to admit that being told that I couldn't have children was the proverbial straw that broke the camel's back. It might have made no difference in the world—look at Katie, Mary Lou, and a dozen others I could name. It isn't always a good idea to stay in a rocky marriage for the sake of children, although I think that can help get couples past temporary troubles. Anyway, in my case, without the kind of foundation we should have had and no other real anchor, it wasn't worth fighting for. I looked in the mirror right after the divorce and asked myself what I was going to do about all this, and I decided that trying to hang on to anger and bitterness just wasn't my style."

"No, that isn't you," Helen said warmly. "Not for a minute."

Phyllis moved closer to Helen and bumped her shoulder. "The party girl and favorite aunt were better fits for me. I wasn't opposed to the idea of remarrying, but when I took stock of everything, I didn't need a man from a financial perspective unless I wanted to significantly elevate my style of living and Wallington isn't exactly overflowing with wealthy men to make that happen. So, why not be what I wanted to be, enjoy what I liked, and if that didn't happen to match with what some guy was looking for, then it was no big deal." Now came the familiar buoyant tone. "And it has been fun. Oh sure, there have been a few boors along the way but not many. Most have had at least one or two worthy characteristics."

Helen leaned into her friend. "Which category does Avery fit into?"

"Ooh, so far, he's definitely neither boorish nor dull. In fact, in some ways, he's perfect."

Helen was startled and drew back a little. "Perfect as in . . . ?"

Phyllis laughed. "Not that kind of perfect. What I mean is that he's fun, dances like a dream, is attractive, actually reads, and appreciates culture as well as does the basic manly stuff. He's a scuba diver, by the way, and skydives. He not only has a good job, but he isn't ready to put down roots.

He keeps a condo in Fort Lauderdale, and as you noticed, that's a pretty quick flight from Atlanta. See what I mean?"

Helen nodded. "It does sound like a nice long-distance relationship arrangement."

"Absolutely," Phyllis said. "We meet wherever, have a good time for however long, then back to our own lives." She tilted her head. "You know, in talking about it, he reminds me quite a bit of Max, except for the settling down part. He—I mean Max—seems to be prepping the soil if not quite putting down roots."

Helen heard the unasked question. Was she ready to answer it? "That's hard to know," was what she chose to say. "He hasn't made any firm decisions. His mamma is, of course, thrilled to have him in town. He gets to be the fun uncle, like you are the fun aunt, and the arrangement he has job-wise suits him. He bought some new, fancy bike last week and joined the cycling club."

Phyllis reached out a hand and patted Helen's arm. "I'm not prying, sweetie. We've been friends since we were kids, and even though you know I think you should officially start dating—and don't bother to tell me that's not what's going on—you have to do this in whatever way works for you."

"Yeah, I know that a lot of people have us linked together. It's just . . ."

"A step that you aren't ready to take yet, and maybe he isn't either," Phyllis finished for her. "There's no reason to rush. I tease you and that's all. You do what makes you comfortable, and from what I know of Max, he isn't going to push you."

"No, he doesn't and won't. I think the whole coming back to his hometown isn't something that he really expected to do, and he's still figuring out how he wants to work that out."

"It's funny in a way, isn't it? Max has traveled all over the world—well, I don't think he's been to the North Pole—and if he does decide to stay in Wallington, it will be because he wants to, certainly not because he doesn't know what else is out there. For him, it will be a conscious choice rather than a choice made from either habit or fear of the unknown. Small-town life comes with its own issues, but there are a lot of plusses, too." Phyllis swept one hand to the darkened water. "I travel more than I used to, although mostly short trips, and I've been to some places that I could see myself living in but never to the point where I was ready to pack up and actually leave. I thought Mexico was great, but there is something special about these islands."

"I agree," Helen said, ready to swing away from the more serious topics. "And speaking of islands, if Avery dives, and you do come back, you really will have to try it. Tommy, who did our one-day course, said there's a computer-based course you can take and between Max being a diver and having tried it now, I just might go for it. Apparently, you take the classes online, then pick a location to finish the sessions in the pool and open water. Tommy said I could even do it in one of the lakes around home, or pick the Gulf, anywhere on the East Coast from the Carolinas to the Florida Keys, or back here in the Caribbean."

"Well, listen to you," Phyllis said enthusiastically. "That's great. You didn't go diving while we were on St. Croix, though, did you?"

Helen shook her head. "I had other things that I wanted to do, and the snorkeling was wonderful." She snapped her fingers. "Oh, that reminds me. You haven't seen the scarves and the bag of fabric that I got from this lady, Mama Marie. If you're not meeting Avery for a while, come on to the cabin. I'll brew us a cup of tea."

"Tea on the balcony would be nice," Phyllis said. They made their way past good-humored crowds flowing in and out of later seatings for dinner, the lounges with multiple choices of music, the movie theater, the disco, and small casino that Helen hadn't stepped foot into other than to see where it was. Not that she was opposed to gambling—it simply wasn't of any interest to her.

"I don't want to make you late for meeting with Avery," Helen said and swiped the keycard through the door.

"The time is fine," Phyllis replied, "and if I'm a few minutes off, that's good for him. Never hurts to keep a guy waiting a bit."

Helen stopped before she responded. The lamp by the bed was on, and she had a sudden feeling that something was out of place.

Phyllis immediately spoke up. "What's wrong?"

Helen turned slowly. "I know this is going to sound crazy, but I think someone's been in the room."

Phyllis glanced at her watch. "Maybe turndown service came early."

Helen stepped around to look at the bed—no prettily wrapped chocolate on the pillow. She rotated and noticed that the wardrobe door hadn't been completely closed. "No," she said, trying to keep her voice normal. "They haven't been here yet."

Phyllis stepped around Helen and looked at the essentially undisturbed room. "Okay, let's take inventory and see if anything is missing. That will be important before we call."

Helen was startled at the comment. Call? Well, of course, she should call if she was correct, but what on earth could she have to be stolen? She'd brought very little jewelry with her and certainly hadn't left a stack of cash lying about. "You're right," she said. "I mean, it's possible that I left the lamp on and didn't close the door all the way. That's not like me, but it could have happened." The inspection was quick, everything in place. It wasn't until she opened the bottom drawer of the dresser that she realized what was gone. She lifted out the pile of beautiful scarves, then gestured for Phyllis.

"Oh, those are gorgeous," Phyllis began. "Okay, what did you find?"

Helen pointed to the empty drawer. "This is crazy—the bag of scrap fabrics is gone."

Phyllis bent closer to the drawer—the sort of reaction when someone knows what they are seeing, but the brain hasn't fully accepted the fact yet. "You're sure that's where you put it?"

"Yes, the scarves were laid out flat and the bag was on top of them." She gently replaced the scarves as they had been. Puzzlement momentarily edged out her discomfort with the thought of having her privacy violated. "Why on earth would someone come in here and take a bag of remnants?"

Phyllis laid her hand on Helen's arm and steered her toward the sitting area. "I haven't the faintest idea, but I would say it's time for you to meet Avery."

"Avery?"

Phyllis nodded. "Look, security of the passengers is very important, and based on what he's told me, they are extremely careful about vetting the employees. You aren't the kind of person to forget to latch your door completely, your keycard was in your possession, and this doesn't appear to be an ordinary robbery. Whatever this is seems really peculiar and rather than go through the regular process of calling Guest Relations, I'll call Avery personally and see what he thinks about it."

"Okay," Helen said, seeing the logic in that. "You call him, and I'll tend to the tea. Or is he a coffee drinker?"

Phyllis flashed a grin despite the circumstances. "Coffee and, yes, I do know how he takes his. Black and strong. That does make it easy to remember."

Helen smiled at such a typical Phyllis response and then felt a frown crease her forehead. There must be a logical explanation for what had happened, but for the life of her, she couldn't imagine what it was.

# CHAPTER TWELVE

Helen wasn't the least bit surprised by Avery's appearance. Aside from the fact that she had a set notion of what a retired military man who kept himself in good shape would look like, he fit the general type that Phyllis gravitated to. The only difference was that his mostly black hair was pulled into a short ponytail and he had a small diamond earring. He was a head taller than she and Phyllis, had slightly hooded brown eyes, and the angular planes of his cheeks made Helen wonder if there was Native American ancestry in his blood. There was no sign of a softening paunch or slump to his shoulders, and his hands were lightly callused across the palms, although he didn't have the half-healed cuts and scrapes of a man who was engaged in physical work with his hands.

"A pleasure to meet you," he said, declining the offer of coffee. His voice didn't carry a hint of a regional location. "Can you fill me in on what has happened?"

"I'm genuinely puzzled," Helen said, as Phyllis guided them to the sitting area. Avery quietly walked Helen through her day. When she mentioned the part about seeing the young woman near the cabin, he held up a finger.

"Would you do something for me? Would you close your eyes for a minute?"

Helen was startled. "What?"

"It's amazing what we store in our brain without realizing it. If you could close your eyes for a minute, and breathe in and out slowly, I'll ask you a couple of questions."

"All right."

"Okay, how many times did you see this young woman?"

Helen almost said, "Once," but paused. "Twice, but it seems like three times and I don't think that's correct." Her eyes popped open, Avery's face was waiting for her thought to finish. "I almost bumped into her this morning up at class and when I did . . ." She turned toward Phyllis, who was sitting in the chair to Avery's left, watching them both. "I know it wasn't, but she looked a lot like the young woman who was with Mama Marie yesterday. That's why it felt as if I'd seen her before."

Avery nodded. "That makes sense. We hire as many local people as we can for staff, and by *local*, that means from the islands where we have ports of call. It will only take a few minutes to find out if she is Cruzan. I have to agree that a missing bag of scrap material seems out of the ordinary, but if it is one thing that I've learned in this business, there are reasons that turn out to be more logical than you think once you discover what happened. We take pride on the ship to ensure the security of our passengers, and I'll get to the bottom of this as quickly as I can." He stood and inclined his head to Phyllis as he shook Helen's hand. "If you ladies will excuse me, I'd like to locate the young woman and see what she has to say."

Phyllis rose and winked at Helen. "I'm betting you'll be done in time for a midnight nightcap. I'll have a cup of tea while we're waiting."

"I appreciate the confidence. We'll see if we can't make that happen," he said and let himself out of the cabin.

Helen knew that look on Phyllis's face. "My goodness, isn't he impressive?"

"In plenty of ways," she said with a mischievous glint in her eyes. "Would you like me to elaborate?"

"No, thank you," Helen laughed. "How about that cup of tea now? You can have caffeinated since it sounds as if you might have another long night."

Phyllis struck a vampish pose. "The quilting has been great, but I did come for the partying, too."

Helen laughed again. "Out on the balcony—you might need to cool down a bit. I'll bring the tea."

Phyllis waved a hand, the teasing gone from her voice. "In all serious-ness, we've had some wonderful conversations, plus he truly is an excellent dancer. He told me it was something he hadn't thought of taking up until his first ship where they were teaching ballroom dancing. A couple of the instructors gave him lessons. Do you know how long it's been since I met a man who could actually foxtrot?"

"A while, I would think," Helen said, handing Phyllis a mug of steam-ing tea and moving to open the door to the balcony. "Going back to the reason that Avery was here, I'm still struggling to understand why on earth someone would take a bag of fabric pieces, especially since nothing else is missing."

"It will be interesting to see what he finds out."

They settled into chairs outside, Phyllis's comments about dancing leading them into memories of high school proms and how neither of them had taken well to ballet lessons when they were in elementary school. Helen was startled to see that over an hour had elapsed when the sound of a knock on the cabin door carried to them.

"I bet that's Avery," Phyllis said, and followed Helen inside, bringing the mugs with her.

She was correct, and this time, he was ready for a coffee after passing the bag of fabric to Helen. She curbed her curiosity until they were arranged in the sitting area.

"First, let me officially apologize on behalf of the ship," Avery said, a touch more formally than Helen felt was necessary. "It was rather straight-forward when we questioned the young lady."

"The one that I thought it was?"

He nodded. "Yes, and the reason she looked familiar to you was that it was her cousin who is at the bottom of it."

Just as when a puzzle piece would elude her until she walked away from it and then came back to look with fresh eyes, the scene with Mama Marie snapped into focus. "The girl at the stall. The one that Mama Marie said was her granddaughter."

"Yes, she and our employee are cousins, born a few months apart from each other. They've always been close. Marie, our employee, was named after her grandmother. Tessa, the cousin, has taken an unfortunate path, shall we say?"

Helen tilted her head. "What do you mean?

Avery's expression was thoughtful. "Those of us who see the islands as paradise, as a wonderful place to visit, are correct about that up to a point. Sadly, the economy of many of the islands is limited and often mishandled, so that jobs and certainly good-paying jobs are limited. Add the allure of drugs that are a fact of life most anywhere that you go, and you have a subculture where crime is the norm."

Phyllis held her mug between her hands. "That's the path the cousin is on, you mean? Or both of them?"

Avery shrugged. "The cousin, for sure. Marie appears to have made a different choice—or at least she had until this happened. It's a common story. Working on a cruise ship opens opportunity, and records show that Marie has been a model employee. From all appearances, she was dragged into this by her cousin. She confessed everything as soon as we confronted her."

Helen felt a stir of concern for the girl. She obviously wasn't some career thief who had eluded the ship's security screening procedures. "Are you allowed to tell us the details? It may be common to you, but it's still very curious to me."

Avery gave a half-smile. "I hardly think me explaining the background will compromise the investigation that will involve her cousin. Tessa apparently has always been a handful, and recently she fell in with the kind of crowd that spells trouble. Through means that aren't important, she gained information that a number of people don't want her to have." His smile disappeared. "She's playing a dangerous game to be honest. She had the information on a small flash drive, and someone either suspected that she had it or at least wanted to be reassured that she didn't have it."

Helen remembered the anxiety of the girl. "She dropped it into the bag of scraps, planning to retrieve it later."

"Exactly. She had no reason to think that her grandmother would give you the bag."

"And since you were on your way to the ship and we were departing, she wouldn't have another chance to get it, so she leaned on her cousin," Phyllis chimed in.

Avery turned his head and gave her a quick smile. "That's right. Marie said no at first, but Tessa convinced her that if she didn't help her, it could be the end for her. For Tessa, I mean. Marie didn't know exactly what it was that Tessa wanted, only that the bag was important."

"A plea like that would be difficult for anyone to resist," Helen said, picturing what it would have looked like—the cousin pleading for help, putting Marie into a moral dilemma.

Avery's expression was guarded. "True, and since unlike her cousin, Marie was not inclined to criminal behavior, she didn't have the skills to steal the bag without leaving a sign or lie well when I questioned her. She literally blurted the story out to us within a few minutes."

Helen's voice was soft. "How frightened she must have been."

"It's still a theft, and we don't tolerate that," Avery said carefully.

Phyllis turned to Helen with her eyebrows raised. "You don't want her punished, do you?"

Helen released a quiet sigh. "Look, I completely understand that you have to have a strict policy, and I agree with that. But I had a few nice pieces of jewelry in the drawer just above where the bag was, and those weren't touched. The girl obviously isn't a thief. If she's been a model employee up to now, doesn't that count for something? When you get right down to it, no real harm has been done." She searched Avery's face. "I would imagine that in doing your job you have experience with people who lie to you, and didn't you get the sense that Marie isn't like that?"

His expression revealed nothing of what he was thinking. "There can be exceptions to rules."

Helen didn't care if she was coming across as some bleeding heart. That wasn't her character, as Phyllis well knew, but this seemed to be clearly a case that should be an exception. "I'll be happy to make any kind of statement that would be required."

Avery's lips curved without breaking into a smile, and he stood. "Let me see what I can do, but I'm not making any promises as to how this will be received." He did allow a full smile when he looked at Phyllis. "I should have everything wrapped up in about thirty minutes."

"See you in the lounge for the late set," she said, standing as Helen walked Avery to the door. She lifted her mug. "Well, it looks like I have half an hour to kill. Want some more tea or are you ready to crash?"

Helen indicated the balcony. "I think another cup is in order. I still need to unwind a bit. What do you think Avery will do?"

Phyllis cocked her head. "It's funny, isn't it? I don't know him all that well, which always seems strange to say when you've been sharing the things we've shared this week. My guess is that he might take up for the girl." She brought the mugs to Helen, going in to rinse the one Avery had used as Helen prepared the fresh tea and they moved outside again.

"Is it good or bad that Avery is based out of Florida?"

Phyllis laughed throatily. "That is an interesting question. You know that these little out-of-town flings are generally just for fun for me. I love living in Wallington, and there hasn't been a man our age lately that I want to do more than have an occasional dinner with." She grinned in the dim light. "Okay, Max could be the exception to that, but it was obvious from about the first five minutes the two of you were together that friendship with him was what I was in store for." Phyllis quickly waved her hand. "I don't mean that in a I-missed-my-chance way—I mean that from the bottom of my heart. Max fits the right profile for me is all. But there was never a strong feeling that I wanted to be with him for anything other than fun."

"I thought we were talking about Avery," Helen said, warmed and not surprised by her friend's candor.

"Yes, well, my point is that Avery is different—he's sparked an interest that I haven't experienced for a long time." She shifted in her chair, her voice dropping into a reflective tone. "We haven't discussed this, of course, although I'm getting the sense that he might bring the subject up. After all, it doesn't take long to get between Fort Lauderdale and Atlanta, and neither of us have children. So it isn't as if we have to take family-related trips. We can pretty much meet whenever and wherever we'd like to."

"Hmm, a cruise where he isn't working wouldn't be a bad idea," Helen said. "Or a few days in Atlanta could be easy to do. Or, really, it looked as if there were lots of direct flights out of Fort Lauderdale."

Phyllis nodded. "Oh, yeah, you can reach all sorts of places from there with short flights. I am most definitely not ready to bring him to Wallington, but we can go to some lovely destinations. He actually job shares his position on the ship and only works six months a year. I have more flexibility in my schedule than I did in the past. So, if he wants to, I think a long-distance relationship would be pretty easy to manage." She emptied her mug, and the flippant Phyllis voice returned. "This is assuming that Avery isn't a Don Juan who picks a new passenger every cruise and treats her in the same way as he has me. If that's the case, then I might as well go enjoy another wonderful evening and forget the rest of this."

Helen laid her hand lightly on Phyllis's arm. "I know which way I'm betting on this one."

Phyllis nodded once. "We'll see, my friend, we'll see. And now, I'm going to dash into my cabin to powder my nose before I meet the gentleman in question. I'll see myself out if you want to linger here for a bit." She stood, taking her mug and leaning in to kiss the top of Helen's head. "It's been a great cruise either way."

"It has been," Helen agreed, waiting until she heard the door close before she turned her head to the darkness the ship was slicing through. What a strange evening it had become! Fatigue began to pull at her, a yawn escaping into the night. Max. How could she not think about Max considering the conversation with Phyllis? She'd been certain that Max would be and was attracted to Phyllis, and she'd been startled to discover that Phyllis had so quickly concluded that she and Max didn't have the compatibility that appeared to be a natural on the surface based on their age, interest in quilting, and shared stories of places they'd visited.

"I'm not saying that he's an introvert—not by a long shot," Phyllis had confided after quilting circle one night. "Let's face it, though—I get to going about some of my experiences and not everyone knows how to take that. Plus, I'm not the kind of person who likes to sit still. Having a crowd around is much more my style, and with all the solo traveling Max did in his job, he developed the knack for being comfortable with his own company. You can tell that more than about one or two nights a week of being out is probably as much as he cares for."

Helen remembered thinking at the time that, as fond as she was of Phyllis, she was in almost constant motion and just being around her could be tiring. Even though Max was involved in a variety of activities, he did tend to like to have his nights at home, reading and watching television. They'd fallen into a pattern, the occasional dinner out, but mostly trading turns making dinner for each other, then settling in with a movie or sometimes simply talking. Ten o'clock usually was their mutual, unofficial end to their dates. Dates. It was silly of her to struggle with the word—she knew that, and yet, she couldn't use the word without emotionally flinching. How long was it going to take her to get past her hesitation? The breeze shifted, lifting the end of her wrap to flap it against her face, and she smiled at the motion. Did she need a slap to snap her out of her reluctance to want to move forward with Max? She was pretty sure she knew what

Phyllis would say if she asked her about it. Fortunately, Max seemed content with the status of their relationship. He had done nothing to indicate that he was expecting more than the easy companionship they enjoyed. That was enough for now.

# CHAPTER THIRTEEN

Helen's pre-dawn rising meant that her morning walk would allow her to be on the upper deck as the ship approached and maneuvered into the port. The party crowd would be sleeping off their late-night revelry, and with the mystery of the stolen fabric bag solved, she was certain that Phyllis and Avery had closed down the lounge. The same early-bird group she'd seen throughout the cruise obviously agreed with her since they, too, were moving briskly, a few strolling instead. One older couple in particular, from Nebraska, always made her smile. They were in their early eighties, veteran cruisers, and always held hands, keeping their leisurely pace steady. They'd had a few short conversations, and Ralph, the husband, said they took one themed cruise a year alternating between his and her choice. So far, they had never been disappointed. He had improved his photography skills on a trip to the Mexican Riviera last spring and was having no problem keeping entertained while Doris, his wife, was in the quilting sessions. Next on their schedule was a history cruise to the Greek islands. Helen had made a mental note to tell her mother about them.

Talking with the couple made Helen think about the wide variety of themed cruises available. There were certainly a lot to choose from, and if they were all as well-run as this one, she might want to check the list just to see what else was out there. The breeze on this final morning at sea was moderate, not gusty enough to be uncomfortable. The ship's flags were in constant motion, and the film of perspiration under her T-shirt was being quickly wicked away. She'd actually come up top a few minutes early in order to stand at the railing in a silent salute to the coral-colored orb of the sun when it was half-way free of the water. Low whitecaps were being generated by the wind, and cotton-looking clouds became more defined as white against blue rather than pale gray.

Two other ships behind them had come into focus, small in the distance but would loom large as they drew closer. They were filled like this one with passengers who would have stories to tell of their Caribbean vacation. She thought of the plane ride home, glad it was a direct flight. She had enjoyed the cruise immensely, but now, the lure of home was rising in her like the sun inching up from the ocean. Her own routine, Russell's giggles, dinner with the kids or Max, even Tawny's enthusiastic welcome were familiarities that she was ready to return to. Her luggage was packed, a plastic bag waiting to put her sweaty clothes into, the tropical tote she'd made nestled on top of the autographed copy of Laura Baker's book. More than the fun of the cruise had been the pleasure of meeting new quilters, some of whom she would keep in touch with. Sincere invitations had been issued for visits and while Helen didn't honestly expect to be in Kansas City in the foreseeable future, it was always possible. She slowed her pace. The end of the course was just around the turn, and she had plenty of time to clean up and meet everyone for the sumptuous breakfast before disembarking the ship.

She didn't immediately recognize the figure standing near the entry to the stairs. It was a woman in a staff uniform. Marie. She moved toward Helen with a furtive glance as if to see if they were alone. "Excuse me, Mrs. Crowder, but may I please speak with you? Please, it's important." Her voice was soft, her face strained in the way of someone trying to hold back tears.

Oh dear. Helen wasn't sure this was a conversation to have outside, but she certainly didn't want to go down the stairs alone with the girl either.

Perhaps she sensed Helen's reluctance. Her shoulders straightened, and her face seemed more under control. "I wish to thank you, miss, that's all."

Helen stepped close enough for them to talk in low voices.

Marie clenched her hands tightly in front of her. "I am so very sorry for what I did, but I want you to know that I was very frightened for my cousin. Tessa, she isn't really a bad girl in her heart. She makes bad choices of friends, especially boyfriends, and that has made things bad for her."

"I think I understand," Helen said quietly. "It was wrong of Tessa to put you in this position."

Marie nodded, her voice filled with sincere regret. "Yes, and I don't know what will happen to her after this, but there is nothing more I can do to try and help her. I—I—thought I would be fired, and then I was told that it would be only a reprimand. I am certain that it is you who did this for me, and I am more grateful than you can know." Her voice was barely above a whisper, her eyes searching Helen's face.

"It wasn't only that," Helen said with a comforting smile. "I was told that your work record was impeccable and that you told the truth immediately when you were confronted. I couldn't imagine what pressure you were feeling to try and help someone you care about, and I didn't think that a mistake like that should cost you your job. I hope you'll take advantage of being given this second chance."

Marie nodded vigorously and stepped back. "Yes, I will, and may you have blessings for what you did. I felt that I should say this to you, to admit what I did was wrong. I can't make choices for Tessa, but I can for myself."

"That's okay," Helen said, "it's how we learn in life." And it was an interesting thing to learn about Avery as well since he was actually the one who would have pressed for leniency. Others might have brushed her request aside and insisted on following the company policy instead of recognizing that there should be exceptions.

"I hope that your journey home goes well," Marie said in parting, and Helen continued on to her cabin, wanting to believe in the girl's good intentions. Wouldn't she feel like an idiot if it later turned out that Marie got into trouble again?

Chatter at breakfast was expectedly lively, and Phyllis gave her a wink when she sat down, no doubt already knowing what Avery had done for Marie.

"I really got on a roll," Becky said, having gone back for a last refill of tropical fruits. "I finished the tote, a table runner featuring tropical fish, and a set of four placemats for my cousin—the other Becky in the family— Becky Red because of her hair."

"Well, if you weren't going to enjoy the nightlife, at least you have something to show for it," Phyllis said with a grin.

Becky cut into a slice of star fruit. "Quilting late into the evening and no hangover to deal with are much more to my liking."

"I have to tell y'all that with no sales tax in St. Croix, I cleaned up in this one jewelry shop," Mary Lou said. "I bought a batch of pendants, earrings, and bracelets in that Larimar and that takes care of sisters and nieces for Christmas."

Helen, who also had bought extra earrings in the beautiful blue stone for herself, her sister, and her mother, said, "That's right, you keep a handy gift cabinet and buy stuff all year long."

"I've been doing that for years," Mary Lou said. "I'm ready for almost any occasion. I pick up killer bargains that way and almost never have to deal with last-minute shopping."

"I tried that once," Becky said and rolled her eyes. "I stuck things on a shelf in the closet, then put more stuff in the closet and forgot I had the gifts in there. I didn't find them until the following Easter."

"I can relate to that," Phyllis said and glanced at her watch. "If you ladies will excuse me, I've got to dash off. I'll see y'all at the transportation spot. We're booked on the eleven-fifteen bus to the airport."

"It's not difficult to figure where's she's headed," Mary Lou said with an affectionate smile. "That Avery is a nice-looking man, and oh my, you should see him on the dance floor. It's a shame that he doesn't live closer."

"Oh, I don't know," Becky said. "Phyllis does seem to like the shipboard romance kind of situations. Have a good time, then say good-bye."

Helen didn't enter the conversation. After all, Phyllis did like to maintain her party reputation and maybe she and Avery wouldn't carry through with plans for other trips. He might indeed revert to being simply a pleasant encounter for her, and their good-bye today would be the end of it.

"We hate to leave you alone, Helen, but I've got a little more packing to do and Becky's going to stop by and see that cute-as-a-bug scuba instructor."

"To talk about Bob and me and maybe the boys getting certified," Becky said quickly.

"There's some kind of deal that you can do of taking classes and finishing the pool work where you live, then going somewhere else to do the actual diving part."

"Yes, Tommy told me a little about that and it sounds like a good idea," Helen smiled. "Go on, I'm fine."

The two women were barely away from the table when Nancy and Yvonne Huckabee, sisters from Savannah, walked up. "May we join you?"

The resemblance between the two women born barely a year apart was almost twin-like, and it was difficult to tell which one was which from a distance. There was only one-inch difference in their height, both being petite, although curvaceous instead of thin. Helen didn't know if their identical jaw-length pageboy hairstyles and almost identical shades of wheat-colored blonde were meant to enhance the look-alike image or if it was because it was well suited to them.

"I'm down to coffee, but do have a seat," Helen said. "Everyone is scattering about with the usual last-minute chores."

"We're all set," Nancy said and looked to Yvonne. "I'm going for one of those delicious omelets and fruit. You?"

"Let me get another cup of coffee in me before I decide," she said as Helen moved the carafe and an empty mug toward her.

Nancy returned with a full plate that inspired Yvonne toward the Belgian waffle station and slid into a seat. "Your group was new to a quilting cruise, too, weren't you?"

"Yes, although Wanda Wallington, a friend of ours, teaches on some of the cruises as a substitute. She gave us a lot of information."

"Well, we were sort of scouting it out for our group, and we'll be coming on another one even if no one else wants to," Nancy said, pausing between bites. "I enjoy the big quilting shows, and this just adds another dimension for me."

"Gives you a balance to Clyde's hunting trips, you mean," Yvonne said lightly, taking her seat. Banana slices spilled over the top of the waffle, and chunks of pineapple garnished the plate. "The man goes all over the country like four times a year, and believe me, it's not the type of vacation you want to tag along on." She cocked her head at Helen. "I suppose I shouldn't make that assumption. You might be an avid hunter and love that kind of rustic getaway, for all I know."

Helen laughed. "No, the extent of my hunting was learning how to handle a rifle shooting cans off the fence at my grandparents' farm."

"Speaking of quilting shows, though, we might do the Atlanta one next year," Nancy said. "We had a wedding to attend last year and couldn't make it."

"There *is* a tradition for the bride's mother to be in attendance," Yvonne said, dipping a small piece of waffle into macadamia nut syrup. "We did have to chide Penny, that's my niece and her daughter, about scheduling the wedding for that weekend. If they had at least held the wedding in Atlanta instead of wanting to have it in Savannah, we could have shuttled back and forth between the festivities and the show. Penny and her husband both have hectic jobs, and they had to sandwich it in between whatever it was they had going on."

"What is it that they do?"

"I can never remember Penny's title. She works for the state in the Department of Community Affairs, runs a string of different programs to help people get housing. She's a big advocate for affordable housing and says home ownership is one of the best ways for a family to become middle class. She's written several papers spouting more statistics than you can shake a stick at."

"Her husband, Alex, does something in the computer department at Georgia Tech. He's sweet as he can be and not nearly as much of a nerd as his job makes him sound," Yvonne said, barely holding back a giggle. "Anyway, let's make sure we have each other's phone numbers, and we'll get together if we come over."

"Absolutely," Helen agreed. "It's been a while since I've been to Savannah, and Mamma loves the garden show."

"One member of our quilting circle has a sister who owns this wonderful bed and breakfast that y'all would just adore," Yvonne said, as they exchanged numbers and e-mail addresses. "It books early, of course, so do let us know if y'all make plans."

Helen didn't tell them that one of the women she'd gone to college with also ran a B&B within sight of Forsyth Park and that was where they usually stayed. Having an extra contact was always a good idea. She left the women to finish their breakfast and was hailed by the young lady — Bethany? Bianca? — who had stopped her that one morning and told the story of her grandmother.

"Hi, it's Brianna," she said helpfully, a wide smile on her face. "Listen, I'm sure you want to get back to your cabin, but I saw you and wanted to thank you again for our talk. I don't go around spilling my personal history to just any stranger."

Helen saw the shade of embarrassment in the girl's eyes. "You didn't strike me as the type that did. Sometimes, we're drawn to people for reasons we don't understand right away. I hope things work out for you."

"Me, too, and I decided that the best thing is for me to send a letter with a copy of that photo and then Gran can be the one to tell me if she wants to see me. I'll do that as soon as I get home."

"Well, my guess is that she'll be calling you as fast as she can punch in the numbers," Helen said with a lift of her hand. "Have a smooth trip back."

There were no other delaying encounters, and Helen made it through the disembarkation process with only a moderate amount of chaos. The line through security at the airport was rather long, but they'd allotted plenty of time. She hated to be one of those rushing through the terminal, muttering for people to get out of her way. She'd much rather wander through the little shops or sit and read a book before boarding. The flight was free of turbulence and the ride home peppered with questions about what they'd seen and done.

Although the house was incredibly quiet when she entered, she realized that she was glad Tricia was keeping Tawny for one more night. After all the adventure and dazzling meals they'd enjoyed, Helen was looking forward to heating a can of soup for a simple dinner and relaxing in her chair, or maybe she would skip that part and watch television in bed instead. She smiled when she saw the organized pile of mail on the end of the kitchen table—newspapers and magazines sorted into one stack, correspondence in another, junk mail in the last and considerably larger stack. She called Tricia first to let her know that everything was fine then checked her voice mail, saving most of them. She and Tricia didn't spend long on the phone—neither of them had ever been the type to have extended conversations unless it was in person. Helen said she would come by early, take possession of Tawny, and drop Russell off at daycare.

The only other call she wanted to make was to Max. Feeling the effect of waking before dawn and the exertion of traveling, she declined his offer of a late dinner. She promised to get together with him the next night and held the receiver next to her shoulder for a moment before setting it into the base. Max said his week had been fairly calm with a couple of things bubbling up that he would tell her about and didn't seem surprised that she wanted to have a quiet night alone.

Changing into a comfy nightgown and propping up in bed with pillows to her back, she scrolled through the on-screen television guide in the mood for a movie, preferably an older one. She couldn't remember how many times she'd watched the poignant *Bridges Over Madison County*, but weeping over the heart-wrenching ending was not something that she was up for—not after the fun of the cruise. The lighthearted comedy *Foul Play* was on, too, and it was exactly the kind of movie that she needed—nothing difficult to follow and scenes that made her laugh out loud.

# CHAPTER FOURTEEN

The first day back was as busy as Helen had anticipated. It began with Russell, who was thankfully cheerful about being dropped off at daycare. He was normally a happy baby, but prone to the same bouts of crankiness that all infants have when teething. Tricia promised they would come for dinner on Monday to hear all about the trip. Tawny's excitement in seeing Helen had been unbridled enthusiasm demonstrated in whimpers of excitement and insisting on squeezing onto her lap while she was driving. This was one of those times when Helen was glad the little chug weighed not quite twenty pounds.

Laundry, grocery shopping, returning one telephone call that generated three more calls, and afternoon coffee with Wanda consumed the rest of the day. Somewhere in the midst of everything, she called and invited Max over for the evening. She had realized that as low-key as it was to be with Max, she wanted an evening at home. He accepted, but only if she made the salad and nothing else; he would bring dinner to her. She certainly wasn't going to argue with that and added running by the liquor store to her list. She hadn't replenished her wine stock before leaving for the cruise, and she wanted to have a white chilled since Max hadn't told her what the menu was.

She set the table in the kitchen, briefly thinking that she really should get the china and crystal out more often and use the dining room. Why was it that everyone seemed to think of those items as strictly for holidays and special occasion? True, her dishware had been handed down through her grandmother and it wasn't dishwasher safe so using it meant cautious hand washing. It was a beautiful Limoges set of pale blue with a silver rim and a single silver fleur-de-lis painted onto each piece. How a farmer's wife had come to have a set of Limoges was one of the family stories: A neighboring farmer originally had bought the set for his wife whom he met in France during World War I. When she tragically died in giving birth to a third son who also did not survive more than a few hours, the farmer was left with two young sons and no female relatives who lived nearby. Helen's grandmother was of great help until the boys could manage on their own, and with little money available, the man insisted that she take the china as his way of showing gratitude. Helen had always been fascinated with the story, and when Mamaw Pierce had asked if she wanted the china as a wedding present when Helen became engaged, she had quickly accepted and selected crystal with the palest tint of blue to match it.

The sound of Max's Explorer in the carport pulled her from her thoughts, and she hurried to open the door, rightfully assuming that his hands would be full.

"I hope that whoever created Crock-Pots with lids that latch made a lot of money," he said, carrying a sturdy box. He set it onto the tiered kitchen island and stepped into the hug Helen had waiting for him, ignoring Tawny's prancing until he had delivered a warm kiss to Helen's cheek. He reached down and hoisted the dog up as she wriggled and lapped her hello.

He scratched her head, then put her on the floor and nodded to the box. "I'll be right back with dessert if you want to plug the pot in and take out the two containers. A short zap in the microwave should be all they need."

"I didn't mean for you to go to all this trouble," Helen said with a smile, thinking of him lugging everything from his apartment.

He grinned. "Piece of cake, and speaking of which, I know how cruises are, so dessert is light. I picked up those chocolate towers you like from Forsythe's."

"That will be perfect." Lisa, mindful that people watching their calories still enjoyed sweets, had a small line of desserts she'd perfected that truly were lower in calories and especially lower in fat. The "Tasty Towers," which came in chocolate or vanilla, were thin layers of cake with an incredibly light mousse in between the layers and a thin ganache topping with fresh strawberries as decoration. It was difficult to believe that something so good was not laden with calories, and she'd told Helen that it had taken months to find the right combination of ingredients to keep the moistness and get exactly the right flavor.

Helen lifted the lid from the Crock-Pot. A covering of a mushroom mélange hid what she thought would be pork medallions—one of Max's specialties. The plastic containers with the sides were at room temperature, one filled with green beans almandine and the second one with a brown and wild rice mixture that they both often used.

"This is all wonderful," she said, gesturing to the bottle of Pinot Noir she'd selected. "I have a Chardonnay in the fridge if you'd rather."

"I like a red with the mushroom sauce," he said and reached for the corkscrew and the bottle of Pinot Noir next to it. He filled their glasses and touched his to hers. "Here's to having you back. I know you had fun, but I'm glad the cruise was only a week."

Helen wasn't ready to tell him how often she'd thought of him and how nice it would have been to have him along. "It is good to get home," she said instead. "You were absolutely right about the scuba, though. Becky and I loved it, and she's thinking about getting the whole family certified. Do you know about taking part of the course in town and then going somewhere else to finish it?"

Max paused before sipping his wine. "Yes, the YMCA has a program, and I think there's an independent instructor here, too. You can actually complete the full certification, but your qualifying dives are in the quarry and, quite frankly, taking a vacation to the Florida Keys or the Caribbean for that part of the course is a more pleasant way to do it." He held up one finger as he took a drink. "If you enjoyed the one-day course, you've done some of the hardest part. I'll be glad to help you with the academics."

Helen took the containers to the microwave. "Let me think about it. Tell me what you were up to all week."

They talked easily through dinner, staying at the table rather than moving into the den.

"I didn't read the *Gazette*—just glanced through the headlines," Helen said after they'd cleared the dishes and were on an extra mug of coffee. "Did I see something about a public hearing later this week about New Day wanting to take over that old section on Tyler Street? And there's some kind of fuss being raised about it?"

Max shrugged. "I don't know too much. I was at Collectibles talking with Wanda about the newsletter, and Lillie had her feathers ruffled about it. She has a connection to the group that I wasn't clear about and was headed out early to a meeting to prepare for the hearing. I asked Wanda what was going on, and she said New Day works with mentally and physically handicapped people."

"Yes, it's a nice facility about half a mile from the hospital. It was founded, oh, I don't know, maybe sixteen or seventeen years ago. Louise Fraiser was the one who really made it happen because her first grandchild, a little girl, was born with a degenerative disease—I don't recall which one—and the closest facility was in Atlanta. Louise had quite a bit of pull with the county, knew some movers and shakers at the state level, and managed to get in tight with a couple of foundations." Helen's forehead puckered in thought. "We've done a number of quilts for New Day just like we do for the hospital, but I haven't been involved with its work. Sarah Guilford and her church are very supportive. She says New Day offers a full spectrum of support from the severely disabled to people who are right on the border. You know what I mean? They're adults and can manage fairly well, but not enough to truly live independently."

Max nodded. "Yeah, and from what I gather, that's what this plan is. For them to buy up some of the houses on Tyler and build a new facility that's an extension of what they already have. That will allow them to have the adults who can function with minimum help in a different environment from the ones who aren't likely to get better."

"It's a group home sort of thing?"

"That's probably it. Like I said, Lillie was talking a mile a minute, indignant as hell—the Hillman name featuring in her rant—and then she left. Wanda said she'd been on a tear for a couple of hours. As soon as Lillie calms down, Wanda said she would talk to her and try to find out precisely what the problem was."

Helen's mouth tightened slightly. "Well, if the Hillmans are in the mix, there's no telling what it's about. You know how I feel about them."

Max chuckled. "Good point. Fred and Deborah can stir things up, that's for sure, and if they're against something, the odds are that's a good reason to be in favor of it."

Years before, Helen had stopped trying to be charitable about the hypocritical Hillmans, who claimed to be good Christians and supporters of what was good for the town. It had become all too evident, to Helen, that the Hillmans' deeds rarely matched their words and their definition of *good for the town* meant they benefitted personally in some way. They might write checks to worthy causes, but they also made certain that any giving they did came with recognition and preferably a photograph in the *Wallington Gazette*.

"It isn't like Lillie to get that upset," Helen mused. "I didn't really have a chance to talk with Wanda today other than to run over the basic points of the trip and thank her for the upgrade she'd arranged for our cabins. I'll go in tomorrow and find out what the story is. Did you get caught up on your to-do list? I know you had that extra newsletter you'd picked up. That was really nice of you—Rita was thrilled in case she hasn't told you that."

"Only about a dozen times," he laughed. "Once you get the sections set up correctly, populating them isn't difficult. Photos are what tug at people's heartstrings to get them to adopt." Max, proficient with computers and social media, had offered to take the monthly newsletter for the local animal shelter and link it to the websites of several national organizations, increasing the distribution regionally. Doctor Dickinson provided thousands of dollars of veterinarian care to the shelter every year, and Rita had thought of Max when she'd been told the woman doing the newsletter was moving.

Helen suspected that it might not be as easy as he was indicating, although she neither understood how all that technology stuff worked nor was planning to do much more than manage her own e-mail. Despite how much she enjoyed Max's company, she couldn't completely hide a yawn, and he smiled at her gently. "Listen, travel takes more out of you than you realize, and I think another early night will fix you right up. Let me give you a hand in cleaning up."

Helen pushed away from the table and waved her hand to the island. "It won't take me long. Thank you even more for the wonderful dinner, plus coming here."

"Not a problem," he said and stood. "Let me know how you want to do the next one— here, my place, or going out." He carried his mug to the counter and repacked the box with the lid firmly fastened on the Crock-Pot and the containers that Helen insisted on washing quickly.

Max's goodnight kiss to her cheek was close to her lips, and the thought of turning her head sparked through her mind even as she opened the door to let him out. Tawny made an appearance to say good-bye, but Helen wasn't worried about the dog running into the street. She predictably sniffed around the front yard while Helen stood on the top step to give a final wave to Max.

Helen rewarded Tawny with her nighttime treat and once again sighed at her mixed feelings in hesitating with Max. Wasn't it always supposed to be the male who was reluctant to move a relationship along? Didn't that have something to do with men usually being willing to achieve a state within a relationship where they were comfortable and not seeing a reason to change it? Where had she heard that? In their case, she sensed that it was a combination of being comfortable with where they were and Max truly understanding that she didn't want to deal with the idea of romance beyond the close friendship that they had. Not yet anyway. Tawny bumped against her calf, taking her away from her reflection and inexplicably reminding her of the first incident when she could remember consciously despising Fred Hillman.

It had involved a dog—a mixed breed similar in color to Tawny although twice the size with wiry hair, indicating there was probably Airedale in his lineage. Old Mrs. Lofton had lived near the junior high school, and like the rest of the house and yard, her fence wasn't in the best of shape. It was a traditional white picket except that the white was dingy gray and several pickets were loose so that the dog, Rex, often slipped out and ran along the sidewalk, nosing kids, maybe hoping for a scrap of sandwich, or more likely a leftover cookie. Helen usually led him back through the gate and sometimes up the porch to let Mrs. Lofton know he was out. One day she and Phyllis were walking to the end of the block to Harriet Healy's house to work on a school project. Fred Hillman and Robby Strickland were far enough ahead of them so they could hear their laughter but not what was being said. Rex was on the sidewalk, and Helen saw him stiffen as Fred and Robby approached. She had never seen the dog behave like that, and something about it made her urgently call to him. At the sound of her voice, the dog swiveled his head, gave the boys a wide berth, and loped toward Helen. She was looking down at him, her hand outstretched for a pat when she caught movement in her peripheral vision. Rex yelped and jumped to her. She hooked her fingers in his collar, and she snapped her head up to see another rock in Fred's hand, the one he'd thrown at Rex now on the sidewalk.

"You stop that right now," she'd shouted.

"He's a worthless mutt that ought to be shot," Fred had called out, tossing the other rock in the palm of his hand. "That old bat can't keep him under control, and I'm telling Daddy that he's a menace."

Phyllis had been rummaging in her purse, unaware of what was going on, but when she realized what had happened, she took three steps toward the laughing boys. "You're the menace, Fred Hillman, and you do one thing against Mrs. Lofton and I'll tell the whole school that you're scared of a dog that wouldn't harm a soul. I'll tell them you ran crying to your daddy for help like some little girl. You just try me and see if I don't."

Mrs. Lofton opened her front door, tentatively stepping onto the porch, and Fred quickly dropped the rock and nudged Robby. They hurried down the sidewalk.

"Oh dear, Rex is out again. I really must see about getting the fence fixed," she said, creaking the gate open, her pace slow, shoulders slumped, a cane clutched in one hand. Her white hair was pulled in a loose bun, strands clinging to her wrinkled face. The faded ankle-length dress she wore hung loosely on her thin frame. Rex scooted through the gate, waiting patiently until she closed it.

Helen looked to see if Fred and Robby were out of sight. "Would you like us to help you inside?"

Mrs. Lofton's smile didn't seem happy. "Thank you, dears, but I'm okay. It just takes me a while to move around. You tell your mammas hello for me."

"Yes, ma'am," they said in unison, walking backward by unspoken agreement to see that the woman made it through the door without falling.

"That rotten Fred and Robby. You can bet they've done that before," Phyllis said fiercely. "If I had another minute, I'd have chunked that rock at his big butt. Couldn't have missed from this range."

"I'm going to talk to Daddy," Helen said. "He and the sheriff are friends. If Fred's daddy does make a complaint, I want to make sure the sheriff knows what happened."

Phyllis grinned wickedly. "Fred won't say a word—he knows good and well that I'll do what I said."

Helen hadn't doubted Phyllis, but her indignation at the boys had worked into full steam by supper and she angrily recounted the story. Her father had been more calm about it than she would have liked, but he looked thoughtfully at her mother.

"Joy, wasn't Ed looking for a project for the scouts?"

Her mother had raised her eyebrows. "Yes, and I would think a little yard work and fence mending would be perfect," she said. "In fact, I haven't seen Bertha at church for about a month now. I think we ladies should pay her a call."

"I'll go, too, Mamma," Helen had said. She was sure that this was to be one of the church lady visits that would include taking meals and offering to do some cleaning around the house.

Three days later, Mrs. Lofton's modest bungalow had been scrubbed, a week's worth of meals left in the refrigerator, weeds were gone from the yard, scraggly bushes trimmed, and half the pickets replaced, although the new coat of paint on the fence made the house look more drab by comparison. Helen had shamelessly eavesdropped on her parents when she was washing dishes the night after the last improvement had been made. She'd caught Mrs. Lofton's name, and by ever so gently handling the plates and silverware, she could hear her mother explaining that the pastor had called the oldest daughter who lived in Covington. She had apparently been surprised to hear about the lack of food in her mother's house and had promised to come the following week. Then her mother's voice dropped lower and any other information remained between the adults. Helen knew it was being prideful to think that she had a hand in getting the ball rolling, but she had. If she was going to take credit, though, then in a way, Fred's mean behavior had also played a part in the good that had come from the unpleasant encounter.

Helen half-smiled in remembering her confusion over that, the concept of paradox not an easy one to grasp for an eighth grader. She picked Tawny up to give her a snuggle and decided that a chapter or so of reading with the soft jazz station on was what she wanted. She wasn't expecting to need much relaxing before she would fall asleep.

# CHAPTER FIFTEEN

"I knew that y'all would have a great time. Phyllis told me about Avery, which didn't surprise me in the least," Wanda said, smoothing the quilt over the wooden stand. "She mentioned the situation with the fabric bag, too. I'm glad it all worked out. What a peculiar thing to happen."

Helen had been happy to come by Memories and Collectibles half an hour before opening to help set up the display of the consignment quilts by local quilters. Lillian McWherter, the only other full-time employee, had an appointment, and Wanda wanted to have the four new quilts ready before the bus of visitors from Montgomery, Alabama, arrived. Word was spreading about the way in which Wanda had transformed the beautiful old mansion into such a charming shop. The group coming in had been referred by a woman who had been in town on business, dropped in looking for a hostess gift, and spent over an hour talking with Wanda about how she'd planned and executed the renovation. Not a quilter herself, the woman told her sister, who arranges specialty bus trips, mostly for seniors, about Collectibles. After leaving the shop, the visitors planned to have lunch on the historic town square and tour three restored mansions that were usually closed to the public except for Christmas.

"That whole fabric bag thing was rather strange," Helen said, "and I think that Avery's willingness to take up for the girl says a lot about his character."

"Who knows, maybe this is one of those long-distance relationships that can work." Wanda unfolded the last quilt, and Helen took the end to keep it from dragging on the floor while Wanda lifted it onto the stand. "Don't you love the color variation in this one?"

"Yes, but I don't think I know the name of the quilter—Leslie Cutler? As in Doctor Cutler?"

"Yes, she's a niece who is following in her uncle's footsteps. That part of the family lives near Valdosta. She'll be going to dental school in the fall and is interning with him for the summer. She said that quilting and dentistry skills are wonderfully matched because finger dexterity is important in both. I suppose she has a point."

"I have to admit it isn't anything I would have thought about," Helen said, admiring the handiwork. It was a full-size bed panel quilt with yellow, blue, and green print fabric for the binding. Squares in the center panel were shades of yellow brightening from pastel to the same sunflower color as was in the print fabric. Leslie had repeated the concept using blues for the left panel and greens for the right. "Is this a pattern or do you think she designed it?"

Wanda stepped back to check the effect. "A pattern that came from a design that one of the women in her old quilting circle created. Don't you love it when the next generation of quilters joins in?"

"Yes, and if she hasn't linked in with a circle and wants to while she's here, we'd love to have her."

"Nelda beat you to it, although I have a feeling that based on what Leslie told me about her schedule, she may be busier than she realizes. She's planning to volunteer at the animal shelter."

Helen snapped her fingers. "Speaking of the animal shelter, Max was telling me something about Lillie being really upset yesterday over this New Day thing."

Lillie and the animal shelter were very nearly synonymous. She was a fervent supporter and had rescue cats of all sizes and types; fourteen at last count roamed the two acres she owned close to the western edge of town.

"It does seem to be brewing into a bit of a mess," Wanda said with one final look at the display. "Lillie's connection to New Day is actually through the animal shelter's pet therapy program."

"I'm not really familiar with how they're set up," Helen said, hearing the back door open.

"Your ears must be burning," Wanda said as Lillie hurried in, her soft-soled flats making little sound.

"Made it before the bus arrived," she said with a grin. "Good morning, Helen, how are you? Shall I assume that the discussion about me had to do with my sparkling personality?"

That was an applicable description of Lillie, who by standing full height might come in at five foot three. Her hair was loosely pulled into a braid that hung over her right shoulder, her outfit a pair of navy blue slacks and a red top with navy polka dots and three-quarter-length sleeves. Had there been a theme planned for today's visitors, she could have easily arrived in a period costume or vintage clothing.

"I'm good, thanks," Helen said but hesitated to mention New Day. Would it spoil Lillie's mood?

"Actually, we were discussing New Day," Wanda said, waving toward the front entrance. "You fill Helen in, and I'll brew an extra pot of coffee. I've decided to put everything in the foyer instead of the classroom. The tablecloths have been taken care of. I used the garden print cloths—I'm feeling floral today."

They moved to the front of the shop, and Lillie deposited her purse under the counter. "I've calmed down a little, and seeing you gives me an idea, Helen."

"What?" Helen asked, following Lillie into the kitchen. Wanda must have been up extra early this morning. Two trays were already prepared: one with stacks of dark green hot beverage cups, the quilting square cocktail napkins that Wanda ordered by the gross, a small round celadon ceramic bowl filled with tea bags, and plastic stirrers in one of the beverage cups. The other tray held bowls with packets of real sugar, sweetener, and creamer. Helen assumed the open space on that tray was for the cookies that Wanda would put out at the last minute.

"Kristen Duluth, New Day's director, has an excellent presentation about the project," Lillie said, lifting one tray. "She was expecting a number of questions, all of which she has answers for, but the level of opposition voiced at the council meeting really took her—well, all of us—by surprise. So, she has to gather more information for the next meeting. She's terrific, but she's relatively new to town having moved here only three years ago. You know everyone on the council. Would you mind talking to Kristen, maybe give her some ideas about how to strengthen the proposal? Then if you wanted to whisper in a few ears about the value of the project, that could help, too."

With the other tray in hand, Helen followed Lillie to the tables in the foyer. "What exactly are we're talking about?"

Lillie put the tray on one table and took the tray from Helen to place it next to the first one. "Oh, that's right, you were on the cruise. Kristen can give you the details, but the point is that New Day wants to purchase four of the houses on Tyler Street in that neighborhood that's gotten kind of run down. The houses will be a group home, or I guess complex since it's more than one, and there will be a garden. It will be a boost to the neighborhood and a good thing for New Day. All the funding was lined up when, out of the blue, Fred Hillman starts raising a ruckus, making claims about zoning and some other nonsense, and Deborah is sliding around talking about 'those people,' if you understand what I mean."

Lillie's voice was rising, and Helen didn't want to see her upset. "Of course, I'll go see Kristen. In fact, if you can give her a call and see if she's available, I'll make that my next stop."

A smile replaced the tightened expression that was very un-Lillie like. "Oh, that's a great idea. I'll do that right now."

Wanda appeared carrying a black ceramic carafe in one hand and a green one in another. "Do what?"

"Call Kristen and arrange a meeting with her for Helen."

"That sounds like a good thing for you to do," Wanda said. "I just need to bring in the carafe of hot water and platter of cookies. Helen, do you want to hang around for the group? It sounds like they'll be fun."

Helen walked back to the kitchen with Wanda. "I'll pass on this one and go see what the problem is with Kristen. Not that Lillie usually exaggerates, but maybe she's misreading the situation."

"Kristen has a window before her next meeting," Lillie said, coming in and reaching for the platter of cookies. "I told her you'd be there in a bit."

"Thanks, Lillie. Have fun with the ladies from Montgomery," Helen said and let herself out the back door.

School traffic had thinned out, and Helen chose the route that took her past Tyler Street. The neighborhood had been built in the 1970s, solidly middle class back then, mostly ranch-style, red-brick homes on lots large enough for a swing set and a small patio. The front porches were narrower than was tradition in older homes, designed as much to provide a covered entryway into the front door as anything. There were carports instead of garages. *For sale* signs dotted weed-prone yards. Other than two neglected houses with boarded-up windows, the short connector street was more shabby than derelict, like the relative who shows up to a nice restaurant unshaven in ragged jeans and a paint-stained, wrinkled shirt.

Could the New Day project help stall the decline and restore the well-kept look that Helen remembered from barely a decade before?

The New Day facility was in a larger neighborhood that was on the back side of the hospital, a short drive if you knew the streets to take. The location had been selected for its original purpose as a nursing home, a one-story building screened behind trimmed box hedges. It had been constructed with four wings that surrounded an enclosed courtyard, an institutional look heightened by its drab gray color. It was difficult to believe that twenty years had passed since a fire had broken out, severely damaging the building, although fortunately the residents had been safely evacuated. In the process of the investigation, however, multiple code violations had been discovered that led to the sad truth that the administrator had clearly been embezzling.

Corners had been cut—delaying maintenance to save money, keeping inadequate supplies on hand, lowering the food quality, and other disgusting practices that could be hidden under a façade of caring for vulnerable elderly people. With the patients transferred to other facilities, the building in need of almost complete renovation, and the administrator and his assistant leaving town abruptly before charges could be filed, Louise Fraiser, active on the hospital board, stepped in. God rest her soul, she found a few members to serve on a board to convert the facility into a place to care for those with special needs. She negotiated deals to bring the repairs in at a reasonable cost and recruited an administrator who was connected with several foundations and government agencies dedicated to working for improved quality of life for the residents and their families. Louise suffered a heart attack and died not long after the fifth anniversary of New Day's opening, and Norman Healy, vice president of one of the banks, became the president of the board out of his respect for Louise. His personality was the complete opposite of gregarious Louise, and New Day became a quiet operation. Unless a family had need of its services or there was a personal involvement such as Sarah's church supporting the facility, few residents in town were familiar with it.

Helen hadn't been to the building in months and couldn't recall having had any conversation of substance with Kristen. She pulled into the parking lot, glad to see that the beige vinyl siding had been replaced with a blue-gray tone and that camellia bushes had been planted in a wide bed that ran the entire length of the front of the building. The entryway had been refreshed, too, with what seemed to be dark blue nonslip paint on the concrete. The four poles supporting the overhead cover were painted in alternating spirals of blue and green. The straight-backed chairs in the reception area had given way to a couch and six upholstered armchairs, none of which matched, although all blended. Helen wondered if these had been donated by a furniture company clearing out its inventory.

"What timing, I was coming out to tell Reba that I was expecting you," Kristen said, passing through the wide opening that led to the administrative wing. Her welcoming smile helped soften the slightly severe line of her square-jawed face. At five foot nine, she easily topped Helen, and the long legs that had kept her in college on a track scholarship were still well muscled. She wore a teal dress and short-sleeved jacket ensemble. Her black hair was pulled into a French braid, and the skin was still smooth around her deep-set brown eyes and on her wide forehead.

"I thought we would talk in the conference room. I've got coffee and water in there unless you'd like to have tea, Coke, or something else."

"No, coffee is fine," Helen said, following her to the rectangular room with an oval table that could seat twelve. There were another dozen chairs placed against the long wall. The white board at the head of the room was wiped clean, and Helen noticed all the photographs on display. They were enlargements of residents engaged in different activities, many wheelchair-bound as was to be expected. All were smiling, and a few shots were with cats and dogs, probably the pet therapy that Lillie had mentioned.

"It serves to remind us of why we're here," Kristen said, sweeping her hand to the images. "We make every effort to provide as much normal life as we can within each individual's capacity."

"I know it's not easy," Helen said, sitting and taking one of the chocolate mini-muffins as they fixed their coffee.

"No, although it is different for those who are specially trained in the field. Our new project is uplifting, and even more so because we have funding from a variety of sources aligned to take us all the way through," Kristen said, pointing to the open laptop computer. "I'll show the presentation to you in a minute, but I don't want to bore you. How much do you know about it?"

Helen blew air across the hot coffee. "You want to buy some of the houses on Tyler to create a complex for a group home and put in a garden. I drove by there on the way over, and I have to admit that I'm not certain that I can visualize it."

Kristen's smile faded a bit. "I've tweaked the presentation, and the concept is pretty simple. There are four houses side-by-side: two for sale and two that the owners are renting and are amenable to selling. One of those has boarded-up windows because the previous tenants did a lot of damage and the owner hasn't decided what to do about it. Those houses also happen to have slightly larger lots. So, if we purchase all four, we can enclose the area with an attractive fence and put in a garden. It would be a produce and herb garden. We plan to sell the goods to local restaurants."

Helen was surprised. "Really?"

"It's a model that has been used in a number of other places. Gardening is a task that our higher performing residents do well with, and it provides a measurable goal for them. Are you aware by any chance that we have fourteen full-time residents in that category?"

"I didn't know the number. The idea is that if you move them to the Tyler Street complex, you have greater capacity here for individuals who require more attention?"

"That's part of the equation," Kristen said. "The other part is that by buying all four houses, the smallest of which will be the office and where the staff members stay, we can increase the residency capacity. Even though those houses are smallish, they were well constructed and can support another floor being added to allow for extra bedrooms upstairs. With the designs that Jeff Lawson generously contributed to us, we'll be able to comfortably accommodate up to eighteen residents. Some of them prefer to have roommates," she added as Helen was trying to make the math work.

"You obviously have put a great deal of work into this. Did you have agreement with the council before you did the presentation?"

Kristen's mouth tugged down. "I absolutely have the support of the mayor and two members, two are undecided, and one as it turns out is now strongly opposed. I had been under the impression that no one was really against the plan and what I needed to do was provide enough information to persuade the undecided."

"Shall I assume the real objections are coming from Rodney Jackson?"

Kristen raised her eyebrows. "Yes. How did you guess?"

"The Hillmans and Jacksons are very tight—Fred, in essence, made sure that Rodney succeeded him on the council. They're of the same mindset on virtually everything, and if Rodney has seemed to change positions, you can bet it's connected to Fred's objections."

A small sigh escaped from Kristin as she opened the presentation on the computer. "I may have been overconfident in what I put together. Will you take a look and tell me if I missed a compelling point that would win over the undecideds?"

Helen suspected that there was not one thing wrong with the presentation, and she was impressed with what she saw. When Kristen showed the final slide of the six-minute show, Helen set her empty coffee mug aside and said, "Let me start with what may sound like an unrelated question. I know you came here from Columbia. Is that your home or were you raised in a small town by any chance?"

"Columbia isn't nearly as big as a lot of state capitols, but it's been well over one hundred thousand in population for a long time. I stayed there to attend the University of South Carolina, so I guess that makes me a city girl," Kristen said. "Am I about to get a lesson in small-town politics?"

"That's what I think we have going on," Helen said with a sigh. "Your presentation is well done, and the financials are especially important. You aren't asking for any more city or county money than you already receive, and Lord knows Tyler Street could use a boost like what you're showing. If Rodney is digging his heels in, there has to be a reason other than what is being openly stated. When the Hillmans make noise, it is rarely a good thing."

Kristen's eyes were curious. "What do you suggest?"

Helen felt the stir of indignation that Lillie had been projecting, and she straightened her shoulders. "We need a multiple prong approach to this. The extra information that Rodney asked for won't be difficult for you to get. Do that and if you can find another example of how a group home has blended into the neighborhood of a town similar in size to ours, add that in, too. In the meantime, I'll check around to see if I can find out what's really at the bottom of the Hillmans' objections."

"I would appreciate that," Kristen said, a glint of humor in her eyes. "You look like you might have other ideas brewing, too."

Helen smiled. "I do, but I need to work through some details." She stood, her next move fixed in her mind.

"I'll walk you out," Kristen said, "and thank you for being willing to help."

"It really is my pleasure. You just keep on gathering the facts. We'll see about managing the politics for you."

On the drive home, Helen thought about what she wasn't willing to say outright to Kristen. Rodney rarely had an original thought in that pea brain of his. He was nothing more than a surrogate for Fred Hillman, who was kept from running for council again because of term limits. What Fred was up to was the question.

# CHAPTER SIXTEEN

"I don't think this is the least bit mysterious," Sarah said, an unusually sharp edge to her voice. "Fred and Deborah Hillman are the walking definition of hypocrites. They don't have a Christian bone in their bodies, and everything they do in the church and anywhere else is for show. If they happen to do good, it's coincidental to doing something that profits them in one way or the other."

Phyllis clipped a thread from the "a" in "Tea." She was seated on the couch tonight, embroidering gold lettering on the scarlet print tea cozy that she'd quilted for a friend who was remodeling her kitchen. "I don't think you'll get an argument from anyone here. I wouldn't put it past Fred to be working an angle, though. Deborah could be in this for no reason other than she despised Louise Fraiser—God rest her soul—and she never liked the idea of New Day to begin with."

"You mean that the facility is sort of tucked away now, but this new complex would bring it more into public view?" Alicia sounded slightly perplexed.

"If you listen to what Deborah is spreading around town, that has a lot to do with it," Deirdre said calmly, lifting her head from her piece. Someone had found a cache of cigar ribbons in an attic and delivered them to Deirdre, who had been thrilled to try her hand at this type of quilt. "She's never been one to pay attention to who she's talking to, and one of my neighbors was in Cut and Curl when Deborah was there. She was apparently carrying on to beat the band about what a terrible thing it would be to have *those* people right out in town. Agnes, that's my neighbor, pretended that she didn't know anything about it and asked what the deal was. Boy, did Deborah let loose then. It's hard to tell if she thinks disabilities are contagious or if she thinks they're all ax murderers waiting to be unleashed. Her kind of nasty attitude is enough to give me a case of the quilting blues."

Eyebrows were raised around the circle. "The what?"

Deirdre gave a half-smile. "It was an expression Auntie Rose used. She always said that when she was really upset or frustrated that the best remedy was to begin a new quilt project, the more complicated the better, to take her mind off her troubles—that the quilting blues had inspired her more than once."

"I can understand that feeling, and this might be one of those occasions," Becky said harshly. "Fred and Deborah haven't dealt with the kind of heartbreak that other families endure when someone has either been severely injured or, heaven forbid, is born with a disability. They have this notion of privilege that they think extends to every aspect of life. The simple truth of the matter is that they would be perfectly happy if nothing in this town had changed since 1960, when their family was a bigger fish in a small pond. They don't want to admit the kind of growth we've had and that, for the most part, it's been managed pretty well. We have more diversity in our population than I ever thought we would, and I, for one, am glad to see that we have an organization like New Day."

"I can't completely agree with that assessment of the Hillmans," Carolyn said drily. "They didn't have microwaves in 1960, and Fred wouldn't want to give up his big-screen television."

Helen was glad that Carolyn had pricked the bubble of tension. "All joking aside, though, let's think about what all of us can do to help Kristen," she continued, basting a butterfly appliqué onto a medallion that was a white arch covered in morning glories against a pastel green background. The quilt, WELCOME TO MY GARDEN, was a twin size to be contributed to the long-term care wing of the hospital. "We can show up at the next council meeting in support, can't we? There's a public comment time where each individual can speak for no longer than two minutes. They try to limit that segment to twenty minutes, but if we had twelve to fifteen people speak for one minute, that could have an impact."

"We could have more people with placards sitting quietly in the audience that stand as a group during the last speaker," Mary Lou suggested. "I can get with Kristen for a design and have a batch printed up. How many does the town hall seat?"

"Right around a hundred," Katie said. "And there are several employers in town that New Day works with. Scott uses two helpers from New Day for site cleanup and repetitive, unskilled tasks. They're good workers as long as you explain what needs to be done and there's a structure to it."

"The grocery store has a program, too; some of the baggers live at New Day, I think," Sarah said. "Mary Lou, please ask Kristen about that when you talk to her."

"We had a program like New Day back home," Rita said. "Some of the people from the program helped out in the vet clinic and animal shelter where I worked, cleaning cages and giving the evening feedings. They were wonderful with the animals." She was at the quilting table, a stack of completed squares to her left, an unassembled one to her right with the goal of finishing the stacks before the circle broke up. The HUG ME teddy bear crib quilt was for her youngest sister who was due two months after Rita. "Doctor Dickinson knows New Day well because he takes care of the pets at New Day at cost. The residents do a terrific job at providing homes for strays, and sadly, they get quite a few dumped out near them."

Alicia was at one of the floor stand quilting hoops. Brushing a bit of dark blue thread from the apron front she was working on, she said, "Social media can have an impact in situations like this, but I need to think about what the best approach would be. If I'm hearing y'all correctly, what New Day wants to do is take a kind of shabby street, buy the four worst houses on it, remodel those houses, add a garden, have staff on-site in one house, and operate the other three as group homes for mentally challenged adults who are able to hold some level of job in the community?" She took a breath and looked around at the group.

"That's correct," Helen said. "Even though Tyler Street was never the nicest neighborhood, it was an attractive area, and in looking at the plans, it harmonizes well with the existing homes that have been kept up. Jeff Lawson is always careful about that. I can't imagine that anyone who owns property there isn't going to appreciate the physical changes. As for how well these group homes fit into the neighborhood, Kristen has examples of other communities where a similar arrangement has worked well for years. Not one of them has reported problems. It helps the individuals in residence live a normal life as much as they can. Plus, Kristen's not asking the city or taxpayers for a big chunk of money. She has funding lined up."

"My cousin Laura's middle son is in a program like that in Gadsen, Alabama," Sarah said softly. "That's part of what has me so riled about this. Bless his heart, the child was born with a condition that I can't pronounce and he's as sweet as he can be, but he will never get beyond the mental capability of a ten-year-old, and he's aged out of the education system. My sister kept him at home until her husband had a stroke. Caring for her husband and her son as well as working full time was just more than she could handle. Neither of her other two children could let Walter move in with them. So when the pastor told her that Walter might be eligible for the group home in town, it was a blessing to them all. Walter is happy, and he has a supervised job with a janitorial service."

"That's the kind of story that I can help with on social media," Alicia said after a slight pause. "Adding to your list of things to ask Kristen, Mary Lou, please see if she has some real-life testimonials from employers. I bet she does."

"Helen, even though money doesn't seem to be a big issue here, having a fundraiser can be for raising awareness, too," Deirdre said thoughtfully. "We haven't had a quilt auction in town for what, four or five years? That would get people out and talking. We always drew in at least a hundred attendees."

Sarah's expression brightened immediately. "Oh my yes, wouldn't that be fun? I mean, it's a lot of work, and if we want to put one together quickly, it will require a real effort."

"Oh, I think we can manage," Katie said enthusiastically. "We could even play on that—make it a spontaneous event of gathering the quilts you have stashed away to bring. You know that most of us have at least one or two sitting around. If we set it for one month from today, that might also allow for unfinished projects to be done. We'd have to get word out quickly."

"That's where the social media comes in," Alicia said. "You give me the details, and between Max and me, it will hit cyberspace in minutes."

"I'll talk to Denise Grigsby," Phyllis added. "She feels the same way about the Hillmans as we do. I bet she'll give us a great article announcing it. She might even agree to a series leading up to the auction."

"We could reach out to the two neighboring counties for sure," Helen said. "Make it a lunchtime event with an early morning preview. We can talk to a couple of the motels about offering a special discount. If Alicia is correct about the reach of social media, we might get groups from farther out."

"We'll set the church ladies in motion, too," Deirdre said with a smile to Alicia. "Nothing against your computers, but we get those telephones ringing among the older ladies and that will get us noticed."

Sarah smiled widely. "Let's make it a Saturday with the preview starting at seven a.m. for we early birds, going until eleven, then lunch served from eleven to one. The auction can start promptly at one o'clock. Depending on how many quilts we have, that allows us to end around four. I can verify tomorrow if the fellowship hall at the church is available."

Becky held up one finger. "Do we try to have contests?"

"With so little advance notice, I don't think we want to do that," Carolyn said. "You know how competitive some of the women can be, and they'll think they weren't given time to respond. Whoever didn't win would swear it was because of that."

Helen turned to Katie. "Can you handle catering for an event this size? If we start that early, which I totally agree with, we'll need at least some refreshments as well as lunch."

Katie shook her head. "I'm not really into something of this size, but I'd like to be part of it from the quilting side. Why don't we split it? I suggest the Ladies Auxiliary of the church for morning snacks and Dorthea for the meal. She'll do a great job and be as reasonably priced as anyone."

"And the Calico Café has that fabulous four-veggie plate with cornbread for nonmeat eaters," Sarah added. "Actually, that dish has been popular since the day she opened; I have it myself as a change of pace sometimes."

Helen loved the flow of ideas that was pouring from the group, the offers of help with no hesitation. While Kristen would no doubt appreciate what they were planning, mere words of description wouldn't explain the strength of the spirit of what was occurring. "Okay then, Katie, will you work with Dorthea on the menu?"

"No problem," she said and her eyes sparkled. "It seems to me that the perfect auctioneer for this would be Max. Remember, Silas Lawson moved to Florida last year, and I don't think we can lure him back quite this soon."

"I agree," Phyllis said quickly. "He's exactly who we need. Max, I mean, not hauling Silas in."

Helen couldn't suppress a smile thinking of what Max's reaction would be. "He does come to mind, and that's what he gets for missing circle tonight." She turned to Deirdre. "You did start this, though—is there anyone else that you would recommend?"

Deirdre didn't hesitate. "I vote for Max, too. He has a great voice, he's not shy about being in front of a microphone, and he certainly understands quilts."

Phyllis brushed her bangs with her fingertips. "This is going to be all kinds of fun. I think this calls for a glass of wine and some yummy treats. I made a rustic onion and tomato pie tonight with a variation on my recipe, and I want to hear what y'all think."

"We have gone almost ten minutes past our regular break," Carolyn said affectionately. "You're right, though, this has been fun."

The rest of the evening was injected with more ideas for the auction and memories of the annual one that had fallen by the wayside when Mabel Wallington passed away and no one had taken over her role as the organizer. Deirdre had them holding their sides with laughter when she reminded them about the year that Old Man Sparks was hauling two sows and piglets in his banged up pickup truck instead of using a livestock truck and how something had gone wrong right in front of the Women's Club where they were having the auction. Maybe it was a blown tire or a failed latch on the tailgate. Whatever the reason, sows and piglets were scurrying and squealing in the street and on the sidewalk. Women lined up to enter were either laughing or shrieking, depending on their personality. Husbands were commandeered along with the deputies on duty to deal with traffic that was fortunately fairly light, clearing Mr. Sparks's truck, and rounding up the pigs. That was difficult, especially when one of the piglets managed to slip inside the main building. Trying to corner it without utterly destroying the quilt displays had been straight out of some slapstick comedy.

Phyllis, who had been scrambling to keep the raffle ticket table from being knocked over, recounted how Silas had cupped his hands around his mouth with the call of *Sooey pig, sooey, pig*! "Who knew that Silas had such talent, and thank God he did. I can still see that little critter squirming under his arm."

"It was graduating from University of Arkansas did that for him," Katie giggled. "It's a good thing Mabel didn't have her pistol with her, or we might have had ham on the menu."

"Actually I think we did have ham salad as one of the choices," Helen said and saw the startled look pass between Alicia and Rita. "That was just a coincidence, but there were several jokes told. Anyway, the pig escapade was truly the strangest thing that we had happened during an auction. We recovered pretty quickly, and everything went smoothly for the rest of the day."

The laughter subsided, and good-byes were more hurried than usual. Helen suspected everyone wanted to get home and write down their tasks. She didn't intend to call Max at this hour, not since he was an early riser like she was. She would send him an e-mail as soon as she was up, and in all likelihood, his call would come within a few minutes. The e-mail exchange was their routine in the unlikely event that one of them slept in and wouldn't want to be disturbed with a telephone ringing at seven in the morning.

"That was quite a discussion," Becky said, pausing at the dining room table, now devoid of dishes. "I can't believe that I had forgotten about the pig year. Uh, listen, if you don't mind, could I stay for a bit and talk to you about something?"

Helen was surprised since Becky rarely remained for the post-quilting chat session. "Of course, please come into the kitchen. I'm sure there's more wine, and I know the coffee pot is half-full. It won't take more than a couple of minutes to heat the water for tea if you'd rather."

Becky gestured for Helen to precede her. "Coffee is fine, and I promise not to keep you up too late."

Helen was curious as to what was on her mind. Did she have another idea about New Day that she hadn't wanted to bring up to the group?

# CHAPTER SEVENTEEN

Becky took a deep breath and smiled shyly at Helen. This wasn't an ordinary expression for her. "What I want to talk to you about isn't really a secret. It's an idea—no, more like a dream, and there are several parts that have to be worked out before I say too much about it."

They sat with coffee, Helen's curiosity not overriding her longtime habit of allowing people to think through what they wanted to say without prompting. In all the years that Mitch had teased her about their kitchen table being part therapist office and part confessional, she knew that most of the confidences were shared precisely because she did listen. Listened with minimal judgment and without jumping to conclusions, without extending clichéd advice, and without trying to one-up the individual with examples from her own life. She hadn't taken the box of tissues from the counter by the telephone and brought them to the table because she had the impression that whatever Becky was hinting at was exciting, not distressing.

"Is it related to New Day or completely different?"

"Related in a way. Do you remember that I've mentioned equine therapy in the past?"

Helen thought that it had been quite some time since the subject had come up. "You visited a program a while back, didn't you? When you were on vacation in Texas?"

Becky smiled. "Yes. The dude ranch that we went to had been recently certified to conduct equine therapy, and while that wasn't a part of the recreation for guests, the owners invited me to attend a session. We'd been talking about horses from the minute we checked in."

"I'm familiar with bringing dogs and cats into the assisted living and long-term care wing at the hospital, but I'm not sure I can translate that into horses," Helen said. "They're very large animals."

"True, and you obviously have to have horses with the right type of personality. There are multiple benefits, though. Research has been done on how the rhythmic nature of the horse's gait provides therapy and how riding helps strengthen a rider's muscle tone. Other physical benefits include improvements in balance, posture, coordination, reflexes, fine and gross motor skills, and hand-eye coordination. The repetition of various activities allows the rider to concentrate on his or her position while trying new activities. During group sessions, participants learn horsemanship of grooming, tacking, and caring for the horse. As the participants interact with the horses, they develop respect and love for the animals, and because horses require a great deal of attention, the riders bond quickly with them during grooming and feeding. That helps develop responsibility, patience, and compassion. The excitement of riding brings new experiences, and according to the research that I've been doing, the individuals build friendships with other riders as well as support and encourage one another as they discover the joys of riding. The directors and staffs of the organizations involved say that participants' self-esteem and confidence soar as they conquer new challenges. By *they*, I mean the participants. It gives them an outlet to focus on their abilities instead of their limitations, and like other animals, horses are nonjudgmental. They love unconditionally." Becky paused, a slight flush on her cheeks. "Oh dear, I sound like a brochure, don't I?"

Helen reached to pat Becky's arm. "You sound like someone who is passionate. What is it that you have in mind?"

Becky tapped the face of her watch without looking at it. "I'd like to give you the longer version if it's not too late for you. I know you're more of a morning person."

"I haven't quite reached the stage where I need to be in bed at nine-thirty," Helen said. "Whichever version you prefer will be fine."

"Okay, well, I've loved horses since I guess as soon as I could walk. Papaw had this old mare that was as much a plow horse as anything, and I would sit on her every chance I got. One of the farms near his began taking horses in for boarding, and that was like heaven for me. I have to admit that after Papaw passed away and Mamaw wanted to sell the farm, I practically begged Daddy to buy the place so we could turn it into a horse farm."

Helen raised her eyebrows. She didn't think that Becky's family came from the kind of money that you associate with a horse farm.

Becky grinned. "Hey, at fourteen, you want what you want. That poor farm barely limped along, and after having been raised on it, the last thing my daddy or either of his sisters wanted was to be tied to it. Mamaw managed to get enough for it to be comfortable through her last years without having to depend on anyone else." She paused. "We never had much money for extras, and owning even one horse was out of the question. The stable where I first worked actually paid me a small salary, even though I would have been happy to do work for free just to be there. Then they decided to leave the area, and I got on with the Richardson stables. I spent every minute I could out there, certain that I was going to be a large animal vet."

Helen saw a flash of regret before Becky lowered her eyes briefly. She raised them again. "I wasn't what you'd call an academic whiz, and even though my parents wanted me to go to college, I needed to stay in state. Being able to do anything more than a bachelor's degree was going to have to be on me. They couldn't afford to help me beyond that."

"Abraham Baldwin Agricultural College is a good school," Helen said, speaking of Becky's alma mater.

"It is, and one of my professors was helping me look for grants and different ways to pay for vet school, but then, for the first time in my life, I suddenly had something to think about other than horses."

"That was where you met Bob."

"Oh, yes, and my Lord, I can still see that look on his face when he sat next to me in microbiology class. He was just so damn cute, and he asked me to go for coffee as soon as the bell rang." The note of wonder shaded her voice. "For someone like me who had hardly given boys a thought, love at first sight pretty much knocked the breath right out of me."

"It can do that," Helen agreed.

"So there I was, my head in the clouds with a guy who fortunately felt the same way. Bob was planning to be a math teacher, and his family was in about the same kind of financial situation as mine. He was on scholarship and not intending to go to grad school." She shrugged. "We talked about it, and it seemed more practical for us to get Bob settled in a job. We weren't really expecting for the best opportunity to be here in Wallington. If we had been someplace with a vet school program, maybe I could have taken at least part-time classes." The faint flush was back on the side of her neck. "The truth of the matter is that, uh, well, I know this will sound so old-fashioned, but we, well, we waited until we were married and then let's just say that we really enjoyed the honeymoon."

"Ah, that makes sense," Helen said patiently.

"What it comes down to is that I got pregnant barely three months after we were married, and, well, the years do slip by faster than you realize, don't they?" She allowed a tiny sigh to escape. "Miriam Cotton bought the stables, and even though she was great, I was so busy with the boys that I couldn't do much except enjoy an occasional ride. It wasn't until about six years ago that I was able to get back into teaching riding." She tilted her head. "I know I'm rambling, and I truly am about to get to the point. Did you follow the piece last year about the abandoned horses they found?"

"Not really. It seemed like a cruel thing to do, and now that you mention it, Miriam did take them in, didn't she?"

Becky grimaced. "Yes, and I tell you, it almost broke both our hearts when they brought the three over. One was too far gone to save, and it took weeks to get the other two healthy. No one ever found out who they belonged to or how they'd wound up at the old Turner place. If that hunter hadn't discovered them, they would have all died. Anyway, in spite of what they had been through, they were as gentle as you could ask for and Miriam was trying to decide whether to keep them when a guy she knows near Gadsen contacted her to see if she would be interested in donating one to his equine therapy program."

"Gadsen? That's where Sarah was saying her cousin lived. The woman with a son in a place like New Day."

"Exactly," Becky said. "It hit me when she brought the name up, and since we're checking into how these different programs fit into their communities, I want to call the guy in Gadsen. Miriam did send one of the horses, by the way, so we have that connection." Her mouth twitched toward a smile. "I'll want to find out all the details, but, Helen, I honestly think that we could start an equine program here."

"With Miriam, you mean?"

Becky nodded eagerly. "She has the only stable that's large enough, although I would do a lot of the work, especially with getting it all organized. We've discussed it in theory, and I'm not as busy at home as I used to be." She leaned in, her voice barely containing her excitement. "It's the therapy part of it I love. Even though that will have the top priority, we can also provide a place for rescue horses, and according to some of the testimonials that I've read, helping animals recover from abuse and neglect can be a type of therapy, too. It's funny in a way. I've been thinking a lot about this for the past few months, checking out some of the websites, looking into how to apply for nonprofit status, sort of working around the edges, you might say." She wrinkled her nose. "I don't mean that I'm glad Kristen is having difficulty getting approval for the project. It's just that, well, it seems this is kind of an omen. Here I've been toying with the idea, and with the attention we'll be bringing to New Day, it seems as if we can build on that to help people see that Wallington is ready for equine therapy." She broke into a grin and leaned back again. "And no, I'm not putting the horse before the cart."

Helen couldn't repress a laugh at the pun. "I wouldn't have said that anyway. Have you and Bob talked much about this?"

"Oh sure. It's going to take a tremendous effort, but he knows how strongly I feel about it. He's being very encouraging and has promised to help in any way that he can." She lifted her mug from the table. "I'm going to call the guy in Gadsen tomorrow and see how much information he'll send me before I bring it up to Kristen. Available funding will be important, of course, and that's something that I have to get a handle on."

"I can't imagine that she won't be supportive," Helen said, "and I would think that she might know about the program. She seems to be well versed in the whole range of treatments."

Becky nodded and stood. "Hey, thanks for listening. By next week, I should be ready to tell the whole circle about the idea."

"I'm always glad to lend an ear," Helen said, walking Becky to the front door. "I have to admit that it isn't something that I would have thought of, but I can definitely see the merit in it."

Becky nearly bounced down the steps, and Helen wondered if she was going to be able to sleep with everything that seemed to be spinning in her head. She released a yawn that she'd been stifling, and when she turned from locking the door, Tawny was waiting expectantly in the archway to the kitchen.

"You've been out, and it's time for a treat, is it?" She lifted the chug into her arms, fleetingly amused, as she often was, by the fact that she had lived for so long without a pet. She'd seen firsthand the value of pets being brought for visits to the residents of assisted living and long-term care, and she knew that the independent living building allowed small pets. Horses, though, horses had been a brief part of Tricia's adolescence and of no interest at all to Ethan. With no personal prolonged contact, Helen only vaguely knew of the horse lovers around town.

She assumed that Becky was correct in that Miriam's stables were the largest, and there were two others in the area that gave lessons. Most people who owned horses did so for personal use, although some people with barns and meadows probably took horses in for boarding to earn a little extra money. There certainly was a fair number of horses visible from the roads as she drove past pastures that connected the small towns. Horse trailers were a common sight on the roads as well, and she imagined that, like all subsets within a community, horse lovers knew each other and had their own gatherings.

Becky was solidly grounded, and if she was researching the means to bring equine therapy to Wallington, she would do a thorough job of it rather than play around with some half-baked idea. Helen replayed the younger woman's comments about giving up her ambition of becoming a veterinarian. This was a situation where the dream she once had and decided not to pursue could play out in a similar manner, especially if they added the part about horse rescue. Not that Helen was an expert by any means and she wasn't denigrating the extensive volume of material that large animal veterinarians were required to learn, but with Becky's lifelong handling of horses and her willingness to study, Helen bet that Becky's knowledge was similar to many assistants. In one sense, perhaps the combination of equine therapy and rescue work would be as emotionally rewarding as if she had received her degree.

In the way that the mind branches, Helen went through the house, switching off lights, and found her thoughts drifting to her choice of study in business administration. It had nothing to do with either a passion or a plan for a career. As high school sweethearts, she and Mitch had agreed to wait until he graduated from college for them to marry. The girls of their senior class had been basically equally divided as to the ones who were attending college and those who were scheduling summer weddings. It had been Helen's mother who urged her to join the ranks of women for whom college was routine rather than the exception. Her parents had viewed Mitch as a son from the moment he slipped his senior ring onto Helen's finger, yet her mother didn't want her daughters to stay at home because they were not employable. Business administration seemed to be a practical option without the need to take the dreaded statistics class.

Like Becky, Helen had become pregnant early in their marriage. With Mitch's job as an engineer, they could meet their modest needs on his single income. A casual conversation with insurance agent Larry Shipley and their desire for a larger home inspired Helen to consider going to work after Tricia's entry into first grade. Helen's mother lived on one of the school bus routes, and it was a simple matter for the kids to take one bus to school in the morning and another in the afternoon. This arrangement left Helen no real excuse to say no to Larry, even though becoming part of an insurance office wasn't anything she had anticipated. Her visions of boredom, however, were quickly dispelled. Larry's philosophy was that, as an independent agent, he had more freedom in how he could advise his clients. He took the time to get to know them and their needs. Helen discovered that much like bankers and hairdressers, an insurance agent was likely to learn a great deal of personal information about people and their businesses. There was little doubt as to Larry's success, and when Mitch was taken from her so unexpectedly, Helen realized that her mother's long-ago admonition to be prepared to take care of herself had been wise words indeed. In her case, it wasn't financial need that drove her. Having a defined reason to get up and go to work in a job that she enjoyed, for a boss whom she admired, and among people whom she liked provided a surprising level of emotional support as life returned to as normal as it could be without Mitch.

She'd felt a tug of sadness when Larry and Alicia announced they were going to sell the business and had been genuinely surprised when they asked her if she wanted to buy it. Larry assured her that she had the skills required, and she had briefly contemplated the idea. Thankfully, she was financially positioned to where continuing to work was an option for her, not a necessity. Despite the solid nature of Larry's business, she knew the tremendous amount of work that was unseen by clients. More than that, the entrepreneurial spirit didn't stir in her, definitely not in the way of

Carolyn with her clever clothing store, or like Edna Birch whose beauty shop was as popular as ever.

Tawny, who sometimes preferred to sleep in Helen's bed rather than in the den, had padded down the hall with her to the bedroom. Helen turned the lamp on and looked at the little dog. "My, life does bring us twists, doesn't it? What do you think—can big old horses make people feel better?"

Tawny waited until she'd folded back the covers to leap up. Helen ruffled the dog's soft ears. "I bet they do, little one; I bet they do."

Tawny settled onto the second pillow with a tooth-showing yawn, apparently in agreement.

# CHAPTER EIGHTEEN

Helen's eyes snapped open at the ringing of the telephone, and Tawny, perhaps sensing her anxiety, moved closer to her. Good news wasn't delivered at 5:17 in the morning.

"Your daddy is stable is what you need to know first." Her mother's voice held a quiver she couldn't completely hide, and Helen felt a knot clench her stomach. "They're getting ready to run another EKG, and Leland says the initial signs are positive." Leland Turner had been the family doctor for years.

"I'll be there in twenty minutes," Helen said, her feet on the floor. "Do you want me to call Eloise?"

"Not yet. Let's see what the situation is, and, sweetheart, don't speed, okay?"

How like her mother to think of something so absurd. "I'll be fine, Mamma." Not knowing how long she would be at the hospital or if they would need to travel to Atlanta, Helen took two minutes to shower, was dressed, and out the door in a total of seven minutes. With no traffic yet, she dashed through the sliding doors of the emergency room eighteen minutes after she'd hung up the telephone.

Her mother was at the nurses' station, speaking quietly with Betty Wallington. She turned, the expression on her face one that Helen knew well—*the, yes, we have an emergency, but there's no need to panic* one. The only thing that gave her away was that her mother was wearing her pink bed-room slippers instead of shoes. Helen doubted that she'd noticed yet.

Joy Pierce stepped forward into Helen's outstretched arms, the hug tight before she broke the embrace and led Helen to the side. Her brown eyes, which had been passed for generations from mothers to daughters, were steady. "They have him on the machine, and then they're going to transfer him to Intensive Care. Leland will be out to talk to us as soon as he can."

"Let's sit then," Helen said. "Do you want me to get you a cup of coffee?"

"Not right now," Joy replied, sinking into the first chair they came to in the otherwise empty waiting area. Despite the upgrading of the wait-ing room the hospital had done earlier in the year, the sense of it had not changed. How could it? New dark blue carpet tiles eliminated the sound of shoes on linoleum, and the chairs with arms that had padded backrests and stain-resistant upholstery in a geometric print of navy, burgundy, and gold were more comfortable. Two new bookcases held a wider selection of books as well as picture books to help distract children who were waiting, yet the reason to be in the room could not be dispelled. In some cases – the ram-bunctious kid with a broken arm that he would see as a badge of daring did not bring great fear with it nor did the careless cut that obviously required stitches and nothing more. The intense fever of an ill child, the collapse of a father—these were what sent pulses racing and worry shimmering around those seated, praying for good news.

"What happened? When?"

Joy kept her voice low. "We're not entirely sure. Your daddy was fuss-ing about heartburn before we went to bed, and he took one of his pills. It was right around four o'clock when he woke up to go to the bathroom. When he was coming back to bed, his knees buckled and he almost fell. We sat him down, and that was when, of all things, he was feeling pain in his jaw. He looked so pale, though, that I didn't care what part was hurt-ing, and I sure wasn't listening to him tell me that he was probably okay. I called nine-one-one and those boys, bless their hearts, were there really fast. They couldn't have been better, coming right in and getting him on the way here." She suddenly looked at her feet. "My goodness, why do I have my slippers on?"

"Maybe because you had more to worry about than finding your shoes," Helen said with a half-smile.

Joy tried to smile, but her mouth wasn't ready to cooperate. "Yes, well, your daddy was conscious the whole time, which I took as a good sign, and the team here couldn't have been better either. I mean, it isn't like we haven't been to this emergency room before, but this time, I mean, this isn't the same."

Helen hid a flinch, thinking of Mitch's collapse that had signaled what became his final days. "Of course, it's not, and . . ."

"Joy, Helen, let me introduce you to Doctor Marcus Fielder."

They'd been focused on each other and hadn't heard footsteps on the carpet. They both rose hurriedly, turning toward the two men. They were quite a Laurel and Hardy comparison. At five foot eleven and a medium build, slightly soft around the middle when he wasn't covered with a lab coat as he was even at this hour, Doctor Leland Turner was four inches taller than the rounded man with skin the color of coffee with a splash of cream. Their eyes were a similar brown, and both had more white than brown in their hair, although Doctor Turner had considerably more than the closely cropped fringe around Doctor Fielder's balding head.

Doctor Fielder's voice was reassuring and his handshake firm. "It hardly seems correct to say that it's a pleasure to meet you under the circumstances, but I do have good news for you. Let's sit for a moment."

They shifted four chairs into a circle as Doctor Turner explained. "Marcus and two other cardiologists have joined together for a new enterprise that we were preparing to announce at the next board meeting."

"Leland, we can fill them in on that later. Frank's condition is what's important right now," Doctor Fielder said and looked directly at the two women. "Frank is stable, and while this was a heart attack we attribute to atrial fibrillation, which is commonly referred to as 'afib,' he is in quite good health for a man of his age."

He paused. Squeezing her mother's hand, Helen watched the relief lighten her mother's face and knew that her expression mirrored that.

"Putting in a pacemaker will be our preferred choice. As we age, our internal electrical system is often not as robust as it needs to be, and a pacemaker combined with appropriate medication is frequently our best option. I will give you the pros and very few cons about that in a few minutes. Will you want me to do that with you first or with you and your husband together?"

"Together," Joy said immediately. "Frank and I have been making joint decisions as long as we've been married, and we aren't about to change that at this point."

"One never knows," he said with a twitch of his lips. "We can go talk with him now if you'd like, and, Leland, perhaps you can speak with Helen about how our new enterprise will provide better service for Wallington. A pleasure to meet you, Helen," he said and stood, extending his hand to help Joy from her chair.

"Uh," Helen started to stand as her mother smiled softly.

"Doctor Fielder is politely telling you that this is between the three of us, honey. You stay with Leland, and I'll come get you when we're done."

Helen cut her protest short—of course, this should be a private conversation. Her parents were fully capable of making whatever decision was necessary.

Doctor Turner—Helen couldn't bring herself to call him Leland—shifted his chair closer. "Doctor Fielder has spent the past twelve years at Emory, and he was at Johns Hopkins in Baltimore before that."

Helen felt her brow wrinkle. Not to make light of Doctor Fielder's credentials, but Wallington was hardly a medical steppingstone up from Emory. "That's impressive. Does his presence here have something to do with this new capability that you're talking about?"

"Indeed it does. Doctor Fielder and two other highly qualified cardiologists who are also in their early sixties have decided that they want to look to smaller, underserved hospitals to help keep people from having to go to Atlanta for treatment. For hospitals like ours that are willing to have the necessary support equipment and staff, they'll provide on-site surgery and follow-up care for what are the more common cardiovascular issues."

"Like with Daddy?"

"Exactly. The strides in heart surgery over the past decade have been remarkable, and for the lower risk surgeries, such as Frank's, it will be easier for him and for you, for that matter, to have treatment closer to home."

"That does sound like a good idea," Helen said. "We do seem to be getting more services here, don't we? Do you personally know Doctor Fielder?"

"I do, and I would use him for myself if I needed surgery."

"Well, I can't ask for a better recommendation than that," Helen said.

They both glanced over at the sound of raised voices at the nurses' station. A woman was pushing a boy who looked to be around age ten forward, a blood-stained white hand towel pressed to his nose, a man half a pace behind, his expression clearly broadcasting that he thought this was not a situation that required borderline hysteria.

"There's your mamma, and I think this is my cue to slip away," Doctor Turner said, shifting his gaze to the left. He stood and placed his hand briefly on her shoulder. "Everything is going to be fine."

Helen could see the springier step to her mother's walk, and that was more reassuring than the doctor's prognosis. She scrambled from the chair and closed the distance to her mother, who was ignoring the scene at the desk. "Mamma, should we go have some coffee while they get Daddy moved?"

She raised her eyebrows. "Were you eavesdropping? Those are almost the same words that he used."

"You know what a cluster there is around a patient when they're doing that, and there isn't anything that we can do to help."

She lifted one foot slightly from the floor. "I do feel a little silly wearing these things, but I suppose it will give people something to laugh about."

"I'll go get some real shoes and whatever else you need, once we know for sure what's going on with Daddy."

"That Doctor Fielder is something," her mamma said as they made their way to the cafeteria, the scent of frying sausages growing distinctive. "Your daddy took right to him." Neither woman felt hungry. They took their coffees to a back table in the sparsely filled room. The morning shifts had not changed yet, and visitor hours wouldn't start until nine. Helen wondered if there was any real way to make an institutional cafeteria look like other than what it was. It was cheerful enough with a paint scheme of yellow, green, and off white, the flooring in forest green carpet tiles. The food line was partially screened by shoulder-height acrylic panels etched with the frosted glass appearance that interspersed magnolia blossoms and woodland birds. Perhaps it was the mere fact that unless you worked there, the hospital wasn't a place chosen for casual dining. It was for function, not form, and the décor wouldn't change that, although several years ago the hospital administrator had determined that improving the food could be done without a major increase in cost. He brought in a new nutritionist and chef, a decision that had proven popular with staff, patients, and visitors.

"I'll call Eloise while you're making the run to the house," Joy said after deeply inhaling the aroma of the coffee. "Doctor Fielder is planning the surgery for early tomorrow morning. He said your daddy should only be in the hospital for two or three days barring any complications."

Her voice hung briefly on the word, and she took a sip, her tone normal when she spoke again. "We've both been blessed with good health up to now, much more so than a lot of people our age. There's every reason to believe this will go smoothly. In fact, your daddy was joking with the nurses when I left."

"You take good care of yourselves, too," Helen pointed out. "You regularly walk around the neighborhood, and you go to the senior program at the Y."

"That does help," Joy said and ran a finger around the rim of the mug. "Tricia is here, of course, but I really don't think that Ethan and Sarah need to come, do you?" Her eyes were steady, the fear that had spiked through her under control.

Helen tilted her head. "Why don't we let them decide? I'll pass on the doctors' confidence, but they haven't visited since right after Christmas so I won't discourage them from coming if they want to."

Joy smiled affectionately. "As busy as they usually are, dropping everything might be a problem for them, and since we do expect your daddy to be home soon, next weekend could be better. Make sure you let them know that."

"Yes, Mamma, I will. Now, what all do you want other than shoes?"

The short list provided, they went upstairs to check on how soon her father would be settled into the room. The nurse on duty in Intensive Care promised Helen that she could go in when she returned. She kissed the top of her mother's head and left. As she exited the elevator on the ground floor, her eyes caught the arrow on the wall directing her to the chapel. She turned without quite knowing why and crossed into the quiet room.

The low light was soothing as it was meant to be. The ten pews, five on either side of a center aisle, were polished wood, devoid of padded cushions. The altar up front with the pulpit to the right was covered with a royal blue cloth embroidered with white lilies of the valley rather than any particular religious symbol. Two stained glass panels decorated the wall behind it, replicas of the famous rose windows in Notre Dame Cathedral and Chartres. The idea behind that choice had been that the beauty of the patterns could be appreciated by all and not denote a specific faith. The dark blue carpeting muffled footsteps, and Helen slid noiselessly into the second pew from the front, her eyes closing in brief prayer. The sense that had been building in her welled upward, relief battling pain that caught in her throat.

"I'm not intruding, am I?"

Helen hadn't heard Father Singletary enter behind her. "Hi, Father. No, it's just that I . .I ."

"I come for early rounds and I saw that Frank had been admitted. I'll go up to see your mother in a minute. I spoke with Betty Wallington and she sounded positive." He sat on the edge of the pew in front of Helen, angled toward her with his arm on the back of the pew, his presence felt without encroaching on her space.

Not able to speak, she couldn't stop the tears filling her eyes.

Father Singletary passed her a handkerchief that had been freshly washed from the softness of it, his voice sympathetic, "It's the memory of Mitch, I assume?"

Helen bobbed her head, allowing the choking sob to bubble out into the handkerchief that she pressed to her mouth for a moment until she could speak. "I'm so grateful that Daddy is okay. I mean, all the signs are good. He'll need a pacemaker, but he should be fine all things considered. I was so caught up in getting here, being with Mamma, and then when I came downstairs, it just, just . . . I saw the chapel and I don't mean that I'm not happy about Daddy, of course, I am, I thank God for that, and . . ."

Father Singletary twisted until he could look into her eyes, his brown ones understanding her babble. "Mitch's loss was unfair, Helen, cruel in the way that life can be, and there are moments like this when the grief comes back as painful as it ever was. Wonderful years that you should have had together were stolen, and that feeling doesn't leave you because more years have passed."

Helen drew in the shuddering breath that comes with releasing a knot of tangled emotions. "I suppose that's what still hurts so much—the unfairness of it, the wondering *why* that I can't seem to get rid of."

"No one who has actually dealt with that pain expects you to," he said gently. "I've never used the phrase, 'God's will' when it comes to death, and I won't. The hard reality is that we lose good people, and that leaves a wound that can be coped with even though the scar remains. In a situation like this, where you rush to the hospital, not knowing what's happening, it's like the scar is suddenly throbbing."

"That's a good way to put it," she said, the ache beginning to recede. Her hand trembled slightly when she offered the handkerchief back to him. "I think I'm all right now. I'm on my way to Mamma's house to pick up a few things for her. She's still in her bedroom slippers."

"Keep it in case you're not quite through dripping," the priest said, matching her brighter tone. "I have a stack of them that I stash behind the pulpit. Pastor Trotter and I swap them out every few days."

He stood with her, and she stretched out her hands to briefly squeeze his. "Thank you, Father, I appreciate it."

"Of course, any time. Is there anything else that I can do for Joy, other than to pop up and say hello? I can let Reverend Harper know about your father. He doesn't usually come by until after lunch."

"Yes, that would be nice," Helen replied, "one less call for me to deal with."

She was able to make it to the car without seeing anyone else she knew, needing another minute to fully compose herself. She had personal issues with a number of Catholicism's beliefs, but that didn't stop her from appreciating Father Singletary's kindness, which was known throughout the community. She had found his predecessor to be much less outgoing, and friends who were parishioners had indicated to her that his reassignment had been in an effort to bring in a more people-oriented priest. Father Singletary had quickly demonstrated that characteristic, moving from outside his office to forge ties with the other churches in town. Reverend Harper, their Episcopal priest, had praised him early after his arrival, and like today, Helen had seen nothing to detract from that opinion.

The distinctive sounds of the Beach Boys' "Good Vibrations" came from the radio when she cranked the car and she turned the volume up, allowing her fingers to beat the rhythm against the steering wheel. A rollicking song was what she needed to help restore her sense of relief.

# CHAPTER NINETEEN

"**M**amma, it could be hours before Daddy wakes up enough to talk. Helen and I can take turns, and we promise we'll call you the second he can carry on a conversation. Won't you please go home and take a nap?"

The look Joy flashed to them was one they knew only too well. "If I went without sleep as long as I did nursing the two of you when you were sickly, then I'm not about to walk out on your daddy just because I've yawned a few times. I may have more years on me now, but that doesn't mean I'm not perfectly capable of sitting right here until he opens his eyes. Y'all want to do something useful? Go home and clean the kitchen. I left it in a mess, and half the neighbors have been bringing food over."

Helen suppressed an I-told-you-so smile and put her arm around her sister's waist, putting enough pressure into the gesture to forestall a protest. "Mamma's right; let's go take care of that for her." She released her grip and glanced around the room, where the monitors were making what seemed to be appropriate sounds and her father appeared to be peaceful if more pale than she would have liked. They had been assured by the doctors and nurses that everything had gone well with no complications.

Helen couldn't imagine that her mother had slept much, and Eloise had rolled into the hospital at 6:02 before the eight o'clock surgery. That meant she'd been on the road not long before four although she was a morning person like Helen. Hopefully, they would all get a good night's sleep once her father awakened and began joking in his usual manner.

"I wouldn't mind you bringing back those brownies that Edna made. I can share them with the nurses," Joy said, giving them swift embraces to send them on their way.

In the parking lot, Eloise motioned for them to take her black Ford Fusion. "I guess I can't blame her," Eloise said. "She can catch up on sleep later. That Doctor Fielder certainly was nice. What's the story on him?"

Helen explained the new service that was to be available to the community on the drive to the home where they'd grown up, part of the post-World War II building boom that had not unpredictably coincided with the baby boom. Mature oak and magnolia trees canopied over yards that had once been green blank slates waiting for the saplings to grow, for flower beds to be dug, for shrubs and bulbs planted. Front porches stretched the widths of the houses, which were basically three different models, all single story until a few people remodeled to add a second floor. Backyard fences were vine-covered hurricane fences, the honeysuckle needing no encouragement to grow. Swing sets and treehouses, forts and castles made from boxes, room to run and catch lightning bugs while parents called out that supper would be ready soon.

Low-maintenance vinyl siding made the way in, and gas fireplace inserts replaced the real ones as older owners no longer wanted to bother with hauling firewood and the mess of ash. Their parents' house, like most, had changed little in exterior appearance. They pulled into the carport next to the fourteen-year-old blue Crown Victoria that was still in showroom condition. Locked cabinets in front of the vehicle were filled with automotive tools, some that had been passed down from their paternal grandfather.

"Good Lord, Mamma won't have to worry about cooking for a while," Eloise said, standing in front of the open refrigerator. "I count a ham, a gallon container labeled Brunswick Stew, and smaller containers of potato salad, chicken and dumplings, and pulled pork."

For desserts or sweet tooth snacking, the kitchen table was laden with two pies, the plate of brownies, and a plate of oatmeal cookies. Eloise reached into the refrigerator and extracted a plate. "And look, sausage and biscuits. Let's zap a couple in the microwave. I couldn't eat earlier—could you?"

"Now that you mention it, not really," Helen said, remembering the yogurt she'd had before leaving for the hospital. "The little mess Mamma was fussing about won't take long to clean up."

The floor that hadn't been swept, countertops that needed wiping down, a smear across the top of the stove, and an untidy stack of mail that had been deposited on the edge of the table weren't normally seen in Joy's kitchen. She might not wash windows every week, yet her strict standards for cleanliness were ingrained and had been passed to her daughters.

"Eat first, then straighten up? You want more coffee? There's juice in the fridge. I'm about at my caffeine limit."

"Me, too," Helen said, taking a paper plate from the cabinet to hand to Eloise. "One biscuit for me, please, and I'll get the juice." She made space on the drop-leaf table among the desserts for their plates. Their mother had not been one to share meal preparation beyond ensuring they were schooled in family recipes. Cleaning up after was a different story, and Helen fleetingly remembered their pleasure when the first dishwasher had been installed. Not that the glasses were allowed in it—hand washing in hot water with immediate drying was the only prevention against water spots as far as their mother was concerned.

When they sat down to eat, Helen nibbled the sausage biscuit to savor the taste and held up a finger in warning. "I don't care how good these are, I'm only having one."

Eloise smiled. "Remember Mamaw's biscuits? These are almost as good as hers."

"Don't be modest about yours," Helen said. "That's why they're so popular at your brunches."

"Unless someone wants a specific theme that doesn't include biscuits, they're always on the menu. By the way, the new van is super. It's easier to get in and out of, and Danny negotiated a decent deal for us."

Helen looked at her younger sister with the love they'd always shared, notwithstanding minor squabbles that had always been quickly resolved. She'd changed hairstyles last year, and the feathered, shorter cut was flattering. The rinse she was using gave a deeper red undertone than their natural chestnut, but it stopped a shade from being auburn. "You do know how proud Daddy and Mamma are of you and the boys, don't you?"

Eloise wiped a crumb from her lips. "Yeah, when they were visiting last month, Daddy took Danny and Sean out for a Braves game and Mamma and

I had a long talk. It wasn't that they didn't think We'll Do The Cooking couldn't work, but they know how difficult any small business is to run and catering is as competitive as anything. Did I tell you that we're going to be featured in the paper for our tenth anniversary?"

"No, that's super. Nothing like free publicity."

"True, and Sean developed a peach mustard sauce that can be used as a glaze. It's great on chicken and pork."

"That does sound good. Is he keeping it a secret?"

Eloise laughed, the sound exactly like Helen's. "He thinks he is, but I am his mamma after all. I got it out of him in nothing flat." She reached out her hand. "It's something, isn't it, to watch your kids turn into the kind of adults you hoped they would be? I mean, I know that our divorce was a lot more civilized than I've seen with other couples, and I wasn't overly surprised when my ex became too involved with his new life to spend the kind of time with the boys that he should have, but it didn't occur to me that they would take to the business like they have. I got them started in catering as a distraction, and it turned out to be one of the best decisions that I ever made."

Helen gave her sister's hand a quick squeeze. "I couldn't agree more. About both—Danny and Sean being in business with you and feeling like your kids are in a good place. And that's what we've done for Daddy and Mamma if we want to pat ourselves on the back a little more."

"And you're a grandmother now," Eloise said with a grin. "I have a while to wait on that one, although Danny is planning to propose to Abby on her birthday. She's a sweetheart, and I couldn't be happier. She's a special education teacher, and that takes such a dedication. Not that I'm taking anything away from what Tricia does," she added quickly.

Helen pushed her chair from the table. "I know precisely what you mean, and it is different from regular teaching. Speaking of which, let me tell you about this idiotic tempest we have brewing in town."

As Helen updated Eloise on the latest with the New Day project, they brought the small kitchen back to full order. "That it so typical of Frank and Deborah Hillman," Eloise said contemptuously. "Do you really think they have enough backing to stop the project?"

Helen tossed a damp paper towel into the plastic lidded trashcan that sat next to the stove. "I hate to admit it, but they do have a fair amount of influence around town. It seems like Deborah may be getting ready to make some kind of crusade out of it. Phyllis has her hackles up about it, and she swears there's got to be something behind their objections other than what they're saying."

"Oh, I don't know about that," Eloise said with a sniff. "If ever there were two people who . . ."

Helen's cell phone rang. "It's Mamma," she whispered, then, "Yes, Mamma, we did—oh great, we'll be there in a few minutes. Yes, we'll bring the brownies."

"Daddy's awake?"

"And complaining about wanting a cup of coffee," she said with a relieved smile.

The day blurred into a stream of visitors, discussions with the doctors, and nurses attending to varied tasks in Frank's room. Helen, Eloise, and Joy rotated from Frank's room to the waiting room, bringing visitors up-to-date on his condition. Helen and Eloise gave up trying to convince their mother to go home for a bit. Max called to see if there was anything he could do to help, and Helen reluctantly told him no. In truth, she would have enjoyed his company, but Eloise was only going to spend one night and she thought it would take the two of them to dislodge their mother from the hospital.

Doctor Turner was actually the one who convinced her. He told Joy that if all the tests were clear the following day, they would release Frank the day after that. However, at this point, if she didn't get some rest, she wasn't going to be much use to him when they got home. The opinion was echoed by their father, whose ghastly pallor was gone and his humor had returned. He joked that the pacemaker might have been a waste of time because if the Braves didn't start to play better, they were going to kill him before the season was halfway through.

"Here's what we're going to do," Joy said tartly after admonishing her husband for the comment. "I don't want anything complicated for supper—salad, Brunswick Stew, and maybe a sliver of pie. We'll need to pick up salad, so you girls decide who will go to the store, then one of you go on to the house to get things ready and the other one stay here with me until after they serve supper."

"Helen, it's been good for me to catch up with people that I haven't seen in years, but why don't you stay with Mamma? Not everyone coming by will know me," Eloise said. "The nice thing about Brunswick Stew is it can simmer for hours. I'll put it on and let it go until y'all get there. It will be like comfort food aroma therapy."

The pace of visitors had slowed, most of their parents' contemporaries having cycled through. The after-work group came by with offers of assistance, and Helen felt as if she was rewinding a tape to play the same phrases over and over. *Yes, we're grateful that it was a mild attack. Yes, isn't it wonderful what they can do these days? No, he should be home in a day or two.* The concerns expressed were genuine, though, and this was the way such situations were handled.

The drive to her parents' house was mostly quiet, her mamma allowing her shoulders to slump with the fatigue that she'd been denying. As promised, Eloise was in the kitchen extracting a pan of hot rolls from the oven. Salad was on the table, and the meaty scent of the hearty stew set Helen's stomach to rumbling.

"My Lord, I wasn't expecting to be hungry, but all of a sudden I'm starving," Joy said crossing from the small den. "You baked?"

Eloise took the lid from the pot. "I brought them with me frozen in the cooler. Everything is ready unless you want to wait for some reason. I can keep the rolls warm."

"Let me put this tote in the bedroom and wash my hands."

Eloise dropped her voice to a whisper as she ladled stew into bowls. "Is she planning to stay and get some sleep or has she changed her mind?"

"She's staying," Helen replied, taking the glasses from the table to fill them with tea. "You know she's going to want to go in first thing in the morning."

"That's fine—we all have that early-bird trait."

The women sat, their hands joined, Joy's words of grace said with a momentary tremble, the pressure of her fingers intense. She breathed in deeply after saying, "Amen," and smiled softly. "We have a lot to be thankful for today." She reached for a roll. "Not the least of which is that Dave Mabry still makes the best Brunswick Stew in town."

"He does now that Mr. Dickinson Senior gave it up. I never did know what it was that he did so special," Helen said, taking a small bite until it cooled a bit.

"Well, he took pride in using only beef, pork, and chicken that he'd raised himself. I don't know if that was the difference, but he was the only one who could say that," Eloise mused. "Speaking of farming, did I see that the Lurleys have added a petting zoo to their farm?"

Helen nodded. "That's the latest, and yes, that means bunny rabbits are at the farm again. There's a calf; a couple of goat kids, of course; a pen for chicks. They've planted a section with a few butterfly bushes. They open at nine o'clock if you want to make a run out there. It's astounding what they've done with the place. They've had to hire another helper, and if I haven't given you a bar of Juanita's soap yet, I'll bring one tomorrow."

Joy circled the salad on her plate with her fork. "I had my doubts when I heard what they were planning. It's almost impossible for families to compete with the big growers, and as much as I like Kyle and Juanita, and Lord knows, it was good to sell the farm, I thought for sure they were going to be in over their heads. Or, I suppose what I really thought was that Wallington wouldn't respond to what they envisioned."

"Times are changing, Mamma," Eloise said. "Farm to table can be very successful if you understand your market, and from what I've seen, they've taken it in the right sequence. Start with the produce that the local restaurants will buy and have a U-pick option before you try to package for retail sales. Having a niche like they did with the goats was another plus for them. Their cheeses are fabulous, and yes, Helen, you did give me a bar of the soap for Christmas. I don't have much left. I want to try her lotion, too."

"I heard Juanita was going to expand their line of mustards, jams, and jellies to help carry them through the winter months," Joy added. "Jeff Lawson has done up a design to use some kind of folding doors that will enclose their open air market so they can heat it."

Helen snapped her fingers. "Lillie was telling me about it the other day. You know how they have the back wall with the three sides open? Jeff is going to add half-walls all around so the lower part can have display space up against it and the upper part will be screened with these huge folding windows. They're like super insulated glass or something and seal tightly enough so that once the heaters are going, the place will stay warm. They're buying those no-vent electric fireplaces that will give a great atmosphere. Then when it's warm again, they'll fold the windows back and the whole place will be screened. I think it's going to work well for them."

Joy looked thoughtful. "There are some women in the Silver Seniors that make food and gift items, and none of them want to do anything on a schedule. I wonder if Juanita is interested in having a 'Get It While You Can' sort of section where the women could drop off whatever they have to sell. Take Dave Mabry's mamma, for instance."

"Oh, her fudge," Eloise said immediately. "Remember how hers always sold out first at the bake sales?"

Joy broke a roll in half and offered the other piece to Helen. "That's what I'm talking about. She hasn't lost her touch, gets into the mood sporadically, and makes a batch that she takes around. A lot of us are cutting back on sweets, though, and if she could drop it off at Always Fresh Farms, that would be a good deal for both of them."

"I bet Juanita will be interested," Helen said. "If she does it on consignment, there's no risk for them."

"I'll put it on my to-do list for after your Daddy gets home, and now, girls, in about five minutes, I'm going to leave y'all to this and take a long hot shower and climb into my night clothes."

"Wasn't there something about a sliver of pie in the menu request?"

Joy dropped her spoon into the empty bowl. "There was indeed. Let's make that ten minutes until the hot shower."

# CHAPTER TWENTY

"In a word, I have been sent out of the house so your daddy and Ethan can have man time together, although I don't suppose either of them will acknowledge that's what it is. Watching the game is the excuse they use."

A burst of laughter escaped Helen's lips before she could stop herself. "That's good, though, isn't it?"

"Especially considering how I felt last week when I thought your daddy might be on death's door," her mother said, lifting the tote she was carrying. "Is the table set?"

"It is. Let's put everything in the other room and get tea. You want iced or hot?"

"Neither right now. I heard about the auction, and I have a little more than two-thirds of the squares for this quilt done. We can get it finished in plenty of time. How are the preparations going?"

"Everything is on track," Helen said as they moved into the quilting room. "The church hall was available; Dorthea is lined up to cater lunch; the Ladies Auxiliary is going to have pastries, fruit, juice, coffee, and tea for the morning; tickets will be printed next week; and between Alicia and Max, notices are being posted in all kinds of places. Deirdre has the telephone trees working among the set that doesn't do computers. I think we're going to have a respectable turnout. We have twenty-six items pledged so far."

"This will give you twenty-seven, and I imagine several more women will donate soon. You know how it is with wanting to be sure you can finish a piece before you say anything. Aside from the fact that I totally agree with the cause, it's been too long since we've done an auction. Maybe y'all will start the tradition again. Anyway, I've had this one sitting around for probably six months. I put it aside while I was working on that set of Easter table runners for The Arbors." Joy quickly unloaded the tote. "I found the calico and bird print fabrics at that store in Lawrenceville, and the blue for the sashing and binding was left over from that last one that I did for Quilts for Valor."

Helen knew that sending quilts to the program for wounded military veterans was a project that her mother and other women in town felt strongly about. All, like her mother, had some experience with a relative serving as far back as World War II. The local coordinator for the program had tragically lost her middle son in Afghanistan. She'd once told Helen that each time they shipped a batch of quilts, it brought her some degree of comfort.

"I've gone back and forth on where to put the birds and roses squares," Joy said, creating a line of the six squares to the left. "My inclination is to place them in a random pattern, or I can use four of them in the corners and save the other two for something else."

Helen looked at the layout, the blank spots not taking away from the design. The main fabric had a field of medium blue with full roses outlined in white with gradients of pinks for the blossoms and the leaves were interestingly in a soft green instead of darker as would be found in nature. Smaller clusters of pink and white peonies were interspersed among the roses. The bird and roses squares gave the impression of stained glass with roses in magenta and shell pink hues, the leaves of palest green, and bluebirds with spread wings in flight superimposed across the leaves.

"It's a double-bed size, right? I like the idea of using all six squares and scattering them. Was this remnant fabric?"

"Yes to both questions. I loved the colors. You know how it is when a pattern catches your eye and it's the end of a bolt. You take what you can get."

"That's true," Helen said, deftly arranging the squares so fewer blank spaces were showing. They worked companionably for almost an hour and a half, caught up in measuring, trimming, and stitiching.

"I think it's time for a break," Joy said, doing a neck roll left, then right. "What's your cookie situation if we do hot tea?"

"Nothing from Lisa's," Helen laughed. "I have those almond crisps we like, though."

"Perfect. Those are thin, and I can have three for the size of a regular cookie. Let's sit in the kitchen. I'll be there in a few minutes. If you have that cranberry and rosehips tea, it would be great. If not, whatever you're in the mood for is fine."

"Enough for a pot and a little left," Helen said. She put the kettle on then set out the cookies, mugs, spoons, and napkins as she waited for her mother. When the kettle gave the first shriek of the whistle, she switched the gas off and poured the stream of heated water into the daisy-motif teapot.

Joy carried the mugs to the table. "By the way, will Max be playing auctioneer for you? That's the word around town."

"He is," Helen said noticing the way her mamma stressed the word *Max*. She knew that tone well, had in fact adopted it when she became a mother. The real intent of introducing the name was amplified by the *we-need-to-talk* expression her mother wasn't trying to disguise.

"Honey, I've kept quiet for months now, waiting for you to decide that you wanted to open up about Max."

"It's not that simple," she tried.

"It's not that complicated," was the rapid response followed by the soft sigh of a mother who knows that a kiss won't really make the pain go away. "I promise that I haven't had any kind of conversation with the kids, so I can't say for certain that they're okay about you and Max. I can only speak for your daddy and me. Don't give me that look. Drink your tea and eat a cookie." A wad of tissues appeared on the table.

Helen sipped tea, wondering if she could swallow. Surprisingly well as it turned out.

"It wouldn't have been possible for your daddy and me to love Mitch more than we did. He was as much our son as you and Eloise were our daughters. Why the good Lord took him from us in the way that he did will forever be a mystery to me, except that tragedy comes to a lot of people when it isn't deserved."

Helen reached for a tissue, the pooling in her eyes fracturing the image of her mother's resolute face. "You can't hardly count those schoolyard crushes you had, so it's fair to say that you loved Mitch your whole life. There's a lot left in that life, though, and for you to think that you should be spending the rest of it alone doesn't make much sense."

"I'm not alone," Helen said weakly, "I have the kids, Russell, the circ . . ."

"This is me you're talking to, or trying not to talk to, honey." Joy's lips curved gently. "I wasn't ready to say it before, but I will tell you that when I was on the phone with nine-one-one, watching the color drain out of your daddy's face, I was praying harder than I had since Mitch died. I was begging to have more time, to not let this be the moment, to not have it end like that with no chance of recovery. If they'd have run an EKG on me for that first hour, I would probably have been slapped in a bed right beside him." She shot her hand out, transmitting her warmth to Helen. "My prayers were answered, and not discounting the good Lord, I'll give credit where credit is due—to the EMTs, the doctors, and the hospital. Frank isn't about to admit how worried he was, of course—I don't expect him to, being a man like he is. He'll pretend that he knew all along it was nothing to worry too much about, and I'll let him act that way because that's what we do." She withdrew her hand and extended another tissue. "My point here is that Max is a fine man, and I imagine that you're the one holding back in allowing this relationship to be whatever it could become, just friendship or more. I think it's well past time for you to find that out."

Helen bit her bottom lip, the tears flowing silently. "It's confusing, Mamma. Widows remarry—I know that. It's been almost four years, and if the situation were reversed, I wouldn't expect Mitch to stay alone. It's funny, you know. I just assumed that Max and Phyllis would get together."

"She's not his type," was said with calm assuredness.

"That's what she told me, and Max did, too. It's true what you're saying about Max. We enjoy being together and have a lot in common. To be honest, when I was on the cruise, I must have turned around I don't know how many times to point out the sunset or a constellation and half the time I'd be ready to say, *Look, Mitch*, and the other half it was, *Look, Max*. That scared me a little." She blotted her eyes, the tightness in her chest lessening as she spoke the words out loud.

"That doesn't surprise me in the least. Sweetie, this conversation is not going to be the beginning of constant nagging. I'm always here to talk if you want to—you know that. But you've been either holding this inside or trying to fool yourself about how you feel, and I couldn't let it go on any longer. I'll listen to anything that you want to say, or you can change the subject. It's your choice."

"It doesn't seem like you were giving me much choice," Helen said as wryly as she could.

"I mean, it's your choice now."

The anticipated fresh tears didn't start, and Helen took a tentative sip of tea that was barely warm. "I don't want to rush this," she said softly.

"Other than probably Phyllis, I don't think anyone would tell you that you should. Of course, most folks who have seen you two together have pretty well accepted that you're a couple, whether you call yourselves that or not."

"The circle has been really good about it," Helen said. "They leave openings all the time for either of us to refer to ourselves that way and don't belabor the point when neither of us takes the bait."

"Are you nervous about talking to Tricia?"

Helen rolled her eyes. "Actually, Tricia has told me on more than one occasion that I shouldn't be reluctant to acknowledge what's going on." She shifted her gaze and stared directly into her mother's eyes, tears threatening again. "I do understand that I'm not betraying Mitch's memory, and yet, I suppose the truth is that I never thought I could feel the way about another man that I did about Mitch."

Joy pushed the last tissue forward. "I have to be careful here because I want this to come out correctly. A number of my friends are widows, and like you and Wanda, not all of them are elderly. I do think that being widowed at a younger age makes a difference. Yes, Mitch was as much of a soul mate as you could have asked for. It isn't that Max will replace him, and I doubt he expects to. What I also think is that you should give him a chance and see how it goes."

Helen blotted her eyes and blew her nose. "Do you know that we've never even kissed? Quite honestly, Max hasn't tried."

"Unless I miss my guess, I suspect you've sent out plenty of signals that you're not ready for that."

"I probably have," Helen said. "I'm not sure how to change that."

Joy arched her eyebrows. "That's a discussion that Phyllis would no doubt be happy to have with you, but again, there's no need to overcomplicate it. I would say to just let your genuine feelings loose. I'm pretty sure that you don't need to go from not kissing to planning a wedding. There are several steps in between, and if the budding romance doesn't bloom, well, it wouldn't be the first time in the history of the world that happened."

Helen felt the giddiness of the emotional roller coaster slowing to a stop. "Good Lord, this is hardly the way I was expecting the afternoon to turn out."

"Remember, we did make progress on the quilt, too. I need to be getting home, though. Ethan is headed out after the game, and I think he wants to swing by and at least say hello to you."

"I'll be here," Helen said, gathering her mother's things and carrying the tote to the car for her. They shared the bond that can only be found in true affection and a deep trust that it's safe to allow another person to see your frailty. Helen knew how fortunate they were to have a relationship with that kind of strength, and their good-bye hug communicated that understanding.

Tawny, awakened from a nap, was wiggling for a show of affection, and perhaps in the way that dogs do, sensing Helen's need to cuddle. "Oh my, girl, we could have some changes coming into our lives, couldn't we?" Tawny's laps to her face brought a smile as it usually did, and Helen thought of the way in which the little chug would curl contentedly on the sofa between them when she and Max watched television together. They did say that dogs were a gauge of a person's character. She set Tawny on the floor, feeling silly for the thought. There was no question about Max's character, not at this stage. True, he was divorced, but from everything she knew of that, it wasn't a situation where Max could be faulted—certainly not as it had been with Eloise, Phyllis, and her friends in the circle whose husbands had either cheated on them or been emotionally abusive. What was the saying? Falling in love was easy; staying in love could be altogether a different matter. Of course, it wasn't as if she'd ever heard Max's ex-wife's side, but she had known other couples who freely admitted that the "Love is blind" adage had applied to them and that their basic incompatibility finally became too burdensome to cope with.

She moved around the kitchen and thought of Father Singletary's gentleness in the hospital chapel. It combined with her mamma's voice as she'd coaxed Helen to express her conflicting feelings. Had she been completely honest when she said that she would expect Mitch to find someone had the situation been reversed? Was that part of her reluctance? Would she actually want another woman to be here, in their house, the house their children had grown up in, the house that they'd remodeled together? That brought a wince to the surface, a mental image that jolted her as she envisioned an undefined figure standing there as she and Mitch had so often done, him perhaps planting a kiss on the back of her neck as she rinsed glasses. The vividness of the scene caused her to sharply take a breath and then, thankfully, the rational part of her brain gave her a mental thump. She wouldn't have wanted him to take up with some bimbo, but what about someone like Carolyn? Someone she respected and who would have loved him as she had? She wiped the counter, forcing herself to play this out, to deal with the question that she had been avoiding. Her mother was right—today was as good as any to tear away the excuses.

She had known widows who clung to their grief, shackling themselves to the past and, consciously or not, using it as a shield against being active in life. She and Wanda had discussed this, and even though Wanda was also still single, Helen knew there was a gentleman in Charleston—Duncan—who she visited regularly. Their respective careers were taking priority, yet from everything Wanda said, it sounded as if the long-distance relationship was satisfactory for them at this stage. Although she carefully avoided asking Helen about Max, Wanda never seemed to pass up a chance to mention some favorable characteristic or something nice that he'd done.

Why shouldn't she? Helen switched off the light over the stove and wandered into the den where she sat and turned the television on, thinking she would tune in some soft jazz. She recognized the movie that was playing before she hit the button to change channels and began to laugh. It was *Chapter Two* starring Marsha Mason and James Caan, a Neil Simon play that had been adapted for the screen. The comedy takes a poignant turn as the character played by Caan, a widower, remarries in what his brother considers too quickly a fashion. The main character then suffers an attack of guilt that stuns his new bride and he is forced to confront how to balance his memory of his wife and how he would face his future.

Tawny jumped onto the chair, bumping Helen's hand that was holding the remote. "Is this an omen or what, girl? Think about all the movies that could be on at right this moment, and I get this one?" The chug cocked her head and didn't provide an answer.

Without disturbing the dog, Helen muted the sound and swapped the remote control for the telephone handset on the table next to the chair. Her schedule had been erratic for the past week, and Max had left the invitation for dinner open. She didn't want to risk going to his apartment in her current frame of mind, but dinner out was something that she could handle. What she did know was that she wanted to be with him for the evening.

# CHAPTER TWENTY-ONE

"I don't quite know what to think of it or if I am being a bit paranoid," Kristen Duluth said after explaining that her updated presentation to the city council had been postponed.

"They didn't give you a specific reason?" Helen shifted the telephone to her left shoulder.

"Not really, only that a new agenda item had to be added and they were going to slide my presentation into the first meeting next month."

"That does happen," Helen said. "I know you want to get approval, but is your funding situation time sensitive or can this wait with no impact?"

"The delay won't derail the project," Kristen conceded. "It did all sound rather bureaucratic."

"There's a lot of that, too. And in one way, it might be a bonus because we'll have the auction the Saturday before the council meeting. That should get you a boost in support."

"Have I thanked you again for doing this? It's such a generous gesture. I especially like the idea you came up with to use the individuals who we want to move into the complex to be there as runners and helpers."

"That was actually Alicia Johnson's idea. She's got a flair for marketing, and she and Max have been posting to social media for us, whatever that all means."

"Well, thanks again to everyone. I've got a staff meeting shortly and I'll bring them up-to-date."

Helen felt her mouth move into a smile at the word "date." Even though she hadn't said anything to Max last night, there had been a sense of lightness the entire evening they were together. Max had made dinner conversation easy by asking how her daddy was doing post-surgery, and they had spun off into conversations about the benefits of medical technology. He'd had to make it an early evening because of a scheduled video conference with Hawaii at ten p.m., which provided the perfect excuse for her to not invite him in after he drove her home. Aside from her mamma's advice to simply let her feelings show, Helen wasn't certain yet how she was going to do that.

The sound of the telephone startled her. It was Phyllis.

"Helen, listen, I'm in Atlanta and will be headed back as soon as the conference is over. I heard something last night that I've got to tell you about. I can't talk now because I have a panel session getting ready to start, plus this is a conversation that requires wine. Are you going to be in around four?"

"Uh, yeah, sure," Helen said, wondering what would have Phyllis in this kind of mood. If it was a new man—always a possibility when she had an overnight trip to Atlanta—she would have begun the conversation with that lead-in. Well, she would find out soon enough, and it was going to be a busy day.

Right on schedule, Phyllis bustled in through the back door a little after four o'clock, with the announcement of, "I don't know if you're going to be upset or happy. I've swung between the two all day." She plopped her purse on the counter and pecked Helen's cheek, her eyes glancing to the table where wine glasses and a cheese and cracker tray waited.

"Let's start with wine—red or white? Then you can enlighten me as to what on earth you've been up to."

"Basic cabernet is fine if that's okay with you," Phyllis said and stooped to rub Tawny's ears. "I'm kicking these shoes off, too. I love the color of these, but they're not the most comfortable pair I own." Rather than her usual flats, the jade pumps with inch-and-a-half heels were the exact match to the jade and navy square-necked print sheath she was wearing. Plain gold ball earrings and a gold chain with a teardrop jade pendant completed the look.

"That's a nice outfit," Helen said, bringing the open bottle and pouring. "Now, what has got you going?"

Phyllis took a sip first, gave an appreciative little sigh, then grinned in a way that Helen knew preceded something exceptionally juicy. "Okay, I have to put this into context, so don't rush me."

"I wouldn't dream of it. I assume it involves a man or a bar or both."

"Of course, it does. Anyway, you know how it goes at conferences. You link up with people during registration at the hotel and gather at Happy Hour with people you haven't seen since the last conference. So, there were about ten of us, including Gary Goldberg from Macon. A real sweetheart, but totally not my type."

Helen knew better than to interrupt the flow.

"We're all talking the way that you do and another guy that I don't know comes up to Gary and apparently, they weren't expecting to see each other because it's a *hey, what ae you doing here kind of thing*. Gary grabs an empty chair to add to the circle and introduces the guy as Steve Conroy. Not bad looking, but not an attention-getter either. Mid-fifties, he was a little chunky even though his suit was good quality. I'm sitting on the other side of Gary and listening to Bianca Martinez talking when I hear Gary say, 'Wallington? Phyllis is from there,' and I turn back around."

Helen nudged the cheese tray toward Phyllis. She put a wedge of smoked Gouda on a cracker and set it on the napkin. "Turns out Steve is a real estate developer, and he was on his way to Wallington. Want to guess who he was planning to meet with?"

"I don't want to spoil your fun."

"Fred and Tommy Hillman."

That didn't sound right. "Fred and Tommy aren't in real estate."

"That's not entirely correct, which I will explain in a minute. Needless to say, I became very interested in Mr. Steven Conroy. I ordered us all another drink, and Bianca left which gave me the excuse to slide over to the other side of Steve. He's never been to Wallington, and I start in about places to eat, that kind of thing." Anger edged her voice. "I probably could have gotten more detail if we'd been alone, but if what he said and hinted at is true, the Hillmans have managed to get some kind of a deal going for the old Jankowsky property on the east edge of town and, more importantly, for the Tyler Street properties."

Helen was glad she'd swallowed her wine. "What? Did I hear you correctly?"

Phyllis grinned triumphantly. "Yep. My guess is that good old Fred has decided to diversify from the furniture business. Deborah actually has a real estate license. You know a lot of women dabble in that. As far as I know, Deborah never really did anything with her license, but back to the main point. The carpet tile factory is scheduled to expand next year, and I had heard that some other manufacturer—one that makes solar roof tiles was looking at moving here, too. That Jankowsky property has been sitting vacant for fifteen years if not more because of some legal tangle involving the heirs who don't even live here. The location is good, though, for the factory employees. As for Tyler Street, that would be a smaller development, but would be done in tandem with the larger one while they have their own builder around. The idea would be to market the edge of town and close to town as options for buyers."

"And if they can pull it off soon, they'll get everything at a cheaper price."

Phyllis nodded eagerly. "That also means that if New Day goes into Tyler Street, they lose the in-town option. I don't have any idea if that would cause them to pull out of the whole deal, but it might."

"Well, I'll be. This begins to make sense."

Phyllis ate the cracker before she continued. "If the guy Steve was being straight with me, they'll need a couple of density variances to do what they plan, and he's been told that Fred has enough influence to make it happen."

"If he can keep everything quiet while he lines up support, he might very well be able to," Helen mused. "Kristen called earlier. Her presentation to the council has been postponed."

Phyllis refilled their glasses. "Aside from the fact that Fred and Deborah probably dislike the idea of New Day's plan because they're narrow-minded and mean-spirited, the real reason would be the money."

"So if you met this guy Steve last night, that means he's here in town?"

"Yes, although I gather that everything is very tentative. It's more exploratory than a done deal."

It was the same sensation as finding the elusive puzzle pieces that you hadn't been able to see at first. "It seems to me that the Grigsby sisters should be our next stops," Helen said thoughtfully.

"Clarissa first, I think," Phyllis agreed. "Town Square is the largest real estate office in town, and Clarissa can talk about property values as well as anyone, plus she stays wired into the council. If the Chamber of Commerce is courting that new factory, she may be in on that, too. She's back on the executive board again."

"Denise has already given us great press about the quilting auction. If what you're telling me is for real, she's going to eat this up."

"You better believe it," Phyllis grinned. "She never passes up a chance to poke at Fred's hypocrisy. Not that I think he's doing anything illegal, but sneaky definitely comes to mind."

"We have to be fair about it—not to Fred, but to Clarissa and Denise. I don't want us to get carried away just because we want this to be true. How comfortable are you that this guy Steve was on the up and up?"

"I've been around my share of guys who are full of crap when they start talking about deals, and I didn't get that impression of him. It sounded plausible, and you're right in that we need to pass on what I was told and let Clarissa and Denise see what they can find out. Both of them are in better positions than we are to follow the threads. I'm sure this will pique their interest."

"What's your day like tomorrow?

Phyllis shrugged. "Pretty jammed actually what with being gone for a couple of days. If you could go see Clarissa, I'll call Denise and take a bottle of wine to her office. She won't be available until late anyway if her schedule is like it usually is."

"That sounds like a plan," Helen said, tapping her finger on the table. "You nailed it about mixed feelings, though. I'm thrilled to find out that Fred may be involved in some scheme, but I'm furious that he and his family keep saying such ugly things about New Day to help put money in their pockets."

"Well, I have no doubt that their prejudice is genuine—it's just that I don't think they would be trying so hard to have the permit denied if it wasn't for the money."

"I suppose we need to keep quiet about this, except for talking to Clarissa and Denise. If it isn't true, that gives the Hillmans an opportunity to be righteously indignant and that's the last thing we want."

Phyllis tapped her wineglass against Helen's. "Here's betting you a bottle of champagne that the Hillmans are in this neck deep."

"That's a bet I'll be happy to lose," Helen said. They turned their conversation to the auction, and after Phyllis left, Helen stared at the business card of Steven Conroy, Senior Associate, Galbraith Development. She wasn't familiar with the company, although towns within commuting distance to Atlanta had been growing with residential and commercial expansion. Wallington was far enough away to be of no interest, or at least she'd thought so until today. She'd known about the factory expansion from Rita, whose husband was in management there. Four or five sites were still available, mainly land where other textile mills had been during the time that was the primary industry in town.

She liked the idea of another low-impact industry coming in with decent-paying jobs and people did have to live somewhere. The Jankowsky property was on a direct route to the commerce park, and she could see developing that. Tyler Street, however, was more limited in space. If someone wanted to transform that neighborhood, it was likely to require a density waiver to cram enough houses in to make it worth the investment. That would be basically the opposite approach to what New Day was proposing. Clarissa would have that information, and she had come out strongly in support of Kristen's plan. Hmm, now that she thought about it, Clarissa was also close to the mayor's assistant and could probably find out why the agenda for the council meeting had been changed.

The slight click of Tawny's nails against the floor signaled that it was dinnertime, and while Helen usually didn't eat until closer to seven or seven-thirty, with half a bottle of wine in her, she needed something more substantial than a couple of crackers and cheese. Wait, there was some leftover soup in the refrigerator. That would be just the thing to hold her over until dinner. She popped the container in the microwave to heat while she portioned out Tawny's food.

The soup was tomato basil and came close to tasting like homemade. In taking the first spoonful, she was reminded of the wonderful soups they had eaten on the cruise—a conch chowder that had been a toss-up for favorite with a lobster bisque, and a pumpkin that was in the running. That thought keyed the memory of her conversation with Nancy and Yvonne Huckabee the morning of their return. Hadn't she said that her daughter worked for the state in some housing office? Helen reconstructed the breakfast, the two sisters talking about missing the Atlanta Quilt Show because of the timing of the daughter's wedding. Then it had been something about the daughter—what was her name?—Peggy?—Pamela?—no, it was Penny—being with the Department of Community Affairs, which managed different housing programs.

Helen didn't have any experience in dealing with state or federal programs other than being vaguely familiar with subsidized housing. There were anti-discrimination laws, of course, but objecting to New Day having a group home probably didn't fall into the category. But what if there was a special program that was supportive of this type of housing? If there was, that could be one more voice to add to the mix. Wouldn't Kristen know about it, though? Maybe, maybe not since she wasn't from Georgia and the members of New Day's board wouldn't necessarily have knowledge of a program either if one did exist. It was certainly a question to ask Kristen in the morning.

Helen paused in eating the soup, a new idea jangling for attention. Maybe Penny was a quilter like her mamma and aunt—that wouldn't be surprising. She had Nancy's card and would e-mail her an invitation to the auction. If by chance she and Yvonne could come, that would be great, and if Penny was a quilter, they would naturally invite her, too. If she attended, Helen and Phyllis would be certain to introduce her around as being an official with the state. Helen couldn't imagine that Penny and Kristen wouldn't hit it off, and it stood to reason that Penny would be excited about the New Day project. Even if there wasn't a specific program in the state to support it, a few properly placed comments would skitter about town, how a state housing official thought it was a wonderful project. That would make its way to at least one or two members of the council. It wasn't like she was planning to put the unsuspecting woman on the spot—there would be no need for her to have any knowledge of the undercurrent that would be set in motion.

Helen couldn't keep from smiling as she spun the scenario, thinking of how gossip flowed and the tendency for exaggeration with each version that was told. Depending on who latched onto the story, by the time it made the circles, Penny might be elevated to being a personal assistant to the governor. Notwithstanding that it was just as likely that Penny was either not a quilter or that she wouldn't be able to come to the auction, it was worth sending the e-mail to at least establish contact with Nancy. That would show that Helen's "let's-keep-in-touch" farewell had been sincere, and she had genuinely enjoyed the sisters' company. Whether Savannah, Atlanta, or Wallington, Helen suspected they would be seeing one another again. That was how friendships were often formed in the quilting world.

# Chapter Twenty-Two

"Isn't it great? The will-calls and outright sales put us at over one hundred tickets." Sarah and Helen were setting up the ticket table in the foyer, staying well clear of the four Ladies Auxiliary women who were putting the finishing touches on the beverages and pastries table. Helen wasn't certain how they coaxed good coffee from their old-fashioned large aluminum pot, and she didn't care. It was somehow devoid of the slightly metallic taste that those usually produced.

"I know. Dorthea, bless her heart, says she's prepared for up to two hundred. Did you take a look at the display area this morning? You remember Nelda's quilt that won third place at the Paducah show? She contributed that."

"I love that one," Sarah said, checking the cash box for change and the roll of door prize tickets. "It really is a piece of art. You could easily make it the focal point of a room's décor."

The quilt, MAGNOLIA MEMORIES, had captured the glossy, deep green of magnolia leaves and the creamy color of the blossoms. The tree at the center was a magnificent specimen that had been photographed and transferred to fabric. Nelda had selected a mottled green batik fabric as a background and in each corner of the quilt she'd appliquéd clusters of smaller magnolia blossoms, some with a pale pinkish hue.

"The place looks perfect," Helen said, surveying the hall that had seen no telling how many different events. Of the six churches downtown that had been built in the late 1800s, First Methodist had maintained more of its historical structure than the others by consciously minimizing modern conveniences in the main sanctuary and having the fellowship hall, offices, library, nursery, and classrooms in a rectangular building that was covered in the same granite stone that came from the local quarry. The original flooring for the sanctuary and pews had been carved from regional hard black walnut wood, which had been sanded, resanded, and carefully finished each time to preserve its beauty. The newer addition to the church, masked behind the stone façade, had been updated through the decades. Photographs of weddings and other celebrations decorated the walls and reflected changes in the town from the early 1900s.

The cavernous room could be set for three hundred, and the stage against the right wall could accommodate a fifteen-piece band. The latest version of flooring in the hall was a high-grade parquet-look engineered wood that was guaranteed to withstand plenty of foot traffic and the scraping of tables and chairs as they were arranged in different configurations. Every caterer in town had praised the efficient layout of the commercial-grade kitchen with the large pass-thru against the right-hand wall.

They had debated between round and rectangular tables, finally settling on ten-person rounds with crisp white tablecloths to show off the beautiful spring bouquet centerpieces that Cheryl Sullivan, who owned the florist shop adjoined to Lisa Forsythe's Bakery, had provided for the cause. The display area for the auction items was set into an L-shape against the left-hand wall where Deirdre, Phyllis, and Becky were double-checking the tags to make sure each item was labeled. The offerings had jumped to fifty-three, and it was a wonderful mix of quilt sizes. The smaller pieces such as handbags and jackets were placed in the silent auction section. Mary Lou had marshaled the Women's Club to create baskets for the silent auction as well, and several merchants and restaurants had donated gift certificates as door prizes.

Kristen ushered in six young men and women who were among the potential residents of the New Day project. She and they proudly wore aqua polo shirts with *New Day* embroidered in gold thread atop khaki colored pants. "There's a line of cars coming into the parking lot," she said after introducing the smiling group, which Sarah led toward the kitchen for their assignments: keeping the trash picked up, serving during lunch, and performing as runners when door prizes were handed out.

"This is bigger than I was expecting," Kristen said, stepping into the hall itself. Her hair was pulled into a French braid, a wide smile conveying the thanks that she had expressed with every new detail that had been added. "I've never seen so many quilts in one place."

"To be honest, this is about two-thirds the size of what we used to do," Helen said, leading her to the start of the display. "I'm not saying that people aren't coming to support you, but it has been years since our last auction and that's part of the excitement. If we'd really had more notice, we would have had a contest and a vendor area set up."

"What handicraft this is. I love the geometry of it." Kristen had paused in front of COLOR SPLASH, a twin size that was vivid with pinks, purple, aqua, and yellow. Four identical large squares that contained a smaller square inside, then a circle with a smaller circle inside it dominated the corners of the quilts. Three squares—one with a starburst, one with a hexagon, one with four triangles—bases not quite touching were aligned between the two corner squares. The pattern was repeated on the bottom and vertically on each side. The intriguing part was the arrangement was used twice more in decreasing sizes and superimposed so there was a stacked effect to the quilt. The placement of the squares had been moved around to prevent exact duplication on each layer.

"And this—how can a quilt look like a painting?"

Helen smiled. "It has a lot to do with the fabric and the patience of the quilter," Helen said, agreeing with the assessment of DAY ON THE LAKE. It was a fall scene, and she suspected that the completion for autumn might have been delayed because she knew the quilter often put her work on consignment with Wanda and this would have sold quickly in the fall. The center section showed a lake with a boat and the figure of two men fishing. The mirror calmness of the water reflected the shores of the lake, which were lined with trees in glorious colors of red, gold, orange, and yellow. The borders were cleverly done in a wood grain fabric that served as a frame, and from a distance, someone might assume they were looking at either a painting or a photograph.

"That's it. I have to bid on this one," Kristen said of the quilt that was a take on Noah's Ark combining the alphabet. "A" was an anteater, "B" a beaver, "C" a cow, and so forth. This time the borders were the alphabet in uppercase and lowercase, block lettering on the top and bottom, cursive on the sides. The quilt was proportioned so that the entire alphabet was displayed on each border. Kristen turned to Helen. "The variety is amazing. I mean, I suppose when I hear the word 'quilt' I immediately think of something in patchwork."

"There are some of those, too," Helen said, pointing to another section of the display. Her face broke into a smile as Max walked up, and she introduced him to Kristen.

"We've got the sound equipment ready to go," Max said.

"Max will be our auctioneer and master of ceremonies," Helen explained. "He'll give a short welcome speech, explain the sequence of events, and read out the door prizes. Kristen, have you decided if you or Norman as the president of the board will say a few words about New Day before we start the auction?"

"We're still going back and forth on that," she said. "Norman is much more familiar to people than I, but he's not fond of speaking in public. I imagine that he won't make his mind up until the last minute. I'm prepared in case he wants me to do it." She put her hand to the holder clipped to her waistband, where apparently her cell phone was vibrating. "Great to meet you, Max. I'll go find a quiet spot to take this."

"You look terrific in that color," Max said, leaning in to kiss Helen's cheek. "Not that you don't always look terrific, and what a great job everyone has done." Her burgundy crinkle slacks were a natural choice, and one day when she was wearing them in The Right Look shop Carolyn had whipped out a blouse in a shell pink and burgundy print that Helen hadn't been able to resist. Since Helen knew she would be on her feet almost continuously, she'd chosen comfortable flats that were woven leather uppers in pink and burgundy.

"Thank you. So many people have pitched in. We have about five minutes before the doors open, then it should be bustling all day after that."

The sound of group laughter and a burst of chatter echoed from the foyer. Max pivoted, and they saw the throng of women splitting into those who were picking up tickets and those who were showing their tickets for entry.

Max grinned, the cobalt blue short-sleeved shirt he was wearing emphasizing the blue hint in his gray eyes. "I would say the show is starting. Do you have a station to man or are you floating today?"

"Pretty much floating," Helen said, scanning the faces. Some she knew; some she couldn't identify. She was glad, however, to see there were three generations from girls to women that she knew to be in their eighties or older and at least a handful of men. She'd had a delightful conversation with Nancy Huckabee, who had enthusiastically passed on the information about the auction to her daughter Penny. Nancy had called back to tell Helen that Penny wouldn't be able to attend. In a way, that was just as well. Helen had felt a tweak of guilt over her planned manipulation of the woman.

Phyllis came over with a clipboard in her hand. "There's a steady line in case you haven't noticed," she said. In keeping with the theme for the day, she was wearing a quilted vest over a short-sleeved red round-neck top and a pair of navy blue slacks. Her feet also were enclosed in comfortable-looking red canvas shoes. The vest was a lightweight red, white, and blue calico that she'd originally made for a Fourth of July event. "In listening to pieces of conversation, I think we're going to get close to that two hundred we've set up for. We can squeeze in four or five more tables if we need to. If it goes like most of these things, we'll have a few groups that come in around ten-thirty. The count will be close to correct after this wave gets inside."

"Are Alicia and Rita doing okay at the ticket table?"

Phyllis laughed. "Yeah, and Becky is standing by to slide into a chair when they have to take the frequent bathroom breaks."

The two younger pregnant women had insisted that they be allowed to help. Sitting at a table did keep them off their feet, and handling the tickets didn't require any sort of lifting or stretching.

Mary Lou hurried toward them, the excitement hard to miss on her face. As usual, her sense of style trumped the need for comfort, but then again, she was younger. The coral surplice dress was a fluid fabric that fell exactly to the middle of her knees. The slightly darker coral enamel and gold pendant and earrings were the same shade as her espadrilles. "Do you see those two women talking to Sarah?"

"I don't recognize either one of them," Helen said. They looked to be maybe a mother and daughter pair, the older one probably in her fifties. They were close in height at around five six. The younger woman's black hair was cut in a pixie style, while the other woman wore hers in a short pageboy.

"That's because they're from Helen. They're decorating a bed and break-fast that they're opening. The daughter—that's Lannie—saw this on some social media thing and told Eleanor, her mother, that they should come see what they could pick up. I mean what goes better in a B&B than quilts?"

"Helen, Lord, I haven't been there in ages," Phyllis said. "That's a ways from here."

"They're actually combining the trip with a business meeting in Augusta on Monday. They thought it would be fun to come here first. Aside from the fact that it's super to get someone from that distance, I have a feeling they've got a hefty budget to work with."

Helen was a favorite tourist spot in Northeast Georgia in the Blue Ridge Mountains on the Chattahoochee River. It was a re-creation of an alpine village complete with cobblestone alleys and old-world towers. Helen remembered the summer they'd taken the kids there and how they'd teased her about having a whole town as a namesake.

"I like that. Helen, you can do the play-on-your-name bit and charm them into spending extra money, I'm sure," Phyllis said in a low voice. "And speaking of people that we do know, we have Mrs. Mayor checking out the silent auction."

"So we do," Helen said appreciatively. It was time to play hostess, mingle with smiles and *thanks for coming*, and answer questions, weaving in the cause of the event as subtly as possible. She assumed that a fair percentage of attendees were there strictly for the quilts and hadn't paid attention to the reason behind the auction.

She passed by the mayor's wife with a short exchange of pleasantries and intersected with Sarah who introduced her to Eleanor and Elaine—please call me Lannie—Bachman, who assured her they were in the buying mood.

"That's terrific," she said and saw Wanda come into the hall. "If bidding doesn't go your way, though, I want you to meet Wanda Wallington. She has the most wonderful shop and carries quilts on consignment that might work for you as well." She finished the introductions and caught Phyllis waving urgently in her peripheral vision. Oh dear, they'd been blessedly free of problems. Was that about to change?

She excused herself and followed Phyllis's path to the opposite side of the room where the second set of double doors led into the far end of the long foyer. As they exited, she nearly bumped into Denise and Clarissa Grigsby, each wearing a suspiciously mischievous smile.

These were not women you automatically assumed were sisters, other than for the same emerald green eyes which Helen always suspected Clarissa enhanced with tinted contacts. Clarissa was shorter than Denise, and within the first minute of a conversation, you would guess that she was a real estate agent. Her short layered cut of honey blonde hair was perfect for her heart-shaped face, and her outfit today was a jacket and belted sheath in celadon green, a scarf of intricately mixed shades of green tied in a loose bow replacing the need for a necklace.

Denise, at three inches taller, wore her usual pants suit—today's was medium blue, with a sky blue, high-collared blouse. Her age of mid-sixties was easier to tell since she'd allowed her hair to go naturally white, the curls framing her strong-jawed face the only softness about her. The same energy that had intimidated opponents on the basketball courts of high school and college had carried Denise through taking over the *Wallington Gazette* from their father.

"We know you've got a lot to do today," Denise said in her husky voice, "and first, thanks for the auction. I hadn't realized how much I missed having one until I looked back at some of the old articles that we'd run about them." She pulled Phyllis into a tighter circle, glancing around to see if they were alone. "More importantly, as soon as we verify one more detail, this business with Fred Hillman is going to get a full-page spread."

Phyllis lifted up on the balls of her feet. "It's juicy?"

"Definitely."

"Not like illegal juicy—more underhanded," Clarissa said. "This developer he's involved with has a pretty shoddy reputation, and Fred has all but guaranteed that the density waiver as well as a couple of others will be granted. He's totally banking on influencing the council to make that happen."

Denise straightened and stepped back. "Anyway, I'll run the piece sometime this week, and I've got young Randy taking photos. We'll do a nice write-up of the auction for Monday's paper, extolling what I'm sure will be a successful day. That will make a terrific lead-in to the other article." She fastened her gaze on Phyllis. "We are keeping this between the four of us, right?"

Phyllis did a quick cross-my-heart gesture. "We're the ones who came to you, remember? It's our little private secret for now."

Clarissa clapped her manicured hands together twice in the way of a teacher getting the attention of her students. "That you did, and the fun we will have with this is icing on the cake of doing what's right for New Day. Anyway, we just wanted to let y'all in on the plan."

Helen was willing to bet that Clarissa either had, or would soon have, the confidence of the Jankowsky property owners for a new deal that she would put together. A fierce competitive spirit was the other characteristic the sisters shared, despite the fact that Clarissa had adopted a smoother style.

Hearing the volume of voices growing louder, indicating the peak crowd might have arrived, Helen thanked the Grigsby sisters for the update and excused herself. She decided to pass by the ticket table to see if they needed help.

The day progressed with few problems, with the final count at 188 tickets sold. The Ladies Auxiliary was happy with their profits. Norman Healy had solved his dislike for speaking in public by simply introducing Kristen, who focused on the helpers who hoped to be able to move into the new housing. She explained that all the proceeds from the day would be held in a special account to be used in furnishing the new residence.

Even if Helen had been completely objective about Max, she would have acknowledged that he was ideal in his role. He sustained the energy of the auction and inspired waves of laughter with his good-natured teasing about designs and techniques of the quilters who had contributed their work. Holding MAGNOLIA MEMORIES until the final item, Max urged on the bidding war that closed with a $625 sale.

Helen, Phyllis, and Deirdre managed the money, while Becky and the other circle members worked with the New Day helpers to ensure the correct items went home with the new owners. Sarah, who had kept running calculations of the combined revenues, slipped Max the ending number of $12,010 as the net take. The considerably thinned crowd in the hall applauded loudly, and Helen stood to gratefully stretch. The Bachmans, when paying for six quilts and a set of four quilted photo frames from the silent auction, told Helen that Wanda had agreed to open the shop for them in the morning before they left for Augusta.

The hall emptied except for the clean-up crew and the circle members. Rita and Alicia sank onto chairs at one of the few tables that hadn't been taken down. Helen had seen the predictable fatigue from such an active day reflected in the small signs the pregnant women had been trying to hide, and she'd promised them a report by e-mail if they would go home and rest. Neither had protested beyond a single "But," which Helen had dismissed with gentle firmness.

Phyllis popped the palm of her hand to her forehead. "Which one of us forgot to bring champagne to celebrate this great day?"

"That would usually be your department," Deirdre said drily and let loose a happy sigh. "These old bones need a cup of coffee, my easy chair, and a footstool. You youngsters go party on your own."

"Actually, I'm meeting Eleanor and Lannie for drinks. They're staying at the Wallington Inn," Phyllis said and spread her hands as invitation. "Who wants to join us?"

Mary Lou was the only taker, and Max fell into step with Helen as they walked to the parking lot. Despite a mild ache in her calves and twinges in her knees reminding her that she wasn't in her twenties any longer, she was in a cocoon of satisfaction with the results of the day. Max's Explorer was in a space near her Taurus, and Max reached to open the door for her.

"Listen, I don't know about you, but I think grabbing a nice hot shower, then letting someone else do the cooking tonight is the way to go. Want to do dinner at the Copper Pot?"

Helen leaned against the back door, looking into his eyes, knowing it was more than wanting to unwind, at least for her and quite possibly for him. They'd been a part of something good today, and she wasn't ready for that shared feeling to end.

"I'd like that," she said. "I need about an hour to take care of Tawny and change. I'll call you when I'm leaving the house." It was a five minute walk from Max's apartment to the restaurant.

Holding the car door open for Helen, Max said, "Phyllis may have been right about the champagne. I'm sure I have a bottle in the fridge. We could have that after dinner—or a glass before and after."

Helen slid into the seat, shook her head, and smiled to soften the rejection. "That part I'll probably have to take a rain check on. I think a glass or two of wine at dinner will be it for me tonight."

He patted the top of the car and winked. "We'll have other reasons to celebrate soon, I imagine. We'll open it then. See you in a little while."

Helen backed the car out, aware that Max was watching her drive away. She wondered if he meant celebrating the approval of New Day's project or if he had something else in mind.

# CHAPTER TWENTY-THREE

Helen almost laughed out loud when she read the write-up about the quilt auction in the *Gazette*. In keeping with the old adage of "a picture is worth a thousand words," there were three excellent photographs, including one of the mayor's wife chatting with Kristen Duluth and another with one of the New Day helpers assisting an elderly woman into her chair. Helen had seen Randy, the paper's photographer, snapping away like crazy, and Denise Grigsby had no doubt personally selected the specific shots to support the article.

It seemed as if everywhere that Helen went for the next two days, someone praised the auction, often expressing hope that it would become an annual event again. That was the main topic at circle on Tuesday as other members revealed that they too had received similar feedback. There was tentative agreement that they would determine which part of the year had the highest likelihood for success for an auction and select a new charity each year to receive the proceeds. The desire to have a contest had been made clear in the discussions, which meant they needed to make a decision soon on a date and a theme. It had been a rare evening with no one staying late. As Helen switched off the porch light, she looked through the front window and noticed that Becky and Max were just pulling away from the curb in their SUVs. They had apparently stopped to have a conversation about something.

Wednesday was her regular day for laundry, and she'd just transferred a load from the washer to the dryer when the telephone rang. Phyllis didn't bother to say hello. "Do you have coffee on? I'm headed your way. You don't have the paper yet, do you?"

"Yes to coffee and no to paper. Denise's article about the real estate deal is in it, I assume?"

"Front page and it's a doozy. Be there quick as I can. I called the office and told them I'd be a little late."

Helen hoped that Phyllis had a run of luck with traffic lights because she was knocking on the door in record time, carrying a white paper bag in one hand and a newspaper in the other. "Denise had left me a voice mail last night so I ran by Lisa's to pick up a copy of the paper and orange cranberry scones. Don't bother with plates; I'll tear the bag open, and we can use it. You read, and I'll get my coffee."

"She had enough facts to run it as an article and not an editorial?"

"Oh yeah. Clarissa dug into this with her contacts. The article is mostly about Galbraith Development, its less-than-stellar reputation, and why letting Galbraith into a town brings a lot of questions. The situations she cites come right from public record consumer complaints about shoddy workmanship of the builder Galbraith normally uses and about an out-of-court settlement over building on property that had not been properly surveyed. Galbraith developers always go in for increased density waivers in order to squeeze in extra houses. Oh, and there was a lawsuit filed on a project where homebuyers hadn't been warned about a special assessment for some road work. Galbraith moved forward with the project, despite the city clearly saying it would not pay for the road, and Galbraith dumped the cost onto the new homeowners for like ten thousand dollars per house."

"Twelve thousand," Helen read aloud, although she didn't want to spoil Phyllis's pleasure in the telling.

"I've got to give Denise credit, although I shouldn't have doubted that she would do this in the best way possible," Phyllis said, waving her coffee mug before taking a sip. "Instead of attacking Fred or Tommy directly, she lays out Galbraith's troubles from a 'source divulged that a new developer is interested in Wallington' angle and goes from there. Oh, to make it even better, it turns out that Galbraith is a New Jersey-based company that's branched out into the Sunshine States. You know how that plays with people here."

Helen couldn't suppress a smile at Denise employing the tactic of the centuries old rancor against real or perceived carpetbaggers. The photograph she'd included of a typical Galbraith development showed single family homes so close together, they could barely be considered as separate.

"Oh, and the way she supports New Day is that she talks about the kind of responsible development that's been going on in town following the established code for density, and then brings up the pending project and all the benefits to it."

Helen broke off a piece of scone. "It really is clever. She hasn't said a single word about who in town is involved, but the message is going to come across loud and clear to anyone reading this. Can you see Rodney Jackson trying to slide approval for Galbraith through? I don't care how much he wants to do what Fred tells him to, the council members who were sitting on the fence aren't likely to side with him now."

"That's not all," Phyllis said happily. "Denise is going to run an article featuring how much New Day has helped the community by having a local facility. She'll time it to come out a few days before the council meeting."

Helen had to admire Denise's approach. "Mary Lou's idea of having a string of people do one to two minutes of support and have the crowd in the audience with placards is still on track, isn't it? We were so busy preparing for the auction that we forgot to talk about that."

"That's easy to find out," Phyllis said and pointed to the telephone. "Listen, I need to get to the office, so can you give her a call?"

"Of course," Helen said. "In fact, I imagine I'll be having a lot of conversations today." Her prediction was accurate. Kristen called as did Wanda and most of the circle members. Max's call had included the news that he had to take an unplanned overnight business trip to Nashville; Helen invited him to dinner after he returned. Helen ended a call with her mother by agreeing to dinner at her parents' house and saying that she wondered if the Hillmans would be having much of an appetite that evening. The surprising call, though, was from Edna.

"I know your appointment is tomorrow, but is there any chance you can come in this afternoon? Say four-thirty?"

"Uh, sure," Helen said. "Is anything wrong?"

"No, no, I just need to shuffle things around a little bit. Let's do the trim today instead of next week."

"Okay," Helen said, recalculating her sequence of errands. Nothing on her list involved buying perishables, and she could make a big loop ending at The Hair Place. With the beauty parlor sandwiched between the hardware store and the medical supply store, it was usually easier to park in the back lot of the shop rather than trying to find a spot on the square. The bell over the door jingled pleasantly as Helen entered, walking past the bathroom on the right and the office and the small storage room on the left.

The central room of the salon had been remodeled when Ginny Johnson originally opened The Hair Place, and Edna Birch had seen no reason to change either the name or layout when she fulfilled her goal of buying the shop. Large plate glass windows in front allowed light in, and the waiting area to the left and right of the reception desk was furnished with comfortable arm chairs that Edna had found at various garage sales. She had reupholstered them into coordinating solid and print fabrics, purple being the dominate color. The four salon chairs were against one wall, the three shampoo sinks opposite them, and there was adequate space for two people to walk down the middle of the room. A single manicurist station was set against the back wall along with a beverage center with dual coffeemakers: one for coffee, the other for hot water. A rectangular black wire basket held tea bags, decaffeinated coffee packets, sugar, sweeteners, and the little containers of nonrefrigerated creamer. A large water bottle on a stand was pushed against the table. The practical high-traffic vinyl flooring looked like walnut planks, and instead of fluorescent lighting, the bronze rimmed fixtures were frosted, nonglare glass.

Edna had wanted the place to feel warm and have softer touches that her older customers especially appreciated. She didn't try to draw the younger clients, and although there was a *Walk-Ins Welcome* sign in the front window, the women who made up the bulk of her business had standing weekly appointments or were at least regular in their patronage. In an almost mirror image of The Hair Place, Al's Barbershop was directly across the square. Neither Edna nor Al advertised unisex service. While they wouldn't have refused such service, they were rarely called upon to provide it. Women flocked to Edna, and Al's was the place where you would find men who wanted a barbershop that didn't claim to have a stylist.

The difference was that Al had taken over the business from his father and grandfather, while Edna had pulled herself out of poverty, determined to at least finish high school, one of the few women in her family to do so.

Education was not valued among her relatives, and Edna had not been the type of student to inspire a teacher to try and point her to a path of academic achievement. The rural town she'd been born and raised in had one beauty parlor in a doublewide trailer, and at age fourteen, she'd offered to be an unpaid assistant and keep the place clean if the woman would take her on as an apprentice. She developed her skills to the extent she could, but some degree of formal training would be required in order to obtain a license. She'd made the mistake of believing Wally Birch's promise that he would take her to the big town of Wallington, where she could attend the nearby community college. He had gotten them as far as Wallington, but that was it. Had he ever been able to keep a steady job and had Edna not become pregnant in their first six months of marriage, there might have been enough money for her to have pursued training. After the twins, a boy and a girl, were born, Edna decided that working in childcare was a start, and she became inventive about hiding money that Wally would otherwise drink up.

Ginny Johnson, who knew Edna from church, had told her about a part-time training program she could take online, and that as soon as she had her license, Ginny would bring her into the shop. Ginny had even contributed an old computer. Edna scraped together the money to afford the Internet connection. With the coveted license in hand, it didn't take long for Edna to become a favored stylist at Ginny's shop. Once she turned Wally from the house to stop the steady drain of finances, she set up a cake baking business on the side and put that money toward her goal of buying out Ginny, who had set a retirement date, with a lease-to-own option.

Helen was mildly surprised to see only one other customer, a woman under a dryer. Maureen Dickinson, the vet's wife, was exiting the front as she entered from the back.

"I'm sorry I couldn't make it to the quilt auction—it's been the center of conversation," Edna said, motioning Helen to a chair at the sink closest to the back entrance. "Let's get you shampooed, and I'll put that deep conditioner on. It can sit for a bit while I comb Reba out."

Edna, a head shorter than Helen, had broad shoulders for a woman and a square face with a wide mouth, but excellent teeth, which may have been genetic consolation for not having been graced much in the way of feminine charms. She kept her hair cut in a style that brought to mind Florence Henderson on the television show, *The Brady Bunch*, and Helen had always wondered if the shade of brown was a combination of colors or maybe there was a touch of henna thrown in.

"It was a good event," Helen said, leaning back as Edna adjusted the water temperature. "Everyone who helped out was great."

"It's nice when people come together like that," Edna said noncommittally and asked how Helen's daddy's recovery was going.

Helen settled more comfortably into the chair after Edna applied the deep conditioner, her hair wrapped in the plastic cap for the five minutes it took Edna to finish working on the other woman's hair. Edna locked the door after the woman left, rinsed Helen's hair, and gave a brisk towel dry before moving her to the stylist chair.

"I would think you've had a busy day today," Edna said, combing the wet tresses. "I imagine you've had time to read the paper, though."

Helen glanced in the mirror and saw the careful expression on Edna's face. The reason for the change in appointment was becoming clear. "Uh, yes, as a matter of fact. Quite a story on the front page."

"That Denise Grigsby does speak her mind, doesn't she? You know both the sisters pretty well, too, I think. They get their hair done at Lila Gentry's, like their mamma did, so I don't know them more than to say a friendly hello."

Helen heard the unasked question. "I wouldn't say we're best friends, but, yes, I've been around them all my life. They do a lot for the community."

Edna snipped, seeming to focus only on Helen's hair, which she could have cut blindfolded. "I think you might know Elsie Thomas, too—Martha Newton's cousin. Like Martha, she does cleaning and ironing—not many women do that anymore what with washers and dryers being as fancy as they are these days. Some things, though, like table linens and sheets—it just isn't the same as ironing. You take Deborah Hillman—she has Elsie come in once a month and do up a big pile of linens for her."

"I see," Helen said neutrally.

Edna stopped snipping and smiled, looking at Helen in the mirror. "No matter what I hear in this place, I'm not one for passing gossip, in general. There are times, though, when keeping quiet isn't the right thing to do."

"I gather that Elsie came to you about something this morning?"

Edna picked up the blow dryer and set it on low as she brushed through Helen's hair. "Not that Deborah Hillman is much for pleasant unless you're the right kind of people, but Elsie said she was close to being downright rude this morning. Elsie was ironing in one room, and Deborah was talking on the telephone in the next room. She was pacing, and she wasn't keeping her voice down. Elsie could hear her clear as a bell. Said Deborah was worked up into a conniption fit like you wouldn't believe."

"About the article, you mean?"

"Oh, yes, and Elsie said the words she was using to describe the Grigsby sisters were the washing-your-mouth-out-with-soap kind. Said it would cost them—that would be the Hillmans—a big windfall. Deborah was saying it was a conspiracy between the sisters. That somehow Clarissa had gotten wind of their deal and had ruined everything. Said they were meeting with their attorney to see about suing."

Helen frowned. "The Hillmans' names weren't mentioned in the article."

"I read it myself, and sure didn't see it either, but from what Elsie heard, Deborah wanted to talk the developer into suing." Edna finished with the blow dryer. "It wouldn't seem like Deborah could make good on what she was saying, but it might be the right thing to do to give the Grigsby sisters a word about it." She unfastened the black salon cape and stepped back. "I'm glad you could come in today."

Helen wasn't worried about Deborah's nasty, empty threat, and Denise was certainly no stranger to potential lawsuits, but the fact that Edna cared enough to want to pass on a warning was touching. "Thank you for calling, and I'm sure I'll see either Denise or Clarissa very soon."

As she left Edna's, she felt a giggle rising for relief. She was picturing what it must have looked like with Elsie trying to iron as Deborah paced around screeching into the telephone. Even though the idea of bringing suit was absurd, it was proof that everything they'd suspected about the intentions of the Hillmans was true, or at least most of it had to be. Why else would Deborah have reacted in the way that she did? In all fairness to Edna's obvious concern, she would contact the Grigsby sisters, set up a meeting, and tell them about what Elsie had heard. She'd ask Phyllis to join them; she wanted to see Phyllis's expression when she heard about this.

The most important point, however, was to protect Edna and especially Elsie as the source of information. The Grigsby sisters had adequate influence in town to be impervious to the Hillmans, no matter how much Deborah lashed out. It wasn't the same situation if Deborah launched a vindictive campaign against the two women whose livelihoods depended on customer service. Edna's clientele probably wouldn't be swayed to change salons, but gossip that swirled in the salon was supposed to be absorbed by the owner, not shared, and Elsie would definitely be out of at least one client. No, this was a secret they would have to enjoy among a small circle, a delicious tidbit that could be entrusted to only the most reliably closemouthed.

# CHAPTER TWENTY-FOUR

Helen couldn't remember how many years it has been since she'd driven to Richardson's Stables—well, Saddle Up Stables now. Mitch and Ethan both preferred horsepower that came under the hood of a car, and Tricia's horse phase hadn't lasted much longer than a year. She'd discovered, as most did, that there was more to horses than merely climbing onto a saddle and taking a leisurely ride. It had been easy to tell who among the adolescents and teens were the true horse lovers; they were the ones who spent extra time grooming, seemed to communicate in a special language, and were completely relaxed when astride. Not that she had minded Tricia finding other interests—horse ownership came with more complications than they had wanted to be involved with.

Becky had sounded so excited when she called that morning that Helen had agreed to come out right after lunch to meet her for whatever this wonderful surprise was. She had the time. The menu she'd planned for dinner with Max wasn't complicated: Swiss steak with roasted fingerling potatoes and roasted sweet peppers. She had enough tomatoes for the salad, although if she wasn't running late, she would stop in at Always Fresh Farms for a small basket of mixed heirlooms.

The county road was two lanes with no center line painted and vegetation growing right to the edge. Road crews had cut back shrubs and small trees so that approximately six feet on each side of the road was cleared to a few inches high. Weeds intermingled with grass so that you didn't want to tromp along unless you were wearing boots or at least sneakers. There was seven or eight houses total along this stretch, most with five acres or more of land. The exception was Mrs. Cook's bungalow, which sat on two acres across the road from the stables. There had been a series of tenants after Doctor Cook had convinced his mamma to move into town, his solemn promise that the house would not be sold in case she decided to return to the place where she had lived for almost sixty years.

In either coincidence or a strong pull of family, the Cook's youngest daughter, Miriam, had reappeared in Wallington a few months prior to her grandmother's passing. Unlike the other Cook children, Miriam had gone to college in Texas, married, and remained in Dallas until her divorce. Childless and allegedly wanting to divest herself of any connection with her ex-husband and the rest of his family, she'd set about remodeling the homestead, gutting it to the studs while agreeing to maintain the exterior with minor modifications. Vinyl siding in bluish gray that gave the appearance of wood kept the look of the original clapboards, and the windows lacking in insulation with rotting mullions had been replaced with replicas using the latest technology. Fortunately, there had always been a metal roof, the only change there was a medium blue color instead of the previous dulled gray. Miriam had kept the rocking chairs on the wide front porch, and the landscaping that had been the true draw of the house had not been disturbed.

The pond to the right of the house was an elongated oval. There were pink and white azaleas on the far side, with dwarf crepe myrtle coming around, and masses of blue hydrangea that made up a horseshoe of natural fencing. A gravel path led through the open part of the "horseshoe" right to the edge of the pond. There were two wooden chaise lounges with a little side table between them and two big old stumps with the tops ground flat to provide additional seating. It was an ideal setting for birding, reading, or sunbathing.

The exact amount of the settlement from Miriam's husband wasn't common knowledge, but when Beau Richardson wanted to sell the stables, Miriam allegedly paid the full asking price and negotiated a deal to purchase the adjoining eight acres with a dilapidated farmhouse and barn. Those buildings were bulldozed and the ground turned into meadow. The modest house next to the stables where Beau had lived was merely reroofed, thoroughly cleaned, repainted, and converted into administrative space.

The single-wide trailer that Beau had used as an office disappeared, and Miriam brought loggers in to cut trails through the woods. They were wide enough for two horses abreast and allowed riders to meander under the trees, cross either of the two meadows, and go into the woods on the other side. Becky had talked about the incremental changes to the property during circle, and Helen suspected that she had influenced at least some of Miriam's choices.

The light rain the night before had thankfully settled the dust around the large barn even though the humidity had not dissipated with the passing rain. It was a sticky afternoon, and Helen had built time into her schedule for a cooling shower before beginning dinner preparations. She'd put on a pair of well-worn jeans, a loose-fitting short-sleeved pink cotton top, and her older pair of walking shoes, not certain of which part of the stables she would be going to. She parked next to Becky's green Dodge Durango, her Taurus the only sedan among the SUVs and trucks. One of Scott Nelson's equipment trailers and two other trucks were to the right of the office, men busy on what was obviously to be new stables, a building at least the size of the existing one. The whine of saws carried across the open ground, and as soon as Helen slammed the car door shut, Becky emerged from the stables, wiping her hands on the sides of her jeans. She waved in a wide arc, motioning Helen to come to the stables. Helen breathed shallowly, the odors of horse, manure, hay, human sweat, and general earthiness taking her back in time.

"Thanks so much for coming," Becky said, her face beaming with pleasure. "I wanted you to be one of the first to know. I'd give you a big hug, but I'm pretty sweaty."

Her unadorned green T-shirt was blotched with damp spots and a wet streak across the hem that she had probably lifted to wipe her forehead. "Come on inside. We've got water in the cooler. I'll be ready for a break as soon as I finish with Nugget. You okay with being inside? No allergies that I forgot to ask about?"

"No, and I was just remembering how I would watch Tricia do this—Beau Richardson was firm about the kids being responsible for the horses."

"He was at that," Becky said, slipping into the stall where a reddish brown mare with a white patch on her forehead waited patiently, her age showing around her muzzle. "You're one of our matrons, aren't you, my friend?" She stroked the horse's neck and looked to Helen. "Nugget was in really bad shape when they brought her to us, and we weren't at all sure we could save her." She picked up a grooming cloth that was draped over the side of the stall. "By the way, I nearly fell out of my chair laughing when I read Denise's article. Not that it's funny, ha-ha—I mean hysterical in how the Hillmans must have been reacting."

"It has stirred up talk," Helen said mildly. "I think Kristen is actually looking forward to the council meeting at this point."

"She should be," Becky said, still grinning as she gently wiped the grooming cloth around Nugget's ears. She lowered her voice. "Okay, lady, you're good for the day."

Helen felt the affection between human and animal, the bond that was no different than when she held Tawny in her arms, aside from the fact that Tawny was only about half the size of Nugget's head.

Becky closed the stall door and gestured to the big white cooler near the rear doors. "We have water, Gatorade, and maybe some bottled tea. What can I get for you? We'll go to the picnic table if that's okay."

"Water's fine," Helen said, accepting a bottle with ice chips clinging to it and following Becky to the backyard that had been turned into a party area. Four rectangular picnic tables weathered with age were arranged in a rough rectangle on the grass. Two huge grills made from fifty-five-gallon metal drums stood side-by-side several feet away, and to the left of the tables was a square brick fire pit with red-stained Adirondack chairs in a semi-circle. Helen could imagine the stars twinkling as marshmallows were being roasted. Mature oak and hickory trees had been left in place when the land was cleared for the house, and their heavy limbs and thick leaf cover would block the sun unless it was directly overhead.

"Miriam has really expanded the place," Helen said, looking around, noticing that the shade from the trees, while the branches did not form a canopy over the tables, did seem to reduce the heat. "Not that it was bad with Beau, but this is so much more organized."

"She had a vision that she's stuck with each step of the way." Becky leaned in, her eyes alight with happiness. "You saw the construction?"

"It's a little difficult not to," Helen said with a smile.

Becky held her water bottle aloft before taking a swig. "True. I don't know if you remember that I was telling you about the rescue horses Miriam took in?"

Helen nodded. Of course, this was why Becky was excited. "I do, and the extra space means you'll be able to accept more horses?"

"Yes, that was the original intent. What it also does, though, is allow us to take the three horses that are being sent to us to begin our equine therapy program."

"Really? How wonderful! How is it going to work?"

Becky literally wiggled on the bench, her delighted laughter spreading like the spray from a hose when it was on a mist setting. "This past week has been incredible, but I didn't want to say anything until we knew for sure." Her eyes caught Helen's. "We're moving fast, thanks to Max."

"Max?" Helen blurted. "How on earth is he involved?"

Becky wrinkled her nose in a way that reminded Helen of Tricia. "Well, it's one of those odd coincidences. I was in Collectibles right after we came home from the cruise. Max was minding the store because Wanda had an appointment or something, and he'd just put on a fresh pot of coffee. We started talking, and to be honest, I'm not sure how the topic came up, but it was kind of like that night when I was telling you about the folks in Texas. I get onto the subject with someone who seems interested, and it all pours out."

Helen nodded, still trying to see the connection between Max and horses.

"I didn't think any more about the conversation after I left, but it turns out that Max knows a guy near Nashville who has this horse farm and he started a therapy program several years ago."

"Ah," Helen said. "The trip he made."

Becky leaned in, still smiling. "Yes, and it's more than the horses, Helen. This guy, who I guess is pretty loaded, was either really touched by what Max told him or Max is very persuasive. He is having his senior therapist bring the horses and she'll stay for three weeks to help us get started. He's also giving us another forty thousand dollars to make sure we can cover transitional expenses, plus he provided the information we'll need to go after other grants. Miriam left yesterday to personally meet with him. All this, and we didn't even know the man."

"Good Lord!" Helen couldn't think of what else to say.

"Exactly," Becky said and leaned back again. "I mean, this is like winning the lottery. I've been pinching myself off and on to make sure that I'm not dreaming." She jiggled the water bottle that was almost empty. "We aren't making any big announcements yet because we're probably two to three months away from being ready, but I just couldn't wait to tell at least a few people and, well, what with Max's help and all, I won't be able to keep quiet about it at circle. I wanted you to know before that."

"Kind of like a soft opening at a restaurant."

"That's a good way to put it." Becky paused, and a note of shyness crept in as her face settled into a somewhat curious expression. "Look, I don't want to pry, but can I ask you something personal?"

"Uh, sure," Helen said automatically.

"This thing with Max—I mean what he's done for us—I always thought he was a good guy and he's lots of fun to be around, but this was such an incredible thing for him to do. I can't tell you how much I think of him now. And y'all, well, I just want to say that y'all do seem so suited for each other."

Her eyes communicated the concern that she had crossed a line, and Helen reached out a hand to pat her arm. "I've been hearing that from more than one source lately. Mamma said something along the same lines."

Becky sighed as if relieved and smiled again. "We all cared deeply about Mitch, and when you look at the marriages that are solid and the ones that fall apart, you can see the differences. I love Bob, and I can't imagine what losing him would be like. I would think it would be difficult to believe that I would find someone else. Oh dear, I'm making you sad. I'm so sorry."

Her face flashed contrition, and Helen shook her head rapidly, pressing a curled finger beneath her left eye to prevent a tear. "No, no, don't feel badly—it isn't that." She sniffed loudly, the sensation passing. "This is a happy day, a happy moment, and I can't begin to tell you how terrific I think it is. You shouldn't feel awkward about having said what you did about Max and me—I truly understand where it came from." She gave one more reassuring pat. "Women can handle these kinds of conversations."

Sounds from the trail closest to the picnic area indicated riders were approaching. Helen stood and held her arms wide for Becky. "This is all great, and it's going to be super. Thank you for sharing it with me." Helen gave Becky a smile of reassurance. "Off you go now to make sure those horses are taken care of properly."

Helen held her emotions in check during their good-bye and until she was away from the stables. She felt the tears pressing and let the car roll to a stop on the side of the empty road. There were no vehicles in sight, the sounds of the woods not penetrating through the closed windows and the hum of the air conditioner. As she yanked tissues from the pocket of her purse in the passenger's seat, the classic rock radio station suddenly started playing, "You Look Wonderful Tonight" by Eric Clapton. Oh, God, how often had Mitch crooned those words when they were getting ready to go out? The torrent of weeping was short-lived, her vision clearing as a thought crystallized, the one she'd been fighting had finally pushed its way forward, demanding to be heard.

"I would think it would be difficult to believe that I would find someone else."

In that single sentence, Becky had unknowingly almost completely defined Helen's reluctance to change the relationship with Max. Could she be so lucky as to find not one "Mr. Right," but two? Becky was correct—looking at the marriages that failed, you could see someone being more careful when they remarried to try and offset whatever mistake had been made the first time. In her case, though, there had been no mistake—not that she and Mitch hadn't argued occasionally. Their marriage hadn't failed; it had just ended. They had been the essence of a teenage romance that worked, that endured. Now, to be offered another chance seemed unfair in one sense. And the fear that lurked behind that question peeked out as no longer a blurry feeling of misgiving, but as a danger sign flashing. What if she and Max were supposed to be together and then she lost him, too? Statistically, wasn't that probable? How long would they have and how could she bear going through what she had with Mitch again? Her life was safe, and wouldn't it be easier and wiser to stay within those boundaries she'd created? The radio's DJ segued to the upbeat "Kokomo" by the Beach Boys, and it was as if snapping a finger to get her attention.

Despite how compatible she and Max seemed to be and how much they enjoyed each other's company, they could not know until they actually ventured into the territory of a relationship beyond friendship. What might happen between her and Max was the stuff of the future, and the simple truth was that they might discover their feelings did not have the depth to carry them past what they currently had. She wadded the damp tissue, stuck it in the empty ashtray, and shook her head. It was time to stop all this fuss and worry. Becky was also correct in that what Max had done was amazing, and she was certain that if those words were used, he would shrug and say that anyone would have done the same thing. He was a good man, and that was what was important. It was time for her to stop trying to prevent or predict what *could* happen and trust that the two of them could manage whatever *did* happen. She hadn't planned to come to this conclusion sitting alone on a country road, but then again, epiphanies had no doubt occurred in stranger places than this.

# CHAPTER TWENTY-FIVE

The parking lot of the town hall had been nearly full, and the crowd inside was in what sounded like a festive mood. Before Helen could seek out Kristen, Phyllis grabbed her arm and tugged her to a somewhat quiet corner. Her eyes were bright with humor.

"This is just too funny. I want to be the first one to tell you." She glanced over her shoulder to see that they were alone. "Council member Rodney Jackson will not be in attendance this evening. He's stricken with some bug."

Helen giggled. "Seriously? That old excuse? That's how he's going to play this?"

Phyllis nodded rapidly. "If you think about it, what other choice does he have? With all the positive publicity about New Day, the article about Galbraith Development, and you better believe he got word about the supporters we have here, he would look like a complete idiot if he tried to stall New Day again. He may be under Fred's thumb, but they have to know at this stage it's a losing battle."

"Not being here is a safer bet," Helen said and turned her head when she thought she heard her name being called. Carolyn was waving to them from the other side of the large entry area.

In keeping with the master plan for historic buildings, the town hall that sat one street over from the town square had preserved the stone 1800s structure and built a newer facility behind it that could be accessed by a connecting hallway or from the side street. The older building with its four small administrative offices had two sets of wooden double doors that were wide open this evening for the capacity audience. The worn planked floors had been refinished the year prior, the few boards that needed to be replaced stained to match the older wood. The trios of tall leaded glass windows on either side of the entryway had originally been brought painstakingly by wagon from Atlanta, and the frescoed ceiling of clouds against a blue sky and spreading magnolia trees in full bloom was a point of interest in the visitor brochures.

Helen turned to a movement she caught out of the corner of her eye. Mary Lou was handing out eight by eleven rectangular placards to a cluster of people. The design they'd settled on was fairly plain—*We Support New Day's Group Home* in royal blue block letters against a white background with a heart in deep red centered below the text. Five individuals were ready with their one-minute speeches, the first of whom would explain what the placard said and the members of the audience would stand silently holding them aloft as each person spoke. She saw most of the circle members and noticed that, like her, they had dressed for the occasion in either business attire or "Sunday best" as Mamaw Pierce use to call it. Deirdre lifted a hand in acknowledgment, not breaking the conversation she was having with Father Singletary. She knew that Max would be fifteen or twenty minutes late and was bringing his placard in case he arrived during the public comment segment. Most of their dinner conversation had been about the horse therapy program as Helen was fascinated with the story of how Max had come to know the generous benefactor. As she'd expected, he was modest about the role he'd played, and Helen hadn't insisted that he take the credit he was due. The evening had been comfortable for her as if by finally recognizing why she worried about might happen with Max, she had lessened the feeling of pressure to *do something.* She would know when the time was right.

Denise Grigsby strode in drawing immediate attention, Randy the photographer one step behind. She was dressed in a dove gray suit with a pencil skirt, the jacket with a single button. The two-inch dark gray heels she wore emphasized her height, and she was carrying a reporter's notebook in her left hand. Helen didn't know if it was coincidence that the mayor took one look at her and disappeared into the main room. If Denise noticed, that didn't stop her movement as she swept forward, dispensing *Hellos,* the remaining throng falling in behind her to find seats inside.

The inner chamber where meetings were held was windowless, the walls lined with photographs of town founders and the city as it changed through the decades. Practicality had won out, and pews had been replaced in the 1950s with straight-backed chairs that had given way to more comfortable seating with black stackable, armless chairs with high-grade vinyl padded seats and backs. Care had been taken when installing recessed lighting to remove as few of the tin ceiling tiles as was required, and antique white decorative rings had been added to keep a period look.

The large table for the mayor and council was set at the front of the room. There was an open space between council table and the first row of spectator chairs and a rectangular table to the right for city assistants and department heads. Wallington had not yet adopted the practice of videotaping its meetings. Instead, it relied on tape recording and the thirty-plus years of experience of the assistant who had allegedly never missed a council meeting since the day she was hired.

In retrospect, the evening was almost anti-climactic. The public speaking segment was met with nods and smiles. The mayor and council, having accurately assessed that further delay in approving New Day's project was not in their best interest, or perhaps devoid of Rodney Jackson's insistence, focused more closely on Kristen's presentation. Dressed in a dusty blue three-button suit, a white blouse with red and navy blue pinstripes, and low-heeled navy pumps, she exuded the air of a confident director, using only one chart to sum up the earlier proposal and concentrating on the answers to the questions that had been raised. The single question that was asked by the mayor reiterated that she was requesting no special funding from the city. Kristen maintained her poise as the unanimous vote was taken, politely thanking the body and all who had supported the project.

Max texted Helen fifteen minutes into the meeting. *Can't make it. Have to run by Arbors. Not to worry, but Mamma needs a hand. Call you later.* Helen suspected that Miss Edith, Max's mamma, had mislaid something and wouldn't be able to sleep until it was located. Max and his sister, Angela, were realistic that Miss Edith's forgetfulness was taking a possible turn into a more serious condition, and they tried to reduce the periods when she would become anxious over a minor situation. They wanted to spend as much time with her as they could, aware that they might lose her to the grip of Alzheimer's or other dementia.

Kristen and New Day's board members were engulfed in congratulations as soon as the meeting adjourned.

"In anticipation of success, I booked the Wine Room at the Wallington Inn," Clarissa said to Phyllis and Helen. "I invited the New Day Board, but they've scheduled a special meeting to work out some details. Mary Lou is coming, and Denise will be along in a bit. I think Carolyn and Becky are in, too."

Phyllis grinned and gave a thumbs-up signal. "It's half-price martini night. See you over there."

Helen was more interested in why Clarissa was making this gesture than in martinis. She didn't think that passing along Edna's information had been that useful. She sent a short text to Max to let him know she wouldn't be home until later. When she arrived at the restaurant, Phyllis was ordering her second martini. The Wallington Inn had been nearly destroyed by a tornado in the early 1960s, and other than salvaging much of the wood, the antique furniture it had been known for had been smashed beyond repair. In the erratic way that tornados can strike, the damage had been confined to a narrow strip of town, and the inn was restored within a year as a reasonable replica of the stone-and-shingle carriage house architecture that featured steps leading to a deep front porch where rocking chairs sat beneath a row of ceiling fans.

The McNaulty sisters, unmarried and childless, had clung to one of the antebellum homes that graced Wallington, and they had fond memories of special occasion dinners at the inn. Much to the surprise of the owners, the sisters offered to contribute as many of their furnishings as the owners cared to have with only the provision that a wing of the hotel be named in their honor. They were present for the grand opening, the photograph on display in the city hall. The sisters sold the McNaulty house as one of the first to be converted to office space and moved to a cottage on St. Simons Island. As best anyone could remember, they never returned to Wallington.

The bar of the inn was to the left of the reception area and opened into the dining room, the ambience throughout that of open beams and polished wood, a piano providing music Thursdays through Saturdays, the Sunday brunch popular with the after-church crowd. The Wine Room was not a misnomer. The room at the back of the restaurant had floor to ceiling wood-clad wine cabinets and two rectangular tables that could seat a maximum of twelve. The glass doors to the room provided privacy without a feeling of being closed in. Denise and Clarissa were favored patrons; the Wine Room was like a secondary office to them.

"I ordered fried green tomatoes and stuffed mushrooms as appetizers," Clarissa said, motioning to the bottle of red wine and a bottle of white in an ice bucket. "Wine, martini, or something else?"

"Wine is fine," Helen said and took the chair next to Becky. Denise hadn't arrived yet. The waiter poured her a white and gently closed the door as he left.

Clarissa pointed to the menus on the table. "Phyllis explained what she'd found out to Mary Lou, Carolyn, and Becky so they know what prompted the article. Denise and I wanted to do something special for y'all because this whole nasty business might have slipped through if you and Phyllis hadn't come to us. We'll fill everyone in after we order."

Curiosity snaked through the room, the women confining their conversation to dinner choices while they waited for Denise, who walked in as Helen decided to have the chicken cordon bleu.

"I'll have my usual and please bring another bottle of white," Denise said, the head of the table being the natural place for her to sit. The waiter nodded, emptying the bottle of white in filling her glass. Clarissa and Carolyn were drinking the red, and Carolyn shook her head when Clarissa asked if they would be needing a second bottle. "First, a toast to New Day and everyone who pitched in to help." After they all gave soft cheers, Denise looked at her sister and made a rolling gesture as if saying, "The floor is yours."

"I need y'all to understand that what we're going to tell you involves absolutely nothing illegal. In fact, considering the outcome, being amused is more appropriate than indignant." There was no question that she had their full attention. "The Jankowsky property has been tangled up for years in a dispute among the heirs, which happen to be two sisters and a brother who are nieces and nephews of the deceased owner. None of them have been to Wallington since they were kids, and as we discovered without too much research I might add, the oldest sister was the holdout to selling. She passed away several months ago. Exactly how Fred Hillman was linked in with them is a little fuzzy and not all that important. The point is that the heirs didn't know about the carpet factory expansion and that the value of their property has an excellent chance of increasing in the next year or two. The Hillmans were looking to take out a loan to buy the property at the last assessed value and resell it to Galbraith." She took a sip as the women exchanged *Aha* looks.

"The connection to Galbraith is actually through Tommy Hillman, although Fred is the one who moved with the idea. Galbraith is the kind of developer that looks for towns on the verge of growth, many of which are happy to waive their building density codes if they have them. The Jankowsky land is an ideal setup for them. As for Tyler Street, Galbraith wanted an additional footprint within the city limits. Because Tommy is the insurance agent for most of those homeowners, he knows the neighborhood well. The existing home prices have been lowered due to the vacant and deteriorating houses, which meant the developers could snatch the area up if the New Day project failed. Deborah would, of course, be the real estate agent. Even with the lesser prices for Tyler Street, she would still make money."

Carolyn, ever the businesswoman, looked thoughtful. "I'm not trying to defend the Hillmans, but if Galbraith did buy up that section of Tyler, wouldn't the other homeowners profit too by selling?"

"That's a *yes, but*," Clarissa said. "If the sellers move away to somewhere less expensive, they would be okay. If they want to move to another part of Wallington, they'd be ten thousand dollars or more short in buying a new home based on average costs. On the other hand, New Day's plans would increase the value of their current homes in less than a year."

Mary Lou cocked her head. "The money was obviously the main factor, but you have to wonder if the Hillmans would have objected even without that as motive."

"They probably would have," Denise said flatly. "They're the kind of people who always do."

Phyllis motioned toward Clarissa with her empty martini glass. "Should we assume that a more reputable real estate agent has approached the Jankowsky heirs?"

Clarissa waved her hand at the waiter poised to open the door, a second waiter behind him with a tray of plates balanced on his shoulder. "That's a fair question, and let's say that a better price for the Jankowsky property can mean more money for the heirs, a good deal for the right developer, and, yes, a healthy commission for the agent who brings it all together."

Phyllis turned her head to Denise. "While I am truly happy to have started this pot to boiling, I don't suppose y'all want to tell us how you found out about all of this?"

"I'm invoking the rule of journalism to never to reveal my sources," Denise said, glancing at the grilled salmon set in front of her. "Let's enjoy our dinners, shall we?"

A sudden silence descended over the group as they all took their initial bites. As sounds of approval for the food and general chatter continued, Becky leaned toward Helen. "I think I want to let everyone in on the news instead of waiting until circle."

Mary Lou paused in cutting her tilapia topped with sun-dried tomatoes and shallot butter. "What news? You're not . . ."

"No, not that," Becky said immediately. "It's sort of related to New Day, and, Denise, I'm going to have to ask that you keep it quiet for maybe a month or two."

"That bargain comes with the guarantee of an exclusive," she said firmly.

"It's a deal, although I don't think we'll be having reporters rushing in for the story."

Becky's description of the equine therapy program and Max's role took them through dinner, and Clarissa offered another toast for what had turned into an eventful evening. Hugs and farewell kisses carried them until after nine o'clock. Helen was startled at the time. In the midst of all the noise, she hadn't heard the signal of a text from Max. *Am beat. Left you a voice mail. Dinner tomorrow, my place? Call if you get in before ten.*

Helen took Max at his word and holding Tawny under her arm to allow the fervent tongue laps of *Welcome home, I missed you*, she speed-dialed Max.

"How is Miss Edith?"

"I stayed with her until she calmed down. This time it was her favorite thimble that had managed to get put in the wrong drawer of the dresser. It assumed y'all went somewhere to celebrate the victory? Denise's photographer sent a Tweet with the news." The tired edge disappeared from his voice.

Tweeting was somewhat of a mystery to Helen. "Clarissa and Denise took us to the Wine Room. I'm sorry you missed it."

"Ah, were you treated to extra details of their maneuverings as well as dinner?"

"As a matter of fact, we were, and it's a story that you will thoroughly enjoy. Oh, and Becky told everyone about the horse therapy program."

"Good for her. Is tomorrow night here okay with you? Or would you rather go out?"

"Your place is fine," Helen said, stifling her own yawn as she set Tawny on the floor. They agreed on the time, and Max told her to not bring any-thing—he hadn't decided on the menu yet, although he was leaning toward lamb.

Helen stood in the quiet kitchen, waiting for the water to heat, defi-nitely needing chamomile tea after all the excitement. Max's use of the word "maneuverings" had applied to more than one group of people. She felt a deep sense of pride in the way that not only the circle had stood up to help New Day, but also the others in the community who had rallied, voicing their support. What she didn't experience was the tiniest flicker of guilt over taking pleasure in having caused the Hillmans to lose out on their underhanded scheme. While the money may have been their driving motivation, she knew them well enough to realize that their ugly behavior regarding the entire project had reflected their disdain for people who didn't fit into their definition of worthy. Not that it was likely they would learn a single valuable lesson from this. No, their attitude toward the Grigsby sisters would simply harden, and there was no telling who else would be added to their list to dislike.

The vibration of the teakettle alerted Helen, and Tawny was prancing for her nighttime treat. She'd spent enough mental energy on the Hillmans. It was time to relax and relish the good deed they had done.

# CHAPTER TWENTY-SIX

**W**hen Max opened the door, the aroma of roasting meat drifted into the hallway.

"Smells like lamb," Helen said, extending a bottle of white and red, stretching on her tiptoes for Max's kiss to her cheek. She loved the aftershave he was wearing, a musky scent without being overbearing. "I know you said to not bring anything, but we do go through a fair amount of wine, and I hate to come empty-handed."

"There are a few open spots in the wine rack, and I have champagne chilled for us tonight. It seemed appropriate. You look terrific."

"Thank you, and I've always liked you in that shirt." Helen was wearing one of the gauzy outfits that she'd bought to take on the cruise. The slacks and tunic that fell below her hips was made of a fluid fabric that didn't wrinkle when packed. Crimson was not a color that she wore as often as she probably should, and she'd accessorized with a shell necklace and earrings that she'd found in one of their port calls. Max's blue print shirt from a trip to the South Pacific featured a pattern of sharks done in a primitive type of drawing.

"The grocery store had a great rack of lamb," he said, leading her to the familiar stool at the breakfast bar that separated the kitchen from the combined den and dining nook. Two forks were tines down on decorative paper napkins that were imprinted with grape clusters. The champagne bottle was nestled in the brown leather-clad ice bucket, one glass partially full. Max poured champagne for her and leaned across the counter, his eyes holding hers as they softly touched the crystal flutes together. "Here's to a great outcome and all the work that went into it."

The timer on the stove beeped, and he smiled. "My taste buds were saying to be French this evening, so it's a preparation of Dijon, red wine, rosemary, and cracked pepper on the lamb. I threw some rosemary in with the roasted potatoes, too, and used a light mustard and honey glaze for the carrots."

"It sounds delicious," Helen said, thinking how there weren't many men in Wallington who would be comfortable in preparing a meal like this. Or maybe there were—Tricia's generation tended to be more food conscious. "You really are pretty handy in the kitchen, you know."

"Have some brie in pastry," he said, moving the plate from the other side of the stove. He'd cut thin slices and removed the first wedge to show the gooey cheese not quite oozing from the golden pastry. "I can't take credit for this—it's the premade from the specialty cheese section of the store. The total skill required is to unwrap it and follow the directions." He cut into a wedge as Helen did, sharing the plate. "I used to travel more than two hundred days a year on average and ate out all the time, which does expand your culinary horizon. After my divorce, I moved into a condo that was close to one of the supermarkets that offered cooking demonstrations. The supermarket had all the ingredients you needed for that particular meal set up along with the recipe card."

"That can inspire you," Helen said.

"It did, and more so because the presenters were a man and a woman who rotated with the demonstrations. The guy was in his mid-fifties and made it his mission to snag men with the line that if they really wanted to impress women, having two or three dinners with a *Wow* factor was the way to do it. That stuffed game hen meal that I do was from him."

Helen edge another piece of brie loose as the timer beeped on the stove. "Was it cooking shows after that?"

"You bet," he said, opening the oven door and extracting a roasting pan. "This needs to sit while the potatoes and carrots finish." He carefully transferred the meat to a wooden cutting board and loosely tented it with foil. "I'm not trying to be sexist, but the number of male chefs on television has gone a long way to getting men to do something other grilling. Once I mastered the techniques of the basic dishes, I gained enough confidence to branch out. I'm happy to say there weren't too many failures in the process."

Helen sipped her champagne. "Well, I can vouch for all the successes in the dinners we've had. Do you want me to put the salads out?"

"Sure. The bottle of Medoc is breathing on the table. You can pour if you'd like, and we'll save the rest of the bubbly for after dinner."

In the refrigerator, Helen found the salads covered in plastic wrap and a small box from Forsythe Bakery.

"Dessert is Lisa's chocolate raspberry cake. Dark chocolate that Lisa does so well with raspberry and chocolate ganache between the layers and fresh raspberries and white chocolate curls on top. It's one of your favorites, isn't?"

"Yes, and I walked this morning anticipating your fondness for Lisa's desserts." The table was set, lemon slices in the pitcher of water next to the bottle of wine.

"I did three extra miles on the bike," Max said, removing the potatoes and carrots. "I'll serve from the stove, if that's okay. I'll put the stopper in the champagne and bring the plates over."

Helen poured the water and wine, a surge washing through her in the gesture. Being here with Max, ready to sit down to a meal like this felt as natural as slipping into a cozy robe. Had she described the way to have a romantic evening, there was not one thing she would change. Could she not see this for what it was?

"I'm all set to hear what the Grigsby sisters were up to," Max said, waiting for her reaction to her first bite of lamb. "I'm willing to bet that Denise had a lot more information than she put in the article."

Helen gave a tiny sigh of contentment at the flavor of the meat. "This is great. All right, I'll give you the full version even though you may have already guessed parts of it."

Max didn't interrupt, taking obvious pleasure in the telling and expressing no surprise at what the women had discovered.

"Well, I doubt the Hillmans will learn a lesson from this, but at least it's over with and everything worked out the right way."

Helen shook her head as he offered the wine bottle. "That's funny—I had the same reaction last night."

His smile was warm, his eyes on hers again. "Great minds do think alike. Why don't I put on the coffee and I'll cork the red? We can have more champagne after dessert."

Helen pushed her chair back. "If you're going to use the French press, let me clear the dishes while you do that and slice the cake. A small piece for me—I didn't walk that far."

It was there again when they choreographed around in the kitchen, a synchronization of movement.

Max sent her to the couch after dessert and coffee, promising to bring the champagne. "Did you want to see what movies are on?"

He had tuned to the Soundscape Music channel, and the melodic flute of some New Age piece was playing. Helen didn't reach for the remote control. Instead, she looked at him as he approached with filled champagne flutes. "Actually, I–I would like us to have a talk." Part of Helen's brain had been formulating what she was going to say all evening. She had envisioned the actual exchange with Max being light and pleasant, steering away from emotional topics until she arrived at the *main point*.

He stopped momentarily and slightly cocked his head. "Do you have any idea how nervous those words make a man? Is this a good 'like to have a talk' or something I should be worried about?"

She laughed softly and held out her hand for the glass. "I hope you think it's good." She was sitting at an angle, her feet firmly on the floor. He sat with his back into the corner of the couch, wariness not completely erased from his face. She took a deep breath, exhaled, and suddenly didn't know where to start.

"Oh dear, I–I–I can't seem to find the words." What was wrong with her?

A smile curved his lips as if her hesitation was all he needed for reassurance. "May I take a guess?"

She sucked in the edge of her lower lip and nodded.

His voice was gentle and low. "Helen, you must know that I care deeply for you. I can't honestly say how much that had to do with my decision to stay here in Wallington, but it has certainly been a big part of it. What I am sure of is that I know how much you loved Mitch and what a great guy he was. Your experience—high school sweethearts who never dated anyone else—is a world apart from what I experienced in a marriage that didn't work out, and while I can't say that I've had a girl in every port, being a bachelor didn't mean I was without companionship."

Helen was having trouble taking full breaths, watching Max's eyes and seeing only warmth.

"I enjoy every minute that we spend together, and for the first time in my life, I've hesitated to so much as put my arms around you because I don't want you to feel like I'm trying to rush anything. Am I on track so far? What there is between us is what you wanted to talk about?"

She nodded again, wanting the tears that were forming to disappear, worried that he would misunderstand. He reached into his back pocket for a handkerchief. "Those are happy tears, right?"

She took the folded square and dabbed at the corner of one eye, then the other. "Oh, yes, happy tears. Let me take a drink. I think I can do this."

"There's no hurry."

The sip of champagne steadied her. "I wish I could tell you how I felt, but the truth is that I can't quite get there. Most of it is because I fell in love with Mitch at such a young age, and I haven't ever been with anyone else. It never occurred to either of us that we wouldn't grow old together, that we would lose all those years that we expected to have. He was in a lot of pain the final week, and with the effect of the morphine, we weren't even able to, well, to say the kinds of things that we might have otherwise." Her voice caught. She paused. Max continued to wait. "Our marriage was as strong as you could want one to be, and he had the chance to see the kids grow into the kind of adults that we had hoped. The look on his face when he walked Tricia down the aisle was something that I'll never forget." Helen wiped the tear that streaked down her cheek, and Max didn't flinch from her gaze.

"I know that the last thing Mitch would want is for me to think that I have to be alone. Between the kids, my friends, and the world that I have, I didn't feel like I was missing anything. And then you came along."

"That's not an accusation, is it?"

Helen smiled at her own choice of phrase. "Not at all. I apologize if it sounded like one. At first, I just thought of how nice it was to catch up on what you'd been doing, appreciating what you were doing for your mamma, being genuinely surprised at you having taken up quilting. I truly thought you would go for Phyllis—that made perfect sense to me."

His eyes shifted to amused. "Phyllis makes me laugh, and I think a lot of her without thinking of her in any way except as a friend. That's not to say that I don't consider you to be a friend."

"Isn't friendship supposed to be the best basis for a relationship?"

"That's a lesson that I gleaned from the unraveling of my marriage. I came to recognize that we hadn't had the depth to get us past the rough parts. That's also why I value what I think that you and I have."

Helen stilled the trembling of her hand by lifting the champagne flute and holding the base against her knee. "See, I'm not sure yet what we do have and that confuses me."

Max shifted forward, although not crowding her. "Helen, I know what I feel for you. I was serious about you being a big reason for why I am staying in Wallington for the foreseeable future. I'm not in a hurry, and I don't want to give you the impression that I am." He flashed a half-smile. "It's no secret that a lot of people think they know what you and I should be doing, and that doesn't matter either. All that matters to me is that you feel comfortable. If you want to spend the next month, six months, a year in the kind of relationship we have now, that's okay. My perception is that whatever reluctance you have isn't about me—it's about resolving your feelings. The last thing you need is for me to try and push you through that. I'm not going anywhere, Helen, and unless you tell me otherwise, I plan to make you a lot more dinners or take you out. Being with you is what's important, and we can do that without worrying about the future."

Helen wanted the tears to not fall. She shakily returned the glass to the coffee table, her eyes stinging. Max gently took the handkerchief from her and leaned in to wipe her cheeks. "Why don't we start with you letting me hold you? You can use this shoulder of mine to cry on."

She placed her hand on top of his and moved it to rest on her knee. "I'm almost done, and in just a minute, I think that I would like a kiss."

"I would be happy to oblige," he said barely above a whisper, and with one last shuddering breath, she lifted her mouth to his.

The End

# WELCOME TO WALLINGTON— RECURRING AND NEW CHARACTERS

**H**elen Pierce Crowder was born and raised in Wallington. She married her highschool sweetheart, Mitch, who tragically died of pancreatic cancer a few years prior to the first novel, *Small Town Lies.* She learned to quilt from her maternal grandmother, Mamaw Pierce, and her mother. She helped build up an independent insurance business for the owner and semi-retired after he sold the business. She lives with a chug (cross between a Chihuahua and a pug) named **Tawny** because of the color of her coat.

**Frank and Joy Pierce**, Helen's parents, each grew up on farms in Wallington, but neither wanted to stay with the farming life. Frank became an accountant, and Joy was a stay-at-home mother. Frank is retired, and they travel a good deal. They live across town from Helen.

**Eloise Pierce Russell**, Helen's sister, is two years younger than she and lives in Lawrenceville, Georgia. After her divorce, she established a catering business. Her two sons, **Danny** and **Sean,** began to work with her as teens and are now actively a part of the business. Danny has a degree in business, and Sean went to culinary school.

**Ethan Crowder**, Helen's son, lives in Augusta with his wife, **Sarah**. They don't have children yet.

**Tricia Crowder Kendall,** Helen's daughter and Ethan's younger sister, is a biology teacher at the high school. She is married to **Justin Kendall,** who is on the police force. She met Justin in Baltimore when she went to visit a friend, and it was love at first sight. They were living in Baltimore when her father was diagnosed with cancer. She returned to Wallington to be near Helen. Justin, born and raised in Baltimore, gave up a promising career on that police force and is definitely confused at times about life in a small town in the Deep South. Tricia and Justin had a son, **Russell Mitchell,** at the end of the second novel, *Small Town Haven.* He is six months old now.

The Quilting Circle is, of course, of special importance in each of the novels:

**Phyllis Latchley** is Helen's best friend. They grew up together, and unlike Helen, Phyllis is divorced. She is a "party girl" and speaks her mind with no hesitation. She doesn't mind shocking people with forthright comments; the women in the circle are accustomed to her.

**Deirdre Carter** joined the circle in *Small Town Haven* because the longtime circle she was a member of essentially died off. She is a sixty-three-year-old retired music teacher and substitute choir director in her church.

**Sarah Guilford** is, like Deirdre, a little older and a teetotaler, but doesn't mind that the wine flows at circle meetings.

**Katie Nelson** is married to **Scott,** who is a partner in a construction company. She left her banking job at the end of *Small Town Haven* to pursue her dream of opening Katie's Kitchen Helper, a take-out and delivery meal service.

**Carolyn Reynolds** is the only member of the circle who has never been married. She owns The Right Look: Ladies and Children's Apparel, a charming and successful shop located on the town square.

**Becky Sullivan** substitute teaches, has always loved horses, and had dreamed of being a large animal veterinarian. Between financial difficulties and falling in love with **Bob** in college, she did not go on to vet school. She teaches riding lessons part-time.

**Mary Lou Bell** is the classic Southern beauty with strawberry blonde hair and blue eyes. She is married to her second husband, **Waylon,** and is a stay-at-home mother who sometimes helps in her husband's car dealership.

**Rita Raney,** one of the youngest members, and her husband, **Steve,** have lived in Wallington for only a couple of years. She is a veterinarian assistant who works for **Doctor Wilfred Dickinson.** She is the one who urged Helen to adopt Tawny. She is expecting a son, **Tyler.**

**Alicia Johnson**, the other younger member and also an expectant mother, joined the circle in *Small Town Haven*. She and her husband, **Hiram**, are also new to Wallington. She works at home in a web marketing, editing, and services business.

**Max Mayfield** joined the circle in *Small Town Haven*. At sixty-two, he is slightly older than Helen and left Wallington right after high school graduation. He traveled extensively in his job, and his marriage ended with no children. He came into quilting because of his mother, **Edith**. He returned to Wallington for what was supposed to be a few months' stay and decided to relocate permanently. He left his "road warrior" job and now works with Click for Quilting, an online company, handles quilting newsletters and does design work. Helen thought that he and Phyllis might develop a relationship, but at the end of *Small Town Haven* he made it clear that Helen was the one he was interested in.

Other recurring characters in Wallington fill the roles of friends, neighbors, and local citizens:

**Wanda Wallington**, a friend of Helen's, was both a member of one of the town's founding families and married into the Wallington family. Only a few years older than Helen, she too was widowed unexpectedly. After her husband's death, she decided to convert the downstairs of her antebellum mansion into a specialty store, Memories and Collectibles, and keep her living quarters upstairs. The main part of the wonderful shop is dedicated to quilting, but she also has space to sell dolls, candles, and other gift items as well as a room used for classes that can be set up for parties. Helen teaches quilting classes there part-time. **Betty Wallington**, a cousin, is a nurse at the hospital. **Ruth Staples** is Wanda's mother.

**Lillian McWherter**, a doll expert, is the other full-time employee of Memories and Collectibles.

**Nelda Nichols**, also a quilter, works part-time at Collectibles, especially during the holidays.

**Susanna Dickinson** is a talented fabric artist who teaches most of the classes at Collectibles. She is the niece of veterinarian **Doctor Wilfred Dickinson** and his wife, **Maureen**.

**Doctor Howard Cotton** is a mostly retired physician who also serves as medical examiner. He is married to **Irma**. **Miriam Cotton**, their youngest daughter, owns Saddle Up Stables.

**Doctor Cutler** is a dentist whom Phyllis works for.

**Doctor Fraiser** is an obstetrician who delivered Helen's children and her grandchild.

**Doctor Leland Turner** is a family medicine doctor.

**Edna Birch** owns The Hair Place, where Helen has a weekly appointment.

**Dorthea Carlton** owns the Calico Café.

**Clarissa Grigsby** owns Town Square Realty. Her older sister, **Denise**, took over the community newspaper, the *Wallington Gazette*, after their father passed away.

**Lisa Forsythe** owns a popular bakery that most of the characters frequent.

**Juanita** and **Kyle Lurley** purchased the farm that Helen's grandparents had owned and have turned it into Always Fresh Farms, a place they keep adding to. Juanita makes a line of soaps and lotions.

**Jeff Lawson** is an architect and also specializes in historic buildings.

**Father Singletary** is the priest of the oldest and largest Catholic Church.

**Larry Shipley** owned the insurance company that Helen once worked for. He and his wife, **Alicia**, own an RV and travel frequently. His decision to sell the business to **Tommy Hillman** was the real reason that Helen chose to retire.

**Fred and Deborah Hillman,** Tommy's parents, are among Wallington's oldest families and hold a sense of entitlement, a status that Helen and others view as inappropriate.

New characters of note for *Small Town Quilting Blues*:

**Avery Lyon** is in charge of security on the quilting cruise. He and Phyllis strike up what might be a long-term relationship.

**Kristen Duluth** is the director of New Day, an organization that provides care for individuals with mental and physical special needs.

**Dr. Marcus Fielder** is a cardiologist who has joined with other cardiologists to offer certain services in the Wallington area as an option to going to Atlanta for treatment.

Made in the USA
San Bernardino, CA
16 May 2016